Project Me

Carol Anne Hunter

CROOKED
CAT

Discover us online:
www.crookedcatpublishing.com

Join us on facebook:
www.facebook.com/crookedcatpublishing

Tweet a photo of yourself holding
this book to **@crookedcatbooks**
and something nice will happen.

For my mum, Helen.
Love you.

About the Author

Carol Anne Hunter lives near the beautiful city of Edinburgh, close to her mum and to her step-daughter and family.

After working full-time, part-time and overtime (often all at the same time) for all of her adult life, early retirement from the Civil Service allowed Carol Anne to fulfil a lifelong desire to write. She went on to take courses at Edinburgh and Glasgow universities and is involved with various writing groups.

Her short story, Bee and Let Bee, was published by Octavius magazine in 2013.

Another short story, A Different Kind of Freedom, was runner-up in the Bloody Scotland Crime Writing competition of the same year.

Visit Carol Anne at **www.carolannehunter.co.uk**

Acknowledgements

The Vendange Wall of Fame

No-one writes a book on their own and I had my very own Claptrap Cavalry to call on while writing this one.

Bookbinding in Monkswood had the sheen of authenticity thanks to Norrie and Janice Linton. Lin Callaghan drew me a picture of working for a national accountancy firm. My friends Emma Mooney and Jo Sulfaro both read the manuscript and gave me valuable feedback. My step-daughter, Heather Lundy-Kelsall, and her partner, Mandy Kelsall, convinced me to keep going. Jacqui Johnson kept my story on the right side of the law.

My editor, Maureen Vincent-Northam, helped make the book better. I received such fabulous support from all the Pen Hens and my friends at the Gorebridge Writers' Group. And my mum, Helen, gave me so much inspiration.

Cheers guys, your portraits now hold pride of place on the Vendange Wall of Fame.

Carol Anne Hunter
August 2014

Disclaimer

Like the folks you'll meet throughout this book, Monkswood and everything in it are figments of an over-active imagination. Please don't try to find the town on Google Maps – it's not there, and any resemblance my characters hold to people of the same name found in the The Phone Book or anywhere else is entirely coincidental.

Project Me

A Natural Conspiracy Theory
by Maggie McCardle, 49.11/12ths

Okay girls, it's time for me to come clean. The night I met Ken McCardle I was off my face on a cocktail of several small Bacardi and cokes and a youthful dose of oestrogen. I therefore cannot claim to have been in my right mind. Plus, it played out like a scene from an old movie – he walked into the pub, clocked me, and made a beeline, which only served to intensify the narcotic effect.

"Hi, my name's Ken," he drawled, his amber eyes glowing, "would you like to go to the theatre with me this weekend?" Not a few drinks down the pub, not even a fend-off in the local flea-pit, but a proper play in a proper theatre, with actors. No chat up lines, no exchange of information, just straight to the bottom line and sort out the niceties later.

And that, as they say, was that.

To my teenage self the twenty-six year old Ken came across as safe and solid. He didn't say much but when he did speak it wasn't with the immaturity I was used to from boys my age. He also had ambition, talked a good game with the compliments and to be honest that was good enough for me. The guy had morals. The guy had principles. The guy had a plan. And all that controlled lust is four star fuel for the flame, don't you think? Well it is when you're nineteen, mid-cycle and pie-eyed (*hic!*). He wasn't the tallest so I ditched my high heels and fell in love. Before long he became my very own action man with gripping hands.

Was I blessed or what?

Ladies, let me explain how this biological honey trap works.

Oestrogen and her co-conspirator alcohol have a similar effect on most women and on me in particular. Handsome Harrys fortunate enough to be blessed with good looks need only one or the other of these mind-altering substances in play to get a ticket into a girl's La Senza smalls. Combined they form a concoction tailored to chemically enhance the attractiveness of any nerd, charmless chav, or spotty Herbert we formerly wouldn't have looked at twice, making them appear very silken and purse-like. This potent brew ensures that those unfortunates who are aesthetically challenged and/or have a personality deficit also get laid from time to time, thereby passing on their genes as nature intended. The end result is that we all get the chance to pair off in a haze of hormones, with perhaps some booze thrown into the pot for good measure. The future success of *Homo erectus* (as it were) is therefore virtually guaranteed.

But there's a downside.

Sad to say, the effects of this wondrous blend can eventually wear off. Booze is short term, causing you to scramble out of bed next morning to search for the jeans you hauled off in a frenzy of booze-fuelled passion the previous night, the ones that still have your lucky pulling knickers inside them. (FYI, *lucky* and *pulling knickers* are, on the whole, a contradiction in terms.)

The oestrogen option is longer term and can cause you to scramble out of bed one morning some several decades later to search out your M&S beige spandex body control armour, now two sizes too small, in the hope that he'll be put off by their spectacular unattractiveness and/or won't want to spend the twenty minutes it takes to painstakingly peel them back off you to do the sweaty deed. Why, I hear you ask, would you do this to the love of your life?

Because you woke up to realise that the balding fart machine on the other side of your bed bears no resemblance to the sex god you hooked up with all those years ago when you were reeling from an overdose of oestrogen, with the possible added exacerbation of the drink.

That's why.

And he's scratching his...oooh, sorry. Didn't mean to shoot that image into your head.

With drink alone the effect lasts for one night only and a week later it's all but forgotten. On the assumption you used contraception, of course.

With the longer-term oestrogen option, yer man himself has inadvertently become your method of contraception. Due to the lengthy delay after the initial hormonal surge, by the time the haze clears you might share a house, a mortgage and several offspring. My rose tinted specs didn't come with a varifocal option, nor were they designed to dangle from the neck by a chain.

So why was I offended to discover he felt the same way about me?

Ken and I were married for – well, forever. We opted for the double income, no kids life. I worked for a Scotland-wide firm of accountants called Manders and Healey – still do. He'd served an apprenticeship with his uncle, who owned a small bookbinding firm in Monkswood, the town we live in near Edinburgh, and had an unspoken promise of partnership. Imagine – me, little Maggie Baxter, married to the likes of Ken McCardle.

There was no 'stop the world' apocalyptic moment where I realised the love had died. It was more a gradual process, like a long, languid emergence from a delicious dream (preferably starring George Clooney as your besotted other half). You don't want to let the dream go so you fight to stay asleep. Eventually you give in, open your eyes, and deal with reality as the very splendid George morphs into He Who Shares Your Bed. In my case, the lust had mellowed into contentment and security. I loved him but wasn't *in* love with him. I could see his faults but turned a blind eye. I figured the good stuff outweighed the bad. This, I thought, is real love.

Until his affair with Busty Babs.

Mind you, I can't speak for everyone. I'm sure there are those of you out there married for years and years to wonderful men who have managed to maintain your oestrogen-induced bliss and you, in turn, have kept them sweet too. To you I doff my derby. And my view of middle-aged marriage might perhaps be jaundiced by my darling husband's philandering. Maybe. Possibly. So whether you agree with my take on things is up to you.

Still.

It's a bugger, isn't it?

Let's drink to our hormones, ladies, where would we be without them.

Saturday, 26th July, 7.30am

Eouww, I can still taste the booze, I must have over-refreshed at old Gibson's retirement do. I've no idea how I got home but here I am in my own bed and, strangely, on the wrong side. I never, ever sleep on the side nearest the door, what's that all about? *Bleuch*, I'm not used to drinking on an empty stomach. Not used to drinking at all, in fact.

Boom-boom-boom. Ugh, my poor head.

I regained consciousness thirty seconds ago, my mouth so dry my top lip had stuck to my teeth. My eyelids refused to open due to mascara-weld but now, when I do manage to prise them far enough apart to peep, I scan the bedclothes jumbled off this side of the bed and it dawns on me that I'm naked. I never sleep naked, not ever.

And what is that pong?

I squeeze my eyes shut and pray – *Please God, make it better and I promise I'll never do it again.*

I can't muster the strength to move and there's a weird rumbling in my head, like low-grade thunder in the distance, rising and falling in harmony with my breath. Whatever I drank it must've been strong stuff. If Ken saw me now he'd be appalled. Ken disapproves of people who drink themselves silly. He also disapproves of women who swear.

Well fuck you, Ken. See? I feel better already.

The rumbling stops, followed by a pause, then a snort before it starts up again.

Oh crap.

No.

I didn't.

I couldn't have.

Oh dear, maybe I did.

I open the other eye; rotate my head one degree at a time. I spy feet, knees, thighs, and...*Geezus.*

I did, I definitely did.

There can't be a man in my bed, there just can't. I don't do one night stands – hell, I don't even do men. But the evidence is there, lying spread-eagled next to me, exuding man-sweat and after shave, all butt-naked and hairy, uncovered in all his glory with nothing but the merest corner of a sheet to shield his pride and joy.

I crane my neck a bit further round, narrow my eyes and focus on a chest, and a neck, and – *good grief, it can't be.*

It is.

It's Gregor the Geek.

Gregor, who at forty-five still lives with his mother. Gregor, whose trousers hang at half-mast. Gregor, whose Mastermind specialist subject is the intricacies of computing. He's only worked at the office a matter of months and is already our resident Johnny No Pals. He is – how can I put this kindly – yes, charismatically challenged. I burrow under my pillow and groan.

A thought jerks my face off the mattress. This will be huge for him. I'm not sure he's ever had sex, far less a one-night stand. He might think this gives him street cred and try to claim his points, or assume I want an action replay and start hanging around my desk. *Shudder.*

Talk about a dear diary moment.

Wait. He works in Finance. We both have access cards to payment programmes. If this gets out, one of us will have to change jobs as per staff regulations and with my luck I'll be banished to post opening in the basement. I cringe.

Ah. I've remembered something – yes, a brandy and port will cure your cold, they said. Have another to make sure, they said.

Bleuch. At least there were only a handful of staff there and chances are, none of them cottoned on since I'm sure we were last to leave the pub. Oh cursed booze, look what you've made me do and, of all people, with Gregor MacAndrew. *Ouch.*

I need to get to the bathroom, regroup my brain cells and formulate an escape plan, which will be difficult given that this tableau is in my house. In my bed. What in hell was I thinking?

Well I wasn't thinking, was I? No, I was getting plastered, and the call of nature is screaming at me now.

*Aoww…*another flashback. I curl up tighter and cringe. I intended to kid myself that nothing happened, that it's a co-incidence we're naked in bed together, but the video clip that just ran through my brain has disabused me of that notion.

Think, woman, think…

Aha! Plan A. I'll creep out of bed, hide in the loo and tidy myself up so I don't frighten him when he does come to. I wouldn't care but my self-esteem's already on the deck and it can't take another beating. I peel back the covers and attempt to slither off the bed in a ladylike fashion, but gravity kicks in and I gather momentum, landing on my dodgy knee.

"Ouch!"

Hand. Mouth. Clamp.

I'm naked, frozen on all fours and praying he doesn't stir. A snort – a pause – normal snoring resumes.

With one eye on his sleeping form I prise open the door as gently as if it's wired to an alarm. I crawl out to the hall, execute a three point turn and lever myself upright but when I draw the bedroom door almost shut and turn towards the spare room – *Aaargh!* Talk about shock therapy. My arms shoot up to defend my eyes from the hellish apparition before me. Who was daft enough to hang a full length mirror right there, opposite my bedroom door?

Oh.

That would be me, Maggie McCardle, 49.10/12ths, and without a detectable brain cell to my name.

Thinking back, Ken and I hadn't done it for ages. Well, a couple of years if I'm truthful. Maybe three or four now that I come to think. We just ground to a halt, like you do over forty-five. Anyway, he always chose a bad time, like when we had an early start next morning. So when he left I considered it the end of the sexual phase of my existence. I figured low expectations = less disappointment and resigned myself to live the quiet life.

The safe life.

The single life.

Now I have a one night stand snoring his head off in my bed and of all people, I've gone and picked on Gregor the Geek.

I don't deserve this nightmare. Don't smoke, don't swear, don't drink to excess (well, except for last night). I pay my bills, don't throw litter out of the car window, and recycle everything in sight. I'm almost a saint, for God's sake, the last of the Goody Two Shoes, a Mary Poppins protégé. Now I've plummeted from grace, never to look down from those dizzy heights again. What if my mother finds out? Or the neighbours see him leave? Thank God I don't have kids or they'd disown me.

Yes folks, one boozy night and I've turned into an ageing Belle de Jour.

I peer a bit closer at my naked form to assess the carnage. There's a definite look of the Alice Coopers about me. My once-plush hair is doing its 'burst mattress' impersonation. Last night's mascara has disintegrated to scatter its sooty remains across my shrunken cheeks. It seems I've aimed for the freshly-dug-up look with huge success – yay me. So I've lost a bit of weight since Ken left – well, two stones to be accurate – but that's the only upside. I heave a sigh. Cellulite makes my thighs look like I've stood too close to the fire and they've started to melt. It's time to admit, my skin's a size too big. I've developed middle-aged droop.

That mirror's a candidate for the municipal tip.

In fact, I'll just bin them all. No mirrors = higher self-esteem.

In these matters, ignorance is the definition of bliss.

You *so* know it's true.

Shit. He must have seen me in the nude. Au naturel. I haven't shaved, plucked or preened for eons and as for exercise – well, I'm allergic.

I want to die.

I creep into the spare room to locate a clean nightie and dressing gown, then pick through a couple of drawers, pocket a hairbrush and hairband, and squirrel them into the bathroom. If I don't pee right this second…

Ooh, relief. Can't risk the flush so I lower the lid. Teeth brushed and face scrubbed clean, I yank the hairbrush through my tangled mane and tie it back. A quick check in the bathroom mirror and – oooh, that's not so bad. If you discount wrinkles, sags, bags and greys, I look almost human.

Maybe it's time to take a seat and work out a plan before he wakes up – *hmmm*, I could take off in the car and leave a note by the kettle – 'Sorry, late for an appointment, let yourself out'. No, he doesn't have a key to lock up and anyway, I don't want to leave him in the house alone. Imagine if he got nosey. My knicker drawer consists of washed-out granny pants two sizes too big which should remain 'sight unseen' in the interests of his mental welfare.

Internal Memo: Buy new nix, effective immediately.

I know, I'll act all nonchalant, as if I do this all the time and it's no biggie. On second thoughts, maybe not – it's bad enough he's in my bed, I don't want to send him off thinking I'm a complete slapper. *Stupid, stupid woman* I mutter, and bang the heel of my hand off my brow; *you're a liability to yourself. I do not recognise you, hung over, dishevelled, and full of remorse.*

A thought hits me. What'll Gregor tell his old mother if she asks where he slept? I can see her in my mind's eye, a tiny wodge of a woman hovering on my doorstep all Queen-Mum-like in a lilac chiffon ensemble with purple hat and handbag, her silvery hair all crinkly and curled. She's waving her walking stick like a weapon and shouting, 'Stay away from one's innocent boy, you geriatric Jezebel', in a Miss Jean Brodie accent while she glowers at me down her peachy powdered nose. Ugh.

Elbows on knees, I drop my head into my hands and groan. Thank God I haven't had a period in ages, so at least I don't have THAT to worry about.

Anybody got any Tramadol? Tamazepam? Ketamine? Right now I'd settle for an aspirin. Anything – anything at all.

A tap-tapping on the door hauls me out of my trance. I squint through splayed fingers and catch sight of his naked form hunched beyond the patterned pane, his hands cupping his cheeky bits.

Zero hour and I'm still trying to pluck a Plan B out of the ether.

"Erm, hello?"

I consider my response and kick off my sparkling dialogue with, "Uh-huh?"

"Sorry, I, um, need in, will you be long?" He shifts to one side so I can no longer see his befrosted outline.

"Nope, just gimme a minute." *Stall for time; stall for time…* I pull the flush, rinse my hands, wipe them dry on my housecoat, anything except open that door.

An idea pings in. I could ask the Universe for help. I read about it just last week and thought, *pheuff*, it's all New Age claptrap but desperate times = desperate measures and I'm all out of ideas so what have I got to lose?

I screw my eyes shut. *"Emergency – Code Red – woman down, send back-up."* I pause, open an eye, cock an ear – nada, zip, zilch. Looks like the Claptrap Cavalry have let me down. I'll just have to open the door and deal with it.

I glance at the mirror. I'm deteriorating again, but there's not a lot I can do about it so I take a deep breath and open the door.

Where the hell's he gone now?

I take a few faltering steps into the hallway and freeze. There he is, in the bedroom, all naked and hopping around on one foot while trying to fit the other into his Deputy Dawg boxer shorts. Stocky with rugby players' thighs, he has the hairiest body I've ever seen with a little beer belly which overhangs… Oh dear, Mother Nature wasn't very generous there. Positively stingy, in fact.

I did not register that tiny detail during our drunken shenanigans.

"Erm, do you want a cup of tea or something?" I manage but I can see he's keen to get those boxers on. He panics and hops half a turn, obscuring my view of his little soldier.

"Ahm, no thanks, I'd better get off, I'm, err, playing golf, in Leith, need to, uhm, go home first. Thanks anyway." He's now completed two twirls and almost fallen on his face, which is red from the neck up.

Now that I look at him, he's not too shabby – in fact he's almost handsome without the jam jar specs. Pale hazel eyes, tanned skin, thick dark hair, good body for a guy in his forties if you can get past the hairiness and the half-mast trousers. But gorgeous smelling after shave – who even knew he wore the stuff?

Luckily, he never refers to a girlfriend so at least I won't have some angry female battering my door down to slap me one.

Except maybe his Queen Mother, of course.

Somehow, though, he's different. Without the geeky grin and the horn-rimmed specs he seems almost like a regular guy in his rush to get dressed and leave.

How ironic is that? Even geeks shag and go.

I don't think he'll tell anyone about our little liaison. He has far more reason to fear what I could reveal about him and his tiny todger. Anyway, I'm exhausted – being a paragon of virtue was hard work and I'm overdue a day off.

Wow – did you feel that? All the power just swivelled round to me. I think I've just had a Pivotal Moment.

Let me explain. Imagine your life is a jigsaw but the pieces don't fit so you cobble them together the best you can. Then you drop one and when you bend down to pick it up, you discover a key piece hidden under the table. You know exactly where it fits so you place it in and wham! The big picture changes completely. Like, when I discovered Ken's affair. I figure it's a syndrome of sorts. Pivotal Moment Syndrome, maybe.

Somewhat more cathartic than your regular PMS and highly illuminating.

So let's recap from my new perspective.

My man-drought is broken. I didn't let my mother down, she'll never know about it. I didn't shock the offspring, I don't have any. I'm a grown up therefore if the neighbours see him leave, so what? It's none of their business and at least they won't think of me as a lonely betrayed woman any more. I don't feel one iota of remorse, what I feel is liberated and, dare I say it, a teeny bit dangerous.

As long as management don't find out, I'm safe, assuming he realises the implications of bragging. If the pub crowd caught on, I'll just have to implement my

Plan B.

I really must start working on some Plan Bs.

Either way, my take on things has altered. Thank you, Gregor, you're a star. Of sorts.

In the time it's taken him to speed-dress and sprint to the loo I've had a few more flashbacks and from what I remember, he was a prize guy when it came to the deed, despite his handicap (and I'm not talking golf). Skilled, I'd say, in making up for it, not the novice I expected at all.

I'm sitting on the top step huddling my knees when he stumbles down the stairs mumbling his goodbyes, catapults himself out of the front door and away.

Six weeks 'til my big five-o and I've been dreading it but something's changed.

It's not a biological clock that's ticking, it's a stopwatch, and I need to find a new sector for my puzzle. Problem is, I haven't a clue where to start.

Suggestions, anybody?

Saturday afternoon, 26th July

As soon as the revolving door propels us into Vickers and Innes's, Mum spots the furniture of her dreams and takes off up the aisle with me scooting along behind her until a text pulls me up sharp. I pluck the phone out of my bag and check the screen. It's from Ken, and the first contact since he left. He needs to talk, ASAP. We haven't been eyeball to eyeball in almost a year. I shudder, clear the screen and cast phone into bag as if it's bubonic.

"I saw it in their telly ad and thought, I'm having that," says Mum when I catch up with her. "Seventy per cent off. What do you think?"

"Perfect," I say, and watch her spread herself across the bed to stake her claim. Keen to find a salesman, I carry out a quick reccie. On any other day they circle the floor, cheetahs on commission who stalk while you browse, but not today. "Stay put, I'll find help," I say, and hot-foot down the aisle but within seconds I'm halted by a disembodied voice behind me.

"Mogs? Mogs Baxter?"

Heart pounding, I swing round on my heel. Dear God, it's him, Johnny Davidson, my Johnny-who-got-away Johnny. I'm amazed I recognise him without his flowing blonde locks and ginger moustache, and it's a bigger wonder he recognises me. I had no time to titivate so to say I'm tatty is to understate.

Maybe if I pretend to be somebody else, or make a run for it – nah, I'm cornered.

"Johnny. Hi." Now, why does he still make my skin tingle, the same way it did back when I was sixteen which is – wow.

Thirty-odd years ago.

"It *is* you," he says, his voice thick with nostalgia. "Nobody's called me Johnny in years; it's just John these days. Anyway, I'm great, how are you?"

"Yeah, really good," I say, but I'm really not. A swarm of centipedes have stormed my ribs, leaping and hopping, spar to spar, from my sternum all the way round to my backbone. Unable to think of something to say that packs any gravitas, the best I can come up with is, "Last I heard, you got married and moved up north."

His head tilts a fraction. "Yup. Then I got divorced and moved back down south," he says, and tags on a token smile. I'd feel less self-conscious if he looked dog-eared like me but despite the fair hair streaked white at the temples, his slate-grey eyes still crinkle when he smiles and he looks good. If only I wasn't decked out in baggy jeans and an oversized T-shirt, had something other than an abandoned bird's nest for hair, and wasn't cosmetic-free.

I call it shabby chic.

You might have a different name for it.

"But that was a couple of years ago," he says to fill the verbal void. "We amalgamated with another company years ago and I became a director, so did my dad. I managed our outlet up there until my old man retired and I came back and took over his end of the business. We've eight branches across Scotland these days." Hands pocketed, he leans his angular frame against the back of a display sofa and casually crosses his legs at the ankle.

"How about you – married?" he asks.

"Uhm, yes, but that ended a while ago. Remember Ken McCardle?" Drat, my voice didn't wobble once 'til I uttered that name.

"You married *him*? He always struck me as straight-laced, straight-faced. What happened?" As soon as the words are out he cringes. He jerks forward, one hand catching me by the

17

elbow, his eyes wide. "Mogs, I'm so sorry – that's none of my business."

Conscious of a pink flush rising, I flex a shoulder. "No, it's fine, I don't mind." To be honest I do mind, but I can't say that. "Mid-life crisis – his, not mine. He still works in his uncle's bookbinding firm. The old man's dangled a share in front of him for years but he never made it legal. When it came time to retire his uncle decided to run the thing remotely and Ken knew he'd never get his hands on the helm. Maybe he felt undervalued, or needed affirmation, so he got himself a blonde ego-boost. No matter, I've moved on since the split, so it's fine."

At this point I issue what I intend to be a chuckle in the hope that I'll sound all laissez-faire about the thing. But when it sallies forth from my voice box it fails to negotiate the bend that leads to my mouth, heads instead for my sinus region and mutates into a horse-like whinny, flaming my cheeks even redder.

I wish I had the bottle to say hey, listen up, Johnny boy. So my halfwit husband did the dirty on me, so what? And I choose to spend my time watching talent shows, who cares? Yes, I stay home and make curtains for everybody and his wife, what about it? I don't need a wild social life so don't hassle me about it, Johnny m'laddo, just don't.

I'm happy.

I am.

I'm sure I am.

Hmmph.

He tilts his head again. "Ah, the old mid-life crunch. Same thing here – her, not me. But you look great," he says, and he almost sounds convincing, "it's so good to see you. Need any help?"

"Oooh, yes," I say, grateful for the change of subject, "my mum wants bedroom furniture." I point to where my mother is patrolling the perimeter of her display, swinging her handbag like some medieval flail.

"Bring her to that desk and I'll sort it out." He signals towards an order station and takes off towards it while I weave through the furniture to collect her, my mind racing.

Every girl's entitled to one bad boy. Johnny 'Harley' Davidson was mine. He rode with a biker gang, smoked spliffs, and strutted with a swagger the young Elvis would've traded his quiff for. Oh, he threw me the occasional 'I'll phone you' – no mobiles or internet back then – and I wasted days glaring at the contraption, willing it to ring.

But see? Then I met Ken and forgot all about him. Lucky me.

Mum and I amble up the aisle towards his station where he's still waiting for the computer to load. "Have a seat, ladies."

"Mum, this is John, do you remember?" I say as we pull up our chairs. "His nickname was Harley." She shoots me a look, turns down her mouth and shrugs both shoulders all the way up to her ears. "From when I was sixteen," I say. "Used to bomb around on his motorbike, always called me Mogs, said I had cat's eyes?" She faces him, lifts her chin and narrows two rheumy brown eyes his way.

"Oh, did he, now," she murmurs, still studying him through slatted lids while he stares at the screen, the thumb of his left hand drumming a tattoo across the desk. "Well her name's not Mogs, it's Maggie." Without warning she lowers her brows, leans into me, and jabs a thumb in his direction. *"Do I know this joker?"* she stage-whispers, her voice hoarse because that means planet earth has stopped spinning therefore I'm the only person who can see or hear her. *"Who the hell is he anyway?"* she adds. Oh dear, a Time Out Moment. I cringe, swallow, and blush to the roots of my fringe.

Embarrassment, thy name is Mother.

"Tell you later," I growl under my breath and widen my eyes at her by way of a silent entreaty to drop it. John smiles at her, winks at me, goes back to his screen.

Bollocks, he heard that.

"Hello, Mrs Baxter, nice to meet you again," he says.

She dips her head in my direction. "She'll be fifty soon, you know."

A flush of colour floods my cheeks. I draw closer, speak quieter, my heart pounding in my throat. "Mum, I'm sure John's not interested."

"Refuses to let me throw her a party, of course," she interjects, paying no heed to me, "doesn't want a soul to know, it seems. What do you think, John, she should let me throw her one, shouldn't she?" I cover my eyes with one hand and choke back the urge to scream.

The next voice I hear is John's. "I'm sure *Maggie* can decide that without my interference, Mrs Baxter." I sneak a look from between my fingers and catch her scowling but before she can say another word he cuts in and takes her in a different direction. "We have some lovely pieces in the showroom at the moment, Mrs Baxter. Which range are you interested in?" Brows tight, she leans towards me and I brace myself for another Time Out. This time she prompts, *"The opera song that gay fella sang,"* in a low voice out of the corner of her mouth.

"Barcelona," I whisper.

She turns her gaze back to John. "The Barcelona," she declares in her telephone voice, concluding her second Time Out of the day. Without moving a muscle, his eyes flash to me, twinkle for the briefest moment, then flick back to Mum.

"Excellent choice, Mrs Baxter," says he, suppressing a smirk, "elegant and a snip at the price. Can't believe they've discontinued it. So, which pieces would you like to order?"

She holds up a hand to count off the items on her fingers while he taps the keys, "I'll have the double wardrobe, the dresser with the mirror, two bedside tables – oh, and the single bed to match." During the lull while he inputs her selection, she presses a forefinger to her lips and stares at the floor, lost in thought. Suddenly she swings round in her chair and dunts her elbow into the soft flesh of my upper arm. "Here's an idea," she says, "why don't you get a single bed?" Then with a wave of her hand she adds, "get rid of yon king-sized thing, it's no use to you now you're on your own." And tops it off with a self-approving nod, as if she's come up with just the best idea ever.

My heart stops. *Time, please rewind so I can interrupt before she says it again.* Too late, it's out there. Fingers poised on keyboard John freezes, moving nothing but his eyes which dart to me for my reaction. It's official, my love life is dead. Forever.

"Mum, that bed's almost new," I garble, and give her my best evil eye. Stop talking, it forewarns. Be quiet, it commands. You're embarrassing me, it scowls. She clocks it, blanks it and keeps going.

"But think of all the extra space you'd have if you got rid of it, enough for another wardrobe, isn't that right, John?" I swear I've turned the colour of lead on a vestry roof.

John remains silent in anticipation of further revelations, his fingertips still frozen to the keyboard.

"But, Mum..."

It begins.

A furnace in my core erupts and blazes into my belly, pulsing and radiating heat. It sears down my thighs then up through my chest wall while I shudder; shake; sweat. Just when I think I'm about to disintegrate the inferno subsides and I'm left cold, clammy and confused. That was less of a hot flush, more of a seizure. Has my cold escalated into the 'flu? I'm self-destructing, aren't I? I'm in implode mode and he can see me, oh God, can he see me.

Shit, here comes the second wave.

This one pushes the heat up over my shoulders, surges it across my neck and *wham!* The fever builds to a crescendo, blazing through my cheeks. Again it recedes as quick as it arose and I'm left shivering, trickles of cold sweat weaving their way down my temples, hair stuck to my forehead in soggy clumps, my damp skin itching. In an attempt to shrink through the parquet flooring I schlump down and further down in my seat but it's useless. I'm trapped in this chair, John and my mother gaping at me as if I've sprouted a second head, me wishing I could sprout a pair of wings instead.

Hang on, an idea is germinating. So what if it didn't work the first time? I pull in a breath and screw my eyes shut. *"Emergency – Code Red – woman down, send back-up."* I count to three and open an eye. Nada. Zip. Zilch.

What did I expect, an SAS-style rescue unit to swing down from the skylight lobbing stun grenades? I lower my weary head into my hands and groan. There is but one certain escape route open to me now.

Erm…beam me up, Scotty.

Sunday, 27th July

"Stop laughing," I plead down the line but Cat's beyond hysterical. "I know you're my section leader and I shouldn't put you in this position but I had to tell somebody."

"I realise your cobwebs needed dusting, but *Gregor?*" She cackles so heartily, I'm forced to create some distance between handset and eardrum. "So, the love potion I bought you at the hippie fair worked?"

"Aye, but Gregor was the best the cosmos could come up with for your three quid."

She chuckles again. "Next time I'll buy you the super-deluxe version at a fiver."

"Ouch, that hurt."

"I'm joking! But I'm glad you've broken your vow of celibacy."

"Only because I didn't know the rules of alcoholic enhancement still applied to me despite my age. I suppose by default those rules also applied to him. Given how much he threw down his neck before we 'got it on' it appears that I'm a fourteen-pinter. Therefore I'm on the lookout for a man with a chronic drink problem who should've gone to Specsavers."

She laughs yet again. "Listen, my friend Winnie's coming over later. Come, you'll like her. Bring a bottle."

"I think not, it's a trot up the twelve steps if I guzzle much more."

Another sigh, this one less tolerant. "Lighten up, Maggie, two nights on the tipple don't make you a boozebag. And anyway, I can't wait to see Winnie's face when she hears about you and Computer Boy, she'll wet herself."

"Just what I need, two thirty-five year olds ridiculing me instead of just you."

Her tone softens. "Sorry. She won't judge, and maybe she can advise. And Maggie?"

"*Mmm-hmm?*"

"Next time you do something this hilarious, forewarn me so I can wear a Tena-Lady?"

Oh hardy hardy harr.

***

I spent an hour scouring the bowels of my wardrobe and the best I could come up with was a crinkle blouse and jeans, both way too big. Then I took a breath, closed my eyes and performed a rite I thought I never would.

I took off my wedding rings.

Now here I am, peering through the floaters to the glass beyond. When my vision clears, a forty-nine year old deadbeat peers back. *Bleuch.*

Anybody got a gun?

***

"Maggie, meet Winnie. Winnie, meet Maggie," says Cat by way of introduction, and Winnie smiles and nods a *hi*. Her white-blonde crop, ankle length gypsy skirt and gold sandals all relegate me to the status of bag lady. "You're two glasses of communal wine behind so if you want to join the convent you've some ceremonial swigging to do." Cat jibes. She dances towards the kitchen, bustles back with a goblet in one hand and a freshly opened Pinot Grigio in the other, and proceeds to part-fill the glass from the bottle. She hands it over and I sip, liquid joy streaming over my tongue, bloodstream-bound, before the rush to my brain.

"How do you know each other?" I ask.

"Church choir," says Cat, deadpan. She shows Winnie the bottle. "More tea, Vicar?"

Winnie giggles and presents her glass. "Thank you, Mother Superior, God Bless You." And Cat tops her up.

God, I feel ancient.

At last the wine soothes my brain and I tell them my story. Somehow I choose the exact moment Cat takes a gulp from her glass to reveal Gregor's shortfall. She snorts followed by spasms of tipsy, tear-stained giggles, white wine sloshing over the knees of her plus-size jeans.

Cat pulls a tissue from her bag. "I'm gonna call him Eminem from now on," she splutters, mopping the wine off her jeans. Laughter converts into stumped looks. "A map and a magnifying glass, *dozies*," she says, bangs a hand against the chair arm and hoots, her hilarity cut short by a hiccup.

Panic mounts. "Cat, you can't say anything, management would have a fit in case they thinks he's sanctioned payments to my offshore account in the Cayman Islands."

Winnie scowls. "Cat?"

"What do you's think I am?" she says, and throws her hair back, so many coppered corkscrews bouncing over her shoulders to bungee down her back. "Unclench. Honest Maggie, you're like, 49 going on 100. *I-would-neh-ver*," she enunciates, emphasising the last three words as if I'm a bit on the slow side, then as an afterthought adds, "and you didn't tell me you had an offshore account in the Cayman Islands."

Oh, for a blunt instrument.

One finger taps her temple. "Think about it," she says. "Of the original ten in Secretarial Support there's only me, you, Della and Esme left, and God only knows when Esme will be back. To be a team leader you need a minimum of four. I'm just a glorified stats collator these days so stop worrying, I won't utter a word. Anyway, the audit team are due to arrive from HQ at any second." She smirks, "Gregor will be too harassed then to spread silly stories."

"I forgot about them," I say, "but I know the new manager's called a staff meeting for tomorrow at nine. Shame Uncle Pete didn't get the job."

"Your uncle works there?" asks Winnie.

Cat and I giggle. "No, everybody calls Pete uncle," I tell her. "He's the best, keeps a supply of choccie bikkies in his desk for emergencies. He's been the assistant manager, like, forever."

"Aye, he carried old Gibson right up 'til he tottered out the door on Friday," says Cat, "but I heard they thought Pete was too much of a softie for the job. This new dame's got a helluva reputation so whatever she says, it'll take precedence over your little peccadillo."

"Dunno how I'll react when I bump into him though."

"Don't act fazed or embarrassed," Winnie chips in. "Smile. Say 'hi' and keep going. Like, *hey, it happened, so what?*"

My glass held snug against my chest, I lean back in my seat and close my eyes. "To top the weekend off I had the worst hot flush in a shop yesterday, and now Ken wants to see me ASAP. Just what I need right now." Given her reaction to the Gregor debacle, I think better of telling Cat the whole Johnny Davidson-and-the-single-bed fiasco.

Cat sketches a finger in the air diva-style and adopts full lecture mode. "What *you* need is a mental makeover. You're not some trainee old duffer, you just think you are. Get yourself some HRT, for God's sakes. And it'd help if you ditched the wedding rings and stopped wearing widow's weeds. Ken didn't die, he left." I waggle my ringless finger in her direction, a smug look on my face. "Oooh, progress," she crows, then announces, "I'm off to the loo." And she eases herself off her chair and out the door.

"Ignore Cat," whispers Winnie, "she thinks if she puts on a tough act, no one will mention her weight. She told me about your ex. Some men are born ratbags."

I smile at her feminine solidarity. "He's such a control freak, and a skinflint," I say. "First date, took me to the theatre – a private box, mind you – and I thought, wow, he likes to scatter the cash. Then I found out he won the tickets in a raffle. Spent years telling me I didn't need to waste money on make-up or fancy clothes or hair dye."

"So what did he spend his dosh on?"

"No clue, his income's classified, which is probably why he didn't want a joint account. Did me a favour, though. By the time he naffed off with a blonde who, by the way, dresses like a hooker, I had a few bob stashed away."

She looks curious. "Her name's not Babs is it?"

"You know her?"

"From school. She's not the brightest but who needs brains when they're bursting out of an 'F' cup? She's always been into older men. If he's dipping his oil stick there, kiddo, I'd be, like, giving him the full body swerve."

I giggle. "How's about you – been married?"

"Yep, we split when Dale was six, ten years ago. He was more interested in going out with his mates than with us. I've had flings, gone on dates, nothing serious. It's tough on one wage but you survive."

"You must be doing alright, look at you. Love the outfit," I tell her, "that must've cost."

She glances towards the door. "Ssshhh, they're vintage." She sees my puzzled look and tries again. "You know, recycled. Don't tell Cat, it gives her the creeps."

"Promise, I won't say."

"Won't say what?" says Cat, bustling back into the room.

"That's between me and Maggie," Winnie tells her, and casts me a wink.

Cat phlumps down into her chair, wiggles herself comfortable and retrieves her glass. "C'mon – dish. What were you talking about?"

"I was saying I haven't been on a date for ages," says Winnie.

"And I haven't dated since I was a teenager," I say, backing her up. "I'd only had two boyfriends before Ken and one of those was all in my head. Who pays these days, anyway – him? You? Go Dutch?"

"You offer to pay your share, but if they want to pay for the lot, that's better," says Winnie.

I shrug. "Dunno why I asked. The chances of me finding out first hand are non-existent."

"Meeting men's a skoosh," says Winnie, and flaps a dismissive hand. "If I see one I like the look of, I give him the glad eye, beam him a smile, then turn away. If he's looking when I glance back, *tah-dah*."

"So you take, what? Brave pills?"

"Nah," Winnie says and swings her glass aloft, 'brave juice'."

"But what if he took the bait and came over, what do they say? What do you say?"

"What did you say on Friday?"

I blush. "Can't remember."

"Well, you could start with, 'I know you from somewhere, what's your name again?' or 'Didn't you go to school with my sister?' Anything to get a dialogue going," says Winnie.

My voice leaps an octave. "*I* could start with?"

"Sure. Century twenty-one, Maggie, equality and all that. It's just an ice-breaker. So long as he doesn't come out with something cheesy or call you Babe, in which case you run. Once you've got him talking, a good way to test his interest is to absent yourself."

"To do *what*?" I ask, my head spinning at how calculated and juvenile it all sounds.

"Make yourself scarce. Go to the loos. If he's still waiting when you come back – game on."

I giggle. "And what if he's gone?"

"His loss," Cat scoffs, chipping in her tuppence-worth.

"But what if your brain freezes and strikes you mute?"

"Use an alter ego," Winnie advises, "go into character. Works every time." I snigger. "I could *never* pull that off."

"It's easy. Mine's called Patsy 'cos if it all goes tits-up, she cops the blame."

I look doubtful. "It's all a bit clichéd."

"That's the game, those are the rules. The problem comes when your mate doesn't fancy his and you have to tag each other to the loo to swap notes."

"Oh, I know the solution to that," I say, "if you fancy yours, you fan your face and ask your pal if it's hot in here and if you're not into him, you shiver and ask her if she feels cold too. Then she lets you know how she feels about her bloke. Job done."

They look impressed and my street cred has just put its foot on the bottom rung.

Winnie turns to me. "Time you put in a bit of twenty-first century practice. Why don't I take you out on the lash?"

A glottal spasm reduces my voice to a witter. "N-n-no, you don't have to do that. I was just curious." But Winnie's already pulling her diary out of her bag. My right hand moves to worry my wedding ring but finds no comfort there.

She mutters as she flips the pages. "I can't do this weekend or next, how's about two weeks from Friday, the fifteenth of August?"

No, I'm not ready. I'll never be ready, there's too much to do and I'm too old to go out with Winnie.

My mind whirrs, clicks, and transmits the call. *Emergency – Code Red – woman down, send back-up.* I pause, close an eye, cock an ear.

Damn.

Unaware of my expanding fear, Winnie notes the date in her diary. "The Abbey Lounge is re-opening as Bar Vendange," she says, tapping her teeth with her pen while she ponders. "I hear it's to have a wee dance floor and everything." From the desperation on my face it must be clear I'm hunting for a get-out clause. "Don't worry" says Winnie, and pats my arm for effect, "we can just go for a quiet drink and a look-see. You can practise your flirting another time." I gulp down a mouthful of wine but it fails to calm me.

If only he was right here, right now, I'd kick Ken McCardle in the cashews for doing this to me.

***

I've sat here in my living room, in the dark, for the last hour. Thanks to my snake of a husband, I'd slithered to the bottom of the board. If I'm going to climb a few ladders and get back in the game, I need to pick up the dice and throw. Today's the twenty-seventh. That leaves less than six weeks 'til the dreaded Five-0 on September the sixth. I need to do a Mary, Queen of Shops – refurbish, rebrand, relaunch – and I need to do it now.

I think I'll call it Project Me.

Monday, 28th July

Staff arrive and hang up their coats, then huddle round the desks whispering, everyone waiting for the big hand to stretch up towards nine o'clock so they can climb the stairs to the canteen and be confronted by the legend that is Stella Veitch.

Given that our section is tucked into a side spur, no one on the main drag can see us from their work stations nor us them, apart from the human traffic through the double doors and the too-ing and fro-ing from the Finance office. While I wait for my computer to fire up I glimpse Gregor wander up the room. What's with the business suit and the shirt-and-tie combo, his beat up trainers replaced by smart black shoes? Where's the tweedy farmer-wants-a-wife get up? He's still squinting through horn rims but they don't look half so bad now. Hopping around my bedroom on one leg he almost looked like a regular bloke and here he is again, looking all competent and sensible. Almost, in fact, like a middle-aged Clark Kent. The implication isn't that he took off his specs and morphed into Superman or anything, and I'm sure the man of steel would be better endowed, but then Gregor *was* a bit of a super-hero between the sheets.

See how your hormones can fool you, ladies? Not to mention the drink.

Wait – is this sartorial display for me? Geez, I hope not. And here he comes, strolling towards the double doors. I raise my head and aim for *cheeky smirk*. Damn. I overshot the mark and landed on *demented old bat*. He blanks me and saunters through the doors without so much as a glimmer. He might have

31

sneaked a glance. For his ego. For my ego. *Pah.*

At five to nine Cat arrives and we tag onto the conga-line snaking its way up the stairs, Cat's management-based diatribe relieving me of the need to say a word. Rumours of take-overs and redundancies are rife so hearts are hanging heavy and now that we're packed into the canteen the tension is palpable. Stella Veitch's summons-by-email specified nine o'clock sharp and although it's ten past she's failed to show, compounding the agitation. Aware of her aversion to clocking in before half past nine I scan the crowd for Della, but she's nowhere to be seen.

My eyes coast over Gregor at the exact moment his skim past me, and my chest thuds. Not even a suggestion of recognition crosses his features. There goes my self-worth, chugging down the drainpipe.

The door swings open and in strolls Della, chewing gum. 'Perky' doesn't do her justice. Every inch of her defies gravity and I would kill for her fashion flair. In skinny jeans and pumps, loose white shirt and waistcoat, her outfit ticks every box right down to the floaty scarf around her neck. She wanders towards where we're sitting as if she intends to join us, which would be a first since she thinks everyone over the age of thirty is decrepit.

"Yo, peeps," she says, and throws a rapper-style hand-flip. I fold in my lips to suppress a giggle.

"You're late," hisses Cat in her best I'm-the-boss tone, and gives Della an unfriendly poke in the arm.

"C'mon, Boss Cat, core time doesn't kick off 'til half nine."

"This was a three line whip, Adele, m'girl. I said be here before nine."

Della peers boss-eyed at a lock of blonde that's escaped her up-do then tucks it behind her ear. "What-eh-ver. And don't ever call me Adele. Cruella's not even shown her face yet. If she can't turn up on time for me, why should I be on time for her? C'mon, don't gimme a hard time." Della moves to stand with the other youngsters at the back of the room and rests a foot on the wall behind her to wait for curtain-up.

At last the door bursts open and in blasts Stella with sufficient force to disrupt the molecules around her. Since we've no face-to-face with the public every day is dress down day at Manders and Healey so Ms Veitch, with her sharp suit and rapier heels, has made quite the first impression. Her ebony pony-tail pulled back from a suspiciously taut face, she's trowelled on enough mortar to lay the contents of a brickie's hod and what's going on with her top lip? That's one hell of a kisser and to ensure it takes centre-stage, she's emblazoned it blood-red. And those eyebrows, like canopies set too high on the wall to provide any shade. With long manicured claws, blood-tipped to match those lips, she's every inch the dominatrix. She's maybe forty, maybe not. When there's a pact with the devil in force, who can tell?

Several staff shrink in their seats but not Della. She exudes boredom, oozes insolence and chews on her gum. I turn back and realise Pete's in the room, standing to Stella's left. I didn't notice him amble in behind her. His face wearing the battle scars of many a campaign, he has more teeth than Allan Carr and loves a pie. His body is a pie temple. After 'caring for pies' his mantra has always been 'caring for staff' but his despondent look infers that today, he could do with someone to care for him.

I glance to the other side of the room and clock Gregor staring at his feet, inspecting his shoes one at a time. Saddo.

Hands on hips, Stella's eyes sleek the room, a text-book tactic designed to amplify the anxiety. "You's already know my name," she announces in a Glaswegian accent, those beady eyes burning, "and if you's don't, then you should." She renews her stance. "As your office manager, I'm here to make a difference." If you take a deep breath, you can smell her aggression. You can also smell fear.

A fit of coughing erupts at the back of the room, a smoker's hack that rasps from the pit of old Jenksy the messenger's lungs.

She folds her arms and glowers him into a petrified silence before she continues. "I want this office to start achievin' targets so make sure you's get your fingers out and pull your weight." An undertow of murmurs follows which perishes in seconds, victim to her steel-sharp stare.

"I'm hands-on, so there's none o' this I-speak-to-your-line-manager-an'-they-speak-to-you nonsense. If I think you're slackin', I'll personally pull you up. Then I'll pull up your line manager for not doing it first." Uh-oh, they've planted a corporate climber amongst us and it's a mass of thorns and barbs.

"I want this office performing handstands and if any of you's are not happy with that, ye can come an' see me. Any questions?" Her eyes scour the crowd for dissent, daring someone – anyone – to go for the gauntlet. Uncle Pete inspects the ceiling. I focus on Della, who's chewing and grinning, enjoying the cabaret.

Renwick Watson raises a lazy hand, which is tame for him – his default has always been to interrupt with confidence. "You seem to think we struggle to achieve our targets," he says in his usual measured manner, "but our understanding is that, on the whole, we meet them." All heads rotate back to Stella.

"I'm not talking about you's meeting YOUR targets, I'm talking about you's meeting MY targets. I want the old objectives exceeded by a mile and I'll do whatever it takes to achieve that. Got it?" All heads turn to our aspiring Mr Christian.

"I take it the union know of your plans?" A collective intake of breath follows and all heads wheel back to Stella.

"I don't care about the union, I'm runnin' this office accordin' to business needs and this business needs to do handstands to keep me happy. Is that clear?"

Renwick's eyes ballot his colleagues for back-up. Several clear their throats as if to speak but, given that at some point he's insulted everyone in the room, they all ignore his appeal.

"Absolutely," he says but rather than let it go, he jettisons all common sense and does the unthinkable.

He sniggers.

Not a full-out laugh, more a derisive snort backed up by an insolent roll of the eyes. Stella casts him a look that reads *Danger – High Voltage*, then draws her eyes off him and ploughs on but something tells me she's filed his one-man-stand away for later.

"A takeover rumour's goin' round and that's all it is – a rumour. Another rumble rolls around the room. She claps twice to silence the drones. "Chop chop. Back to your desks and get on with it. NOW!"

At that she swooshes out through the canteen door, Uncle Pete ambling along behind her, his head dipped in despair. Cat and I trudge towards the exit in ominous silence. If I thought this was scary, how will I cope if she finds out about Gregor?

Oh God, what have I done?

Monday, 28th July, 5.10pm

Rolls of buckram and cloth, packets of leather and an old Singer sewing machine languish on the floor of Ken's office alongside piles of antique books, some worked on, some waiting. On a shelf a half empty cup is quietly cultivating a greenish fungus across the surface of the cold, stale coffee within. Charlie's, probably. While I linger in the office to let Ken demonstrate his gold leaf skills to a customer in the workshop, a wave of nostalgia engulfs me. It's the tang of cut leather mixed with glue and paper dust combined with the eggy whiff of bookbinder's paste.

It's Ken's smell.

It ingrains into his skin and his hair, lingers on his clothes and the sheets he sleeps in, and when we were younger it lingered on me.

I used to adore that smell.

Does she come here? Does she sit in this, his swivel chair? Use his keyboard, his calculator? I drape my jacket over the back of the chair, sit, and try to swallow down the threatening storm. He was *my* husband, *my* territory, for thirty years.

Ken picks this moment to strut through the office door. He's thinner, his face a shade greyer than I remember, his worry lines deepened into crevices. I also take in the stubble on his chin and the wrinkles on his t-shirt.

This isn't Ken; not my Ken.

"Sorry," he says, leans his weight against the edge of the desk and flicks the kettle on, cool as you like, as if the last year never happened. "New client. I tooled a thistle onto the spine for

him. Found the gold leaf work fascinating. He's minted. Wants
Charlie to replace the leather inlay on his antique desk top. It's
lucky the specialist stuff still attracts enough custom to keep the
three of us busy. Coffee?"

"No, thanks," I say and flash my eyes at the mug on the
shelf. "I see Charlie's still using the crockery to develop new
strains of bio-warfare so I'll give it a miss. Where is he anyway?"

He unscrews the lid of the coffee jar, sprinkles some into a
clean mug and adds the newly-boiled water. "Tenerife with his
brother. Stewart left early so it's just me."

"So. Why did you want to see me?"

"Right," he says, peering into his mug, swirling the contents
around and around. "Here's the thing." He looks up. "We need
to get it sorted." He hoists the mug to his lips, blows on the
steaming liquid, tests it with his lips then takes a blood-curdling
slurp.

"Get what sorted?" I ask and he looks at me as if I'm stupid.

"The divorce."

The word hits me like a hammer. A section of my heart, the
corner where my pride used to live, half hoped he felt remorse,
might even ask for forgiveness. But it never thought he'd want
me to divorce him. Batter him, maybe; murder him, definitely;
but not divorce him.

My eyes launch an angry shot across his bows. "Where did
this come from?"

He offers the ceiling a wearied look, scratches his balding
crown and sighs. "I just think it'd be neater all round and it's
difficult for Babs, me still being married to you." He picks up
his mug and takes another shuddering slurp.

It's several seconds before my anger lets me speak and even
then I can only squeeze out eight words past the tightening in
my throat. "And this has *what*. To do. With her?"

The stern face suggests I'm overstepping the line, the same
look a parent might give an errant child. "She won't get
involved with the business while we're still married. Our book-

37

keeper got pregnant and stopped work. We can't afford to take someone on." He twists around and jerks his thumb at the teeming in-tray. "Babs refuses to tackle this lot until we've at least set the thing in motion. We want to get on with our lives, Maggie."

He said *we*. That used to mean him and me. Now I'm me, singular, standing on the outside looking in.

"Really?" I say, "Babs does bookwork?"

"Don't start. She took a course."

"And now that two-bit trollop is blackmailing you into this? Oh *p-leeease*. Since when did you listen to anything but the voice in your own head?"

Fists balled, his eyes scowl around the furniture as if canvassing support from the filing cabinet, the shelves, the desk. "It's not like that," he says, the tell-tale muscle in his jaw tightening, a sure sign I'm about to exhaust whatever temper he has left. This is *my* Ken, a man who can shift from tiptoe to putting in the boot in a blink. My eyes flash and threaten to sear a welt clear across the back of his retinas. "Don't give me that look," he says, "I just need it done and quick."

A neuron lights up, then another, and another, *click, click, click*.

"It's not Babs who wants this, it's you." The failure to blink accompanied by a *tsk* of denial is intended to intimidate but today, I'm not buying.

"Now, you listen to me," he says, and bangs his mug down hard on the desk. A tidal wave of burning hot coffee leaps out, scalding his fingers, saturating an expensive roll of hand-made paper, and dribbles off the edge of his battered old board cutter. He jumps up, whips a polishing rag from his pocket and blots before he gives up and throws the dripping rag in the bin.

Frustrated that his bid to strong-arm me failed, he leans once more against the edge of the desk and drops his voice to a growl. "Cut it out, Maggie. It's over so what does it matter? My uncle's talking about selling up. We're dependant on Babs to get the books up to date before that happens. I want this sorted, and now." He pauses to let me respond but I'm mute, my mouth dry as tinder.

"Look. There's no point paying lawyers," he says through clenched teeth, "I checked the internet, and it's simple. Our pensions are what they are, there can't be much difference in value. We sold the flat and split the profit when we moved to Etta Place. Under Scots law, I can't touch the house, you inherited it, it's yours. I don't want any contents, nothing, I just want out. All we need to do is say we've agreed a settlement, submit the quickie divorce papers to the court and wait for the rubber stamp. The law requires a year's separation, and it will be by the middle of next month, so what's your problem?"

"How kind, what can I say? No. Why should I? Not even a hint of an apology in your attitude."

He treats the back of his neck to a hard rub before he changes tack with no attempt to disguise it. "Maggie, it's ridiculous to stay married under the circumstances." He nods at the burgeoning in-tray. "Maybe if we start the process then Babs might clear some of this backlog, pull in the money we're due and help get the business up to scratch."

Hang on – I consulted the internet too, just after he left. I try to remember… I'm sure he's entitled to some compensation for the house, since he contributed to its upkeep for nine of the last ten years and he's such a tightwad, I can't believe he'd walk away. Yet here he is, acting as if he's casting me a few crumbs when really, it's his entire share of the cake and he's in one hell of a hurry to dump it.

He knows something that I don't.

What if there's a problem with the construction of the house, or an expensive-to-correct subsidence he doesn't want to cough up for?

I realise he's staring, his eyes searching my face for a response. "I'll think about it," I say, to buy me time to delve deeper. "But no pressure – don't phone, don't write, don't come to the door."

His face betrays an impatience but his silence says he needs me on-side and it hits me – for the first time, I've got him in a chokehold and it's exhilarating.

"Don't drag it out to get back at me, Maggie," he pleads.

"It'll take however long it takes." I stand, throw the strap of my bag over my shoulder and stroll casually out of his workroom, out of the building, my car keys jingling in my hand.

My act might have fooled him but it didn't fool me.

Wednesday, 30th July

"You have to start somewhere, so why not with this?" says Cat, and my heart drops. There she goes, Little Miss Duracell, banging on that drum. I should've sat at my desk and kept my oh-so-brilliant life changing plan to myself, but did I? No, I blabbed. Within seconds of me bragging about my scheme, she'd dreamt up an equally brilliant, non-negotiable, pain-in-the-arse counter-plan.

She'd decided to stage-manage Project Me.

And before I could argue, she'd roped me into Rory's annual staff shindig at the Ship Inn this Friday.

Panic Mode, Level 3.

"There's a DJ on Fridays so you can dance your socks off," says she, hands on hips, and pitches me a determined look. It says: *you're not getting out of this, missy.* I mean, the Ship Inn? It's not exactly The Balmoral.

"But it'll be staff only," I say, thinking I've found my get-out-of-jail-free card.

"Rory's their star employee since he landed that contract so he can invite anybody he pleases and since I'm his better half, I say he invites you."

Panic Mode, Level 5.

"You going, Della?"

"Not a chance, McCardle," says Della, her lip a sneer. "Wouldn't be caught dead in the Ship."

I shake my head. "This is way too soon, I need to refurbish and rebrand before I relaunch. The new me isn't due until my birthday – two months away, Cat, not two days. I don't have

41

anything to wear, my hair's a mess…"

"Oh, give it a rest with the whole *woe is me* routine. You've spent way too much time watching talent shows and peering at the world through your ready readers. You say you want a life, well here it is, gift-wrapped."

"I had to lay low to get to this point," I cry, my breath so fast it's making me giddy. "I'll get a life, give me time."

"You won't if you don't make the effort. It's time to chuck the Cinderella syndrome." Her face lights up. "Here's an idea – I'll be your fairy Catmother."

Panic Mode, Level 7.

"How's about I make a concession," she says, "meet you halfway."

I'm panting now, a combination of panic and anger constricting my airway. "*You'll* make a concession?"

"I'll get ready at your place and chivvy you along, 'cos I know you, you'll back out. And I'll pick out your outfit and do your make-up. "Can't wait to get my tweezers into those brows."

Della grins. "It's not tweezers you need, it's an industrial strimmer." And I throw her a scowl.

Cat barges on. "So whadyu think? Deal or no deal? It'll be *fu-u-un.*"

"But—"

"No buts. Deal or no deal?

"No, but—"

"I said no buts."

"For the love of God," cries Della, "say yes before I slit my wrists. You know you're never gonna get peace until you do."

I turn to Cat. "Okay, you win, but no makeovers, I am not going anywhere looking like Aunt Sally." And Cat gives me a *we'll see* arch of one brow.

Panic Mode, off the scale.

"No, Cat," I wail. "I've got nothing to wear, my hair needs a cut, and I was gonna see the doc about some HRT."

Cat rewards me with a snappy look. "So book a day off."

The conversation is halted by the shrill of Cat's phone. Five seconds later she claps down the receiver, gets up and walks out through the double doors leaving me wishing I was someone else, someone more confident, more assertive; wishing I was someone who could stand up for herself.

Wishing I was Della.

She revels in a confidence I never had at her age. I worried over every detail; hair too dull, legs too skinny, boobs too small. And yet, salesmen arranged free delivery on my day of choice; policemen waved me off with a warning for a dodgy tyre; bartenders served me first despite the row of blokes waving tenners at them. I took it for granted, that was the system – men were courteous to women. It never occurred to me they found me attractive. Now I've become the Amazing Invisible Woman and Cat wants me to take the spotlight, centre stage. *Bleuch*. I want to fold up my wings, climb into my crumpled chrysalis and zip it up.

Look out Level 10, here I come.

It dawns that Cat's back at her desk, her face sombre, eyes focussed on her pen.

Finally she looks up. "Maggie, we need to talk. In the training room. Now." I swivel my eyes to Della who looks down and shuffles some papers into a pile then play-acts reading the top sheet to avoid my gaze. "Maggie?" Cat's already at the double doors, waiting. My gut wound tight, we head in silence along the corridor.

The door closed behind us, we wheel a couple of chairs around to face each other and sit. "I've just been called into Stella's office," she says, and I almost stop breathing. "But before I tell you about that, I met Renwick Watson's admin assistant in the ladies loo. Stella's transferred him from Head of Corporate Tax upstairs to managing the messengers in the basement. He's raging."

"*What?* But they rely on his expertise up there; it was a

shambles before he took over. Has he approached the Union?"

"Aye, but she quoted 'business needs' and the Rep couldn't argue. He's still the same grade but his prestige has gone and all his power with it. We need to tread wary, Maggie, she's a vindictive bitch."

I squirm. "How does this affect me?"

She studies the floor for a moment then looks up. "She wants to commandeer you as her general dogsbody."

I swallow hard. "Why me?"

"You're more experienced than Della, and I'm too busy between my own work and covering for Esme. You'd still be on the section, but giving her work priority. It's up to you, but she wants to know, today." A glum look is sketched across her ashen face.

"There's something else, isn't there?"

Her eyes latch onto mine. "Sorry, confidential."

"Does it mean more dosh?"

"Nope."

"Brownie points?"

"Unlikely."

"What's my incentive?"

"There isn't one."

"It's a done deal, isn't it?"

Cat shrugs. "I'm surprised she's asking rather than telling."

I sigh. "Then I'm obliged to say yes," I concede for the second time today and her face brightens.

"Thank you, Maggie, and if she overloads you I'll pitch in. If she's reliant on our wee section, she might give us a break."

An image of the outcast Renwick cast down into our brick-walled basement slams into my head and I cast her a cynical look. "I wouldn't hold your breath, Cat, just don't hold your breath."

Friday, 1st August, first thing

I should get my butt out of bed and kick-start my mission but I couldn't get an appointment at the health centre until Monday and I'm not due at the hairdresser until half past nine so I can lay a while longer. My to-do list had already grown arms and legs, now it's sprouted horns, a tail and a pitchfork. Ugh.

Hang on – I don't have to do it all in one day, do I? I just need to make a start. All I need is one outfit and a bit of make-up. I'll treat the whole experience as a test drive; an evaluation exercise to jumpstart the planning phase of my project. Do you know what? I'm gonna haul myself off this bed and get my backside into gear.

***

It's three o'clock and I've declared the day a disaster.

I showered, then searched through my wardrobe for an outfit with a bit more pizzazz than my usual over-sized clobber. I chose my tightest jeans (baggy), a t-shirt (also baggy) and a casual jacket (baggy baggy baggy). Then I set off for the salon.

My bob sharpened, I hit the Gyle retail centre and it all went downhill from there.

At what point in life does your Fashion Fairy flounce off and desert you? No I don't mean Gok Wan, I mean the one who lives in your head. In your heyday she guided you through the rails whispering sartorial advice in your ear. 'Not those, with your thighs they smack of jodhpurs; yes, the frilly blouse makes you more boobilicious; *STEP AWAY FROM THE LEOPARD*

PRINT CAT SUIT!' Then one day you see some old biddy in the street sporting a sludge-green quilted gilet and think, '*Hmmm*, that's practical, I bet it would keep my back warm. Now, where can I buy one of those?' And before you know it, you're zipping up a lilac anorak and cruising Frumps-R-Us for elasticated waistbands. Not that I shop in Frumps-R-Us, nor do I possess a lilac anorak. Or anything with an elasticated waistband. I don't. Honest.

So, minus my resident stylist I admitted defeat and am now wending my way home, as soon as I've popped into Tesco to pick up milk and tea bags.

I know, I should devise a Plan B, but one per week is just about my limit at the moment.

Geez, I'm knackered.

***

Aren't supermarkets brilliant? I wandered into the clothing aisle and picked up a blue kaftan top, *el cheapo* – my favourite price after *gratis*. They only had skinny jeans but at six quid, they were a snip. *And* I've dropped two dress sizes – yay me! In the shoe aisle, I spotted a pair of flat silvery sandals that are perfect for me. Now I have an outfit, all I need is a new head and a confidence transplant.

Happy face, happy dance, happy happy happy.
Who said this would be hard?

***

Dammit, I can't do this make up thing and I need to finish the job before Cat arrives and takes over. I couldn't be bothered buying cosmetics so I've revived my '80s make-up box and it's not good. Practice makes perfect, Catriona said. Try different looks, Catriona said.

Pah.

My first attempt borders on Pantomime Dame. Attempt number two makes me look anaemic. I decide to postpone make up in favour of a spot of eyebrow topiary. The first pluck smarts so much, my eyes water so I abandon that idea too. Anyway, what if I pluck them into an unnatural shape? Or two different shapes? Imagine – me, at my age, running away to join the circus.

I squint into the make-up bag again. Did I read somewhere that less is more? Or was it more is less? I slap on a slick of cream and apply the minimum of foundation and use an old lippy as blusher.

There. I still look like me, just perkier. A sweep of translucent powder and a couple of strokes of mascara later and I'm done. Uh-oh, there's the doorbell.

Wish me luck, I think I'll need it.

Friday evening, 1st August,
the Ship Inn

I've been struck by lightning.

I bimbled behind Cat into the function suite and without so much as a by-your-leave he struck me down. There he stands, leaning on the bar, all gorgeous and God-like and chatting to some random bloke. Here I stand, in the middle of the floor, all gawky and gawping and glued to the spot. Curlicues of dark, collar length hair wisp around his face and I can see his blue eyes sparkling from here. Think – David Essex, circa 1975. I should know. His poster hung on the wall opposite my bed right up until I met Ken.

"Come to mama," Cat yells to Rory, and he strides over to hug her five foot three, ten and a half stone frame. "Is this a great reward for all your hard work or what?"

"You betcha," says he, "and wait till you get your hands on my bonus."

"Well done, Rory" I shout over the din of the disco and he grins, his shiny scalp a kaleidoscope of colours under the flashing lights. "Thanks Maggie. Hope you enjoy yourself, I realise you don't know many of my workmates."

"Don't worry, I'll get talking to somebody," I assure him, the music pulsing through me from the floor up.

Cat grabs my arm and yells in my ear. "We're in luck, we missed the speeches. *Bo-ring.* Come and meet some people." She drags me by the arm across the dance floor to the far side of the lounge.

But my gaze is drawn back to David Essex and his high

voltage sparks. If I hadn't been disabused of the notion, I'd swear I'm ovulating. I'm almost sniffing the air for his scent.

"This is Julie and her partner Mark; here's Joanne and Denny and – Maggie?"

Her eyes track my gaze.

Damn. Cat's unstoppable. If she works it out she'll drag me over, introduce us and walk away, leaving me to suffer a full-blown personality bypass.

"You minx, that's Eddie over there talking to Rory's mate, Gus. He's one to watch out for, but our Ed's M.W.K. so eyes off."

And now I know his name – Gus.

"M.W.K?"

"Married with kids," she yelps, delighted I fell for her ploy, and Rory laughs too.

"Eddie?" I shout into her ear and wonder what on earth this crumpled sales-type has done to make him worth the watching. "My mistake. For a sec there he looked like one of Ken's customers."

"Forget him," she says, "let's push this table over and tag it onto the end." Rory rushes to help her and drags the table into place. "I'll get us a drink, then I need to circulate with Rory for a bit. You alright?"

"I'll be fine," I insist and scuttle behind the table as soon as her back's turned so I can face the bar, keep him in my sights, and harvest those heavenly darts.

I get a sudden vision of my once-over in the hall mirror before we set off. I remember thinking, are these jeans too tight? The kaftan too bright? The sandals too flash? *And* I congratulated myself on fobbing off Catriona and her makeover.

Now I wonder if the jeans are too baggy, the top too staid, the make up too light. I wish I'd let Catriona airbrush me after all. And I should've bought heels, why didn't I buy heels?

As the booze flows, the chatter becomes louder and more

loud. I've downed three rosé wines now, and from here I have the perfect view of him at his vantage point at the bar. I've chatted here and there with the crowd at my table but the music makes conversation limited and they spend a lot of time on the dance floor, freeing me up to study him.

And believe me, I'm studying him.

Seems he's a charm-school graduate and quite the party boy. A steady stream of people, male and female, gravitate towards his bar stool with much air-kissing and backslapping. Collar open, tie loose, he dispenses little parcels of attention to all who enter his orbit, every man jack of them on the receiving end of that lopsided grin. And the more he grins, the more my heart squirms.

I like the cut of his gib.

My heart sinks. He's a ten who probably hasn't seen thirty-five yet. I'm somewhere between a one and a two and wishing I was twenty years younger. But then, he'd be fifteen and I'd be under arrest for what I'm thinking.

Catriona's voice brings me back with a crash. "Come on, let's refurbish our faces," she says, and hauls me by the arm across the dance floor and into the toilets where she staggers into a stall. I peer into the mirror and shudder. Every one of my trillion and nine years is on display and he'd never be attracted to the likes of me. I squint at my mono-brow. Well, maybe not so much mono as conjoined. If only I had let Catriona attack me with the tweezers and been more adventurous at the hairdresser, maybe changed my style…

I hear a flush and Catriona shimmies out of the cubicle, cheeks bright with the booze, gyrating to the base beat pounding through the walls. She catches my expression in the dim of the glass and tuts. "Oh Maggie, you should've let me do those brows. You argued so much, we ran out of time. A bit of preening would've made all the difference."

"I did my best."

"This is your best?" She stares me up and down. "You did

look in a mirror before you left the house, yes?" She turns to check herself in the mirror.

"But I'm not ready for a big change," I whine, "and I hate taking all that slap back off." I run my wrists under the cold tap to diffuse the hot flush that's trying to break through.

"I see your problem, lady. It's, maybe you'd have to deal with some man or other chatting you up. Confront your insecurities. And you'd rather play safe. You've got to get back out there sometime." My confidence sinks through the soles of my silver sandals.

"Rory's having a good time," I say, my mind bereft of anything to talk about except wonder boy at the bar and I daren't mention him.

Influenced by several white wine spritzers, she goes with the change of direction.

"He is," she slurs. "I'm just thinking, maybe I should've sat you at the far end of the hall with my two single cousins and their pals. I say single – one's divorced, the other's widowed. You're all in the same boat, although they're a wee bit older. They brought a couple of friends they met through their church fellowship group. Come to think of it, I can't believe I sat you with a bunch of couples. Come on, I'll introduce you." She picks up her bag and heads for the door, dragging me by the sleeve. A spike of dread shoots through me; she wants me to sit with the God Squad and with my eyesight I won't be able to see him from way over in the Bible belt.

"NO," I shout and strain against her gorilla grip. She stops and stares, the force of my refusal arousing her suspicions. "Uhm…I'm fine," I garble, "where I am. We're having a brilliant time. Isn't Julie a great girl? She's so interesting to talk to, and that Joanne, she's a hoot."

"OK," she concedes, her addled brain still trying to work out what's going on, "but if you want a change of scenery later…"

What, swap my vantage point to sit at the back of the hall with a pair of fifty-something bible bashers and their pulpit pals? If you anaesthetised me, Cat, you'd still need to drag me kicking and screaming from my spot. No, I'm staying put.

Back at the table Julie and Joanne get me up to dance and I start to enjoy myself, so much so that I can't believe it when they announce the last dance. Everyone floods onto the floor to sing Auld Lang Syne, cheering when Rory and two of his team take centre floor to attempt a drunken highland fling. Conscious of the advancing time, my eyes search for him from the anonymity of the crowd but he's not on the dance floor. When the lights go on I sneak a peek towards his bar stool to steal one last look.

His jacket's gone and so has he.

But wasn't it brilliant while it lasted?

***

In the grip of a hot flush, I toss my keys at the hall table and sit once again on my spot at the bottom of the stairs, my clammy face cupped in my hands. One man, a man who didn't even look at me, has convinced me that I'm alive.

I'd love to turn my life around but I can't. It's not that I don't want to, it's Cat. When Ken left she did what she always does; she took over, and I was so distraught, I let her. Now if I take my plan to the next stage she'll see it as me giving her an inch.

So how do I snatch my life back without losing her?

Monday, 4ᵗʰ August

Umbrella dripping on the carpet, I push through the double doors in mid-curse at my GP for her late-running clinic, and nod a hurried *hi* to Cat. No sign of Della yet but it's only nine o'clock – the crack of dawn on Planet Adeline. I shirk off my jacket, give it a shake then drape it on the coat stand.

"How's it going?" Cat asks, "did you get the HRT? Make an appointment with the Estate Agent?"

"Yep and yep, took the first pill ten minutes ago and the valuator's coming tonigh—" The thwump of the double doors interrupts me and in stomps Stella, an inferno in her eyes fit to set the carpet ablaze.

"Maggie McCardle, my office – NOW!" she rages, and jabs a crimson nail in the direction of the corridor before she turns to charge out again, leaving the doors bouncing on their hinges.

Cat makes a *what the…* face. "Gregor?" I suggest, my teeth clenched so tight I think my jaw might crack, and I almost hear her inward groan.

When I trudge past his open door, Uncle Pete peers at me over the rim of his specs and sends me a tight-lipped smile coupled with a helpless shrug. Deep in my brain a bell tolls.

It's official – I'm dead woman walking.

When I edge through her door a seated Stella jabs that same blood-tipped finger towards the hot seat front of her desk without taking her eyes off her computer screen. I'm doing everything I can to quash the heat mushrooming in my gut but none of it's working. Wait – anything's worth a go. *Emergency – Code Red – woman down… Acht*, there is no sodding cavalry.

If only I'd thought to 'phone in a bomb threat before I ventured along the corridor.

"Is th-there-a p-problem?" I witter as I lower myself into the chair of doom, knowing the solitary replacement hormone I gulped down an hour ago won't have enough muscle to hold back the impending heat wave.

"I would've thought that was obvious." A billiard ball is lodged in my throat and no amount of swallowing will shift it. She draws her black eyes off the screen to pin me with a penetrating glare. "You are aware that trading within the office is a disciplinary offence which can result in dismissal?"

Unsure where this leading, I stare. "S-sure, I've r-read the emails. What does that have to do with m-me?"

"I think you know," she says, her face darkening. This is even worse than the time I was summoned to the headmaster's office after I dunked Potty Pam's head down the loo.

"I hear you're runnin' a part-time self-employed business from work."

Come again?

"I've g-got no idea what y-you're t-talking about." Bugger, I've developed a stutter and I can see her fury mounting.

"Don't you dare insult my intelligence," she thunders. Oh God Oh God, hot sweat; fear pulsing; can't breathe. She rises to her feet, kicks back her chair and plants both hands on the desk, looming like a bird of prey.

I flinch. I shrink.

She goes for the kill.

"I believe your operation is called The Drape Doctor and you do work for your colleagues."

The dragging in the pit of my stomach intensifies. "It's not a b-business, it's just a h-hobby. I do r-repairs and alterations, that's all. Esme nicknamed me The D-Drape Doctor years ago as a joke and it stuck. I never ch-charge."

Stella throws back her head and forces out a contemptuous laugh. "So you're tellin' me you provide this service for nuthin'?

Oh *pl-eeeease*, don't insult ma intelligence. Nobody does work for nuthin'."

"Did you just call me a *liar*?" I boom. Dammit, I didn't mean to sound so aggressive but she poked one of my pet hates and righteous anger overtook the fear. To my surprise she backs off a little.

"Ah'm just sayin' it's no my experience that folks do things for nuthin."

Bolstered by her tiniest of retreats, my voice steadies. "I'm telling you the truth, Stella, and I'm surprised you didn't check your facts before confronting me. Who told you this nonsense?"

"Ah'm not prepared to divulge my source," she says, her voice more bluster than conviction now, "and believe you me, if I EVER find out you're runnin' a business in office hours, you'll be suspended pendin' dismissal. AM-I-UNDERSTOOD?"

I swallow, and hard. "Loud and clear."

"Good. Now I like to keep my eye on all the comin's and goin's along that corridor so you can leave the door open on your way out." She sits, grabs for the mouse and directs her main beams at her screen.

And just like that, I am dismissed.

My mind fogbound, I stumble to the toilets and lock myself in a cubicle. Within seconds the blistering heat of tears stings my cheeks, my vision blurred by the tears pulsing down my bright red face.

The main door to the loos creaks open and I hear Cat's voice. "Maggie?" I let out an involuntary sob as I unlock the cubicle door.

"What the hell…"

"Sh-she handbagged me. Accused me of r-running a business from work," I babble, "the curtains…"

"*Aaargh*, that cow. I could happy-slap her. Any clue where she got this idea?"

"Nope, but she knows it's codswallop. It was as if she'd found an excuse to Rottweiler me and was loath to pass up on the opportunity."

She shakes her head. "Honest to God, it's like Bedlam on a bad day since she arrived. Can I get you something, tea maybe?"

"Tea? Are you kidding me?" I say, and sniff through the tears.

"You're right. Tell you what – go get yourself out of here for a couple of hours. I'll fetch your coat and bag in case you bump into her. No way is she getting the satisfaction of seeing those puffy eyes. If anybody asks, I'll say I sent you to Remote Storage."

Five minutes later I'm heading out of the main entrance in the direction of the shops but all I can think is, I don't think I can cope if she finds out about me and Gregor.

***

I crawled into my car and drove to Musselburgh harbour where I sat on a bench for an hour to detangle my frazzled nerves. I watched a ship crawl lazily across the Firth of Forth, gulls swooping the water for titbits, mums perambulating their babies, but I couldn't see any of it properly through the wall of hurt and the harder I tried to dismantle it, the higher it grew.

Then I spotted them – bees, bizzing in and out of an airbrick within the harbour wall. And the more I studied them, the more my admiration for them swelled. I fancied the little ones were on their maiden voyage; a test mission to ransack the nearby flowerbeds and bring back their plunder in the hope of attaining their 'wings'. Poised on the latticed concrete grid calculating ambient temperature and wind speed, they waited for their in-house air traffic control to signal the all clear for take-off. This was no long lumber-up-to-speed, more a dodgy diagonal ascent, their bumbee tartan bouncing on the breeze, each a mini-paraglider struggling to stick to the flight path.

Then came the jumbos; the 747s in their black and yellow corduroy. Maybe they were scouts setting out on a mission; to seek out uncharted blooms; to boldly bizz where no bee's buzzed before.

Landings were almost synchronised. Their panniers full of pollen I watched them bob and weave, circling the imaginary runway, waiting for clearance to land. Then it was one in, one out as another launched itself through the lacework lattice and up over my head. And not once did I witness a mid-air collision.

Their hypnotic buzzing distracted me; entertained me; soothed me. This is how it should be, I thought, all working as a unit towards the greater good. But their queen doesn't control the hive, oh no. It's a co-operative and she has her job to do, same as the workers, and if she fails then they take a vote, bump her off, and elect a new queen. No regal ramping of expections, no aggro or disapproval, just every co-worker doing what's best to keep the colony going. Live and let live. Bee and let bee.

If the system works for them, why can't it work for us?

***

Three o'clock and no sign of Stella since I got back, but she's left me a huge report to type by tea time and between the phone ringing and Della yattering I'm beginning to panic. I'm busy spellchecking what I've typed so far when the phone rings yet again.

I pick up.

"Maggie? It's me, dear, your mother," as if I'm a bit dense in the voice recognition department. "Wait 'til I tell you this." I glance at the clock and cringe. She prefers to dispense her stories via intravenous drip and the big hand's already doing double time.

"Oh. Right," I say, paying the minimum of attention, and wedge the handset between shoulder and ear in an attempt to keep going with the spellcheck. "Mum, I'm a bit busy."

"Well, I thought, I'm going to treat myself," she says, cutting me off, "you know, like you did. So I went into John Lewis's and bought myself an outfit for the sequin dancing."

"*Mmm*…great," I say, only half listening. "Mum, I'm up to my ears in it, the sequence dancing isn't until Thursday so I'll pop in tomorrow and have a look."

"That awful Daisy Dundas, goes every week," she rambles on, taking no notice of me, "you know the one, tarts herself up like a Christmas tree, has the nerve to look down her nose at *me*, if you please. Has a high opinion of herself, why, I don't know. She's the one who told everybody her grand-daughter was joining the Bolshie Ballet. Huh," she huffs, an expulsion of sarcastic air, "as if any of us believed that tosh. Anyway, I'll have something to say if she's there this week, her husband had a big heart operation and I heard they've put him into one o' those seduced comas. Mind you, hard as nails she is, I wouldn't put it past her…"

"*Mum*," I interrupt, and it comes across snappier than it's meant to. "I'm really busy here."

"Right, sorry, where was I – oh aye, it's black," she cuts in again, still by-passing my got-to-go signals, "with a long skirt and the fitted jacket has a wee mandarin collar and shiny black tube sequins in a flower design at the front. Wait 'til you see it, you'll love it. And there's more…" I close my eyes and swallow. I know the drill: she's rehearsed this conversation in her head and refuses to be deterred from replaying me the full, unabridged version.

"Aye, it sounds lovely but…"

"It was all in the sale," she interjects, ignoring me yet again, "so I thought, to hell with it, treat yourself and guess what? I bought the parasol as well."

Whoa, back up, spellcheck suspended. I straighten up and press the phone a bit tighter to my ear to make sure I'm not mishearing her. "The parasol?" I prompt, my curiosity spiked, and just to be sure, "you bought the parasol?"

She tuts and I just know she's making a nippy face at the

handset. "Yes dear, were you not listening? The *PAR-A-SOL,*" she enunciates, as if I'm not only deaf but dumb as a sideboard to boot. "I bought the par-a-sol. It's identically similar to the rest of the outfit. It's got shiny black tube sequins dangling along the edge and they jiggle when you walk." I visualise her in Victorian garb, long grey hair in a bun, strolling along Portobello promenade twirling her parasol as she goes.

"Mum, are you sure you mean a *parasol?*"

"For goodness sakes, *yesss,*" she says, the words sharp with frustration. "Have you never heard of a parasol? Honestly Maggie, what is *wrong* with you today?"

"Sorry, Mum," I say, "not sure I have. Can you tell me what you do with such a thing?"

"Of course, dear," she coos, delighted to hear me bow to her superior intellect in such matters. "It's the wee strappy vest top you wear under your blouse."

Monday, 4ᵗʰ August, 6pm

"Mrs McCardle? Mr McQueen, Webber and Grant Estate Agents." He taps his watch. "Sorry I'm late." My guilt-o-meter soars since I've no intention of selling. Bald and with feet permanently set at ten minutes to two, he squeezes his Buddha-esque bulk through the front door, his briefcase and clipboard bumping off the wooden jamb.

"Feel free to look around," I say, and stifle a yawn. At somewhere around five foot two the man's a quart in a pint pot. The button of his jacket straining to hold back his girth, he trundles into the living room, deposits his briefcase on the carpet and pats his pockets to locate his electronic measuring device. While one hand is busy blotting his florid face with a hanky, his eyes explore the skirtings, the four corners of the ceiling and everything in between. "The windows need replacing to meet the current standard," he says, his voice coming in puffs, "but it's very sellable. I checked with the local authority and inspected the outside before I came in. The house has no structural problems that I can see and the décor is in good order."

Did he say…?

"Sorry, estate agent-lingo is all mumbo jumbo to me. So it's solid? Not built over mine workings or made of plywood?"

He looks bemused. "Absolutely not. Why ever would you think that?"

At last the God awful cloying in my stomach might stutter to a stop. I shrug a shoulder and try to look indifferent. "Just checking."

60

He goes back to measuring the room and notes down the results while beads of sweat join forces to run down his face and over his various chins. I almost join him in a celebratory flush but thankfully it downgrades into a sort of pinkish glow. "I see no collections of ceramic animals or plates which bodes well for selling, and your drapes…my goodness, they're exquisite." He takes a step back to admire the view, still dabbing his face with the hanky. "I assume you paid the earth for those, I'm aware of how much these things cost, you know."

Oh boy, an unintentional compliment – I can't let that sail pass without planting a flag on it. "I made them myself," I say, and fail to resist a smug little head shimmy. "It's my hobby."

"I'm impressed. My niece is a talented interior designer but she can't sew. She pays a fortune for people to convert her ideas into reality. You're very creative."

I give him my warmest smile but still he's distracted by the curtains. "I have an idea," he says. "If you like, I'll speak to my niece and see if she can put some work your way. It would be marvellous for her to know someone who designs and sews too. Does that sound like something you'd be interested in?"

What, me? Working hand in hand with an interior designer, formulating ideas, bringing them to life? It takes all my resolve not to skip on the spot until a vision of Stella flashes into my head and my glee evaporates.

"I'd love that but I can't, my boss is already giving me gip about the curtain-making, accused me of touting for trade at work this very morning. I don't want to attract any more strife from her."

"But this is separate from your day job, Mrs McCardle, and strictly between you and my Felicity. Most of her work is commercial so it's unlikely your colleagues would be customers, so your boss need never know. I'll pass on your details anyway and you can see what you think."

Clipboard in hand he shuffles from room to room, measuring and taking notes as he goes. "You'll appreciate the market is slow since the recession and most properties are advertised as 'fixed price'," he says when he's completed a circuit of the house. He scribbles some numbers on the back of a card and hands it to me. "Your beige bathroom suite is a bit old fashioned, but if you give the walls a coat of emulsion…" Wow, the handwritten figure on the back of the card is a chunk more than I expected and I realise he's staring, hoping for a positive response.

"Oh," I say and screw up my lips, my face working hard to look disappointed. "This is the most I'd get? I figured at least ten thousand more."

He considers this for a second before he speaks. "I promise you, that's the going rate," he says. "It's not in my interest to under-value and it's the recession, you see. It's in attractive condition but the garden is small and as I said, there's the coloured sanitary ware. Now, all that remains is the paperwork." He bends to rifle through his briefcase. "You'll need a Homeowner's survey done, of course, but I foresee no problems there. I have an authorisation form here somewhere."

Ah.

I didn't think to work out an escape plan. Panic mode, Level 3 hits town and I spout the first feasible thing that comes into my sorry noggin. "Sorry, I need to discuss it with my ex-husband first." The rifling stops dead, his eyes darting up to snag mine.

"But the house is in your name, Mrs McCardle."

I feel my conscience twang. "That's true, but legally we still need his say-so."

He looks at me, suspicious. "I see," he says, and my heart lurches to think that maybe the games up. "Then you have my number, my dear, do get in touch when you've spoken to him."

"Of course. And you'll talk to your niece?"

He nods. "I will." I should have the decency to blush at my own gall, but I'm way too euphoric for that. He makes his excuses, walks out the door and waddles up the path and away, but despite his reassurance about the house, a cold pall of dread descends on me.

The house is sellable, the house is mortgageable, the house is worth a pretty penny, so what's Ken's game? For some reason he's requested express delivery on the divorce, and financial hari-kari isn't his style, not his style at all. I'm being hoodwinked, but why?

I think it's time I went to see a lawyer.

Wednesday, 6th August, 11am

"I didn't know you were coming in today," I say when I see Esme mosey through the double doors. Did I read somewhere that clashing's the new matching? If so, her purple anorak teamed with a baked-bean-blue beanie hat and red sweat pants place her bang on-trend. Her snarl of peppered hair tethered by an alice-band, she's as sturdy as a snowflake at the best of times but since she lost Stanley she's withered away to a wisp.

"You shouldn't be here so soon, should she, Cat?" I say and give her arm a friendly rub.

She shrugs a shoulder. "Had to come in," she says, her voice as thin as a thread, "to hand in my new sick note in person."

"Whyssat?" asks Della, her bubble-gum giving her jaw its daily workout.

"Yon Veitch woman made a big fuss about my doctor writing 'bereavement syndrome' on the last one. Says there's not such a thing. Cat told her it was self-explanatory but would she listen?" She pivots her eyes to Cat. "Did you not tell them?"

"No," I cut in, "we might be pals but she never discusses anything confidential. How can that cow be so callous?"

Esme sighs and looks downcast. "I've never even met the woman and she's giving me grief. Then her royal highness phoned me in person and demanded to know, since I'm not physically incapacitated, why I couldn't hand in my sick note personally. I said I'd given it to you when you came to hang those curtains you altered for me. Dunno why but all she talked about was the curtains after that. She asked me all these questions about them and I got so *confused.*"

64

My squeal startles her.

"Wh-what?"

"Stella accused Maggie of running a business from work, that's all," Cat says and mugs a cease-and-desist face my way. "Don't worry, Esme, Maggie put her straight."

"Sorry, Esme," I say, "I thought somebody was trying to daub me in it, that's all. I know you wouldn't do that."

"But she asked how much I paid you and I told her you didn't charge, honest I did," she protests, mortified that Stella's cast her in the role of snitch.

"Don't worry," I tell her, "she probably needed to chew somebody out and I pulled the short straw."

"Bloody Cruella," scowls Della, "bawling you out when she knew she was talking through her arse."

Esme shakes her head in disapproval. "There's no need for that kind of language, young lady."

"Fine. What-eh-ver. I'll tone it down."

Esme turns her attention back to me. "I only risked coming because Cat said the woman had an all-day meeting upstairs so I sneaked in and handed the thing to Pete instead. I'll stay and go to the canteen for lunch with you before I head off, if that's alright."

"Sorry, Esme," I say. "Can't today, I'm seeing a lawyer at twelve, in fact I'll need to leave in a minute. Maybe Cat and Della…" She's not listening. Something over my shoulder has caught her eye and caused her jaw to fall slack. A knee-jerk reaction, I glance around for the merest second to see what's spooked her and cringe. It's Gregor, strutting towards us looking all full-witted and nerd-free, and with the gait of a man in a too-small truss. He could double for the Managing Director in his get-up of grey suit, pink shirt with toning tie and trendy new specs. Barriers up, blinds down and with a stick up his shirt tail, he's hugging a buff folder to his chest doing his damnedest to avoid catching my eye.

Cat and I exchange the merest of glances. Della folds her

arms, chomps on her gum and smirks. He struts up to Cat's desk, opens the folder and lays it down in front of her. Puzzled, Cat scrunches her brows in a request for clarification. "Petty cash," he says, his voice tight, "you forgot to sign it."

While he runs a hand down his tie, Cat mutters a stilted 'sorry', signs her name, closes the file and hands it back. He strolls off on stiff legs towards the Finance room, the folder under his arm, and I'm sure I heard him let out his breath when he reached the corner. Esme's eyes despatch a silent query to Cat; Cat punts it to Della; Della transfers it to me; I turn to Esme and complete the relay.

"He turned up at work dressed like 'Man at C&A' last week and that's been him ever since," I tell her, "and the new version's had a personality upgrade. No more techno-talk, suddenly he's geek-chic. At least, that's the goss from Smoker's Corner in the car park."

While Esme's befuddled brain processes this, Della blows a bubble till it pops, making Esme jump.

"Still gives me the heebie geebies," Della mumbles. "Rumour is he uploaded the new persona via flash drive. Probably in suppository form, given the haemorrhoidal walk." She sniggers under her breath at her own joke. "Either that or he's shat himself." Esme is so fazed by his renovation that this lapse in language skates past her unnoticed. She stares after him with a beatific look, as if receiving divine direction. After a lengthy silence she clears her throat, and all three of us wait for her reaction.

Her face is still thunderstruck. "Well, well," she declares, "fuck me."

Wednesday, 6th August, just after noon

Surely this acne-embroidered youth can't be a lawyer. The limp handshake doesn't inspire me and with a name like Brady Bannister, he sounds more cartoon character than legal eagle.

Intros over, we've just sat down when the door opens and in strides a mature man, propelling the flame-haired boy off his chair. "Simon Scobie, Senior Solicitor," says he, offering a firm grip. "Young Brady here is my intern so, if you don't mind, I'll take the lead."

Now, this guy looks the part – commanding, distinguished, and sharp of suit, he oozes affluence right down to the Rolex glittering on his sun-baked wrist. Mr Scobie unbuttons his jacket, pinches his trousers up by the knees and sits on the chair vacated in his honour by his understudy. Just to reinforce that I'm batting out of my league, he flashes me his Hollywood smile, the one that probably cost him the price of a Mercedes Roadster, while Baby Barrister pulls up a chair alongside.

"So," says he, clasping his hands and resting them on the desk, "how can we help?"

I explain my husband's pushing for a quickie divorce – there has to be a catch. I say, he seems happy to walk away – out of character. I tell him, there's something he knows that I don't – I need to know what, preferably before I sign the dotted line.

I hand him the box file containing all the official documents I could find plus a note of the house valuation and Baby Barrister makes a pretence of reading over the boss's shoulder while his elder scans through the pages, separating them into two piles as he goes. Voices lowered, they mumble back and forth, Senior Solicitor pointing to this and that, each scrawling notes for the other to read. All I can hear are murmurs, the rustle of paper and the ticking of the grandfather clock in the corner.

After what seems like an eternity, Senior Solicitor speaks. "As you thought, he is entitled to half the contents, not to mention compensation from the house due to his financial input. It's not much but he does seem to be losing out for the sake of speed."

"His reasoning is, he doesn't want expensive legal bills. He says the one would offset the other so there's no point."

He smiles and nods this way and that, an indication he agrees with Ken to a degree, then goes back to his deliberations. Baby Barrister waits while his mentor stares again at the sheets and strokes his thumb along the square edge of his jaw. His acolyte is waiting for the magician to pull a rabbit out of the hat and I can see that Mr Scobie doesn't want to disappoint his pupil. A tense minute later he sits back and at the very last moment delivers me a congenial smile.

"Do you have insurance?"

"Nope, he didn't believe in putting his money where his mouth couldn't get at it."

Frustrated, he abandons his chummy pretence and returns to scouring the sheets, his tanned fingers tapping the desk. A few moments later his eyes light up. "What about your pensions?"

"Can't be that, they're almost equal," I say, oblivious to the lurking danger.

This time the smile is victorious, verging on a non-verbal *gotcha*. "No, they are not, Mrs McCardle. Yours is final salary, his isn't. According to these forecasts from last year, his pension has a value of around a quarter of the sum yours will achieve."

Why has the room gone suddenly cold?

"Has he requested his share?" he enquires, his black eyes glowing victorious as he moves in for the kill.

What, Ken's due a slice of the pension that I've worked for thirty years to build up while he refused point blank to buy a personal pension and did God only knows what with his income?

I don't think so.

I shift in my seat, uncross my legs, clear my throat. "Uhm... no, he seems to think they're on a par."

With a triumphant flourish, he throws the pages at the desk, relaxes back and meshes his fingers across the front. of his waistcoat. "But they're not and it is his right," he says with a smirk of self-satisfaction. "If he were made aware, he might consult a solicitor after all. His share of your pension combined with his compensation for nine years of contributing to the upkeep of the house and the value of half the contents could come to a pretty penny. More than enough to justify any legal fees he might incur."

God, he's good. As hoped, he's uncovered some hidden meat on the carcass and the fact that it's not Ken's end of the carcass but mine doesn't stop him chasing a chunk for himself. "Once we've apprised him of the situation, you can go ahead and divorce with a clear conscience that everything is above board," he says, imperious, as if I have no choice in the matter. "Mrs McCardle? I see you're perplexed but I assure you he is entitled to it. I'll get in touch and ask whether he wants to go ahead and stake a claim. Now, if you could just authorise me to make contact..." The words waltz off his tongue, issued no doubt in the same, casual way Dr Shipman might have said *if you could just roll up your sleeve*; a directive disguised as a request in the empirical knowledge that the recipient will acquiesce to their natural, God-given authority, and do what they're asked – nay – told to do, with no thought for themselves.

Think, woman, think.

I catch my breath as a vision of Monday's curtain crisis flashes into my head. I rise to my feet, plant both fists on his desk Stella-style and stare into his heartless eyes for a moment longer than even he finds comfortable.

He flinches.

I'm in.

"I came here to get advice on my situation," I scowl, contempt seeping through every syllable. "I don't think informing my husband of his rights against me is part of the deal."

Baby Barrister moves to block me but his idol holds up a hand, his signal for the boy to hold fire, and smiles a humourless smile. "But he should be made aware," he continues, reproving me, "he has a legal right." Damn, what is it with me, men, and betrayal?

"You are not my moral compass, Mr Scobie," I inform him, astonished that this is the first phrase to pop into my head since it seems to fit the situation. "I need time to weigh up my options. If you contact my husband, I'll report you to the Bar, or the Ombudsman, or whoever you people answer to." My mind devoid of anything else intelligent to say, my voice trails off and the next thing I hear coming out of my mouth is a wobbly, "So thank you for your time and goodbye."

Dammit, I've lost the plot and with it my credibility. But when I turn to flounce out I realise my paperwork, complete with Ken's work's phone number, is still there on the desk in two piles in front of him. Hands shaking I swing back around, grab them up, and high-tail it out of the room, along the hall and past reception to hurl myself out through the glass front doors, down the steps and onto the street, not taking time to watch where I'm going.

Wham! I collide with a passing pedestrian, throwing her up against the kerbside railings, my paperwork exploding out of my shaky hands and up into A4 confetti, a one woman tickertape parade aided and abetted by a sudden gust of wind.

"I'm so sorry," I yabber, my heart pounding in my throat, and grab the woman by the arm to help her upright. "Wasn't watching where I was going." She bends to slap street dust off her knees while I make a flustered attempt to gather up the sheets before they're carried away by the breeze.

"No worries," she says, "I was in a daydream myself." She smiles up at me.

"Don't I know you?" she asks. I'm staring at a grey-haired woman who's dressed like the leader of the Women's Guild and she does look familiar.

Her eyes spark. "It *is* you," she says, "Maggie Baxter, from school. It's me, Fran Henderson."

I gasp. "Fran? Well, fancy that, how are you?"

"Great," she says, "and you haven't changed a bit."

"Neither have you," I say, repaying the fib, and compound the lie with yet another porky. "It was your hair that threw me. What are you up to these days? You went off to Uni after sixth year and I lost track."

"I'm in Management Consultancy. Did a degree in Personnel at Glasgow Uni, moved to London, got married, raised two boys, went back to work. What about you – married? Kids? Where do you live?"

I take a moment to work out how to apply a positive spin and decide to parrot her potted history. "Still here, in the People's Republic of Monkswood, in a semi on Etta Place," I tell her. "I was married, but we split up last year. Never had kids so I'm on my own now."

Her attention is split by the honk of a car horn from across the street, the driver waving to her through the open window. "Got to go, but I'd love to get together before the job finishes up here. If you're free Friday night, I'm staying with my brother in town. We could meet up for a drink."

"Absolutely," I say. "How's about The Dome in George Street, eight o'clock?"

"It's a date," she says, and spins around when the horn honks again. "*I'm coming,*" she mouths and turns back to me. "Better dash, my lift's getting impatient – see you Friday." And just like that, she's gone.

Geez, that took me back.

At age eleven, my notion of high school being promotion to

the big league crash-landed on day one when a feral second year bruiser decided me and my lunch money were fair game. I know, poor me, break out the violins, what can I say. But along came Super-Fran, a sixth form prefect who chased her off. After that Fran became my champion.

And after Mr Scobie's performance today, I think I'll need a champion.

Wednesday, 6th August, 1pm

"Maggie, I'm so sorry," says Cat, "the firm represented Rory's mum when she sued her builder and she fairly sang their praises."

"Not your fault," I mumble through a mouthful of tuna sandwich, and take a swig of coffee to help wash it down, all the while keeping one eye on the Mint Aero winking at me from my open drawer. "I'm sure if I rifled through his designer crimp I'd find three sixes."

Della's face depicts the extent of her tedium. "He's a lawyer, what did you expect?"

"What are you gonna do?" cuts in Cat, "it's a lot to lose."

"Dunno. Ken's legally entitled but what about morally? I know he can be a bit slapdash on details but it's not like him to lose out. I'd love to know, what's the rush?"

"Why should you care?" says Cat. "Ask yourself, If the wellie was on the other foot, what then?"

Della makes her are-you-stupid face. "All you'd see is his heels kicking up dust, that's what. When did he last crack a smile, for Gawd's sakes? The guy's a straight-up, double-dyed, torn-faced control freak. Why play fair with him, he never played fair with you."

"Aye, and what about me?" I demand, latching onto the anti-Ken vibe.

"*Yesss*," says Della, and punches the air, "about time, McCardle. Get those papers filled in, signed and sent to the court," she commands, the tap of a fingernail underscoring her every word.

"But I don't want to look too keen after fobbing him off. He's daft, not stupid."

I hear the double doors thwump open and spot Della's eyes brighten when she sees one of the young auditors currently housed in the training room – a baby-faced boy with a shy smile. Pink of cheek and blue of eye, he strolls past our section towards the Finance office. She lowers her head and pretends to be writing but her radar is tracking his every move. I glance at Cat who's leafing through her desk diary, oblivious to the ritual scene playing out before me. Three strides in he chances a glance Della's way and they lock eyes for the merest moment before his pink turns to red and he looks away. Della smirks and adds another scalp to her overcrowded belt.

"Here's an idea to cheer you up," Cat shrieks, tagging my attention. "Rory and I are going to Mr Chow's this Saturday with his team. It's time you took Project Me to the next level so why don't you join us?"

A pulse throbs in my gut. "Erm, I don't have anything new to wear yet and I feel like such a frump and…"

What if he's there? What if he speaks to me? What if he doesn't? I can't, I just can't…

She gives me a smug look. "I was gonna suggest this soon anyway so I'll just bring it forward. I'm off this Friday, and the section's up to date, agreed?" I nod, the knot in my stomach tightening. "And Stella won't be here, she has a meeting in Glasgow with the District Director. Maybe it's time we gave Project Me a push. We could take Friday off, pamper ourselves, get dolled up for Saturday. Me and Rory are off on our hols a week on Friday so I need some new holiday gear anyway."

My heart shifts up a gear. "You've already been away this year, how many holidays are you two having?"

"Don't change the subject," she says. "We can get our hair done, our brows waxed, buy new make-up. It'll be *fu-u-un.*"

"B-but I've just had my hair trimmed and I coloured it myself last week."

"What shade do they call that, *Hint of Carbolic*?" I'm tempted to mention her rust-ridden locks but elect to hold my tongue. "Go on, you'd so suit a lighter colour," she says, "get highlights. Go blonder. What do you think, Della?"

"What-eh-ver, Kitty-Cat. I'm not getting involved," says Della, without so much as glancing up from her screen. Undeterred by this lack of support, Cat keeps going. "Here's the good part. I'll pay for the hair, the beauty treatments, the make-up – call it an early birthday pressie."

"My birthday isn't for another month yet," I wail, "don't bring it any closer. And I can't let you pay for all that."

"Rory's landed a few good contracts recently and he gets his bonus next week," she says, "five figures, we're flush. How do you think we can afford this last minute jaunt to the Maldives?"

"For Chrissakes, let her do this or you'll never get any peace," skirls Della, "none of us will. Me, I'd grab with both hands..." And she fires a hopeful grin in Catriona's direction.

"I need you to hold the fort, Della. Come on, Maggie, it's just one day..."

"Let me think about it," I say to give me time to dig a tunnel but she's already on her feet and starting her victory dance.

"I'll take that as a yes and get right onto making the appointments. I just *lurve* girlie bonding," she says, and picks up her phone to make the calls. My shoulders droop – she's taking over again, putting pressure on me again, making my decisions again.

How the hell do you stop a one-woman steamroller?

Five minutes later she's back at my desk counting off the arrangements on her fingers. "Nine o'clock – hair at Blow on George Street, half eleven – brow wax at Elements on Rose Street, half past twelve – lunch at L'Amuse Bouche. After that we hit Princes Street." In the depths of my purse my credit card lowers its head and groans. Bang on cue her desk phone shrills and when she picks up to deal with the call, Della flashes me a might-as-well-give-in smirk.

Bleuch.

As a distraction, I try to picture myself post-makeover. Blonde, eh? Maybe not, but a few highlights could work. And as you know my brows are as nature intended – not full hairy angel status; not even Madonna-in-the-eighties, but in need of attention.

Stop... What am I doing, talking myself into this? The moment she drops the handset back onto its base I swivel in my chair, resolved to tell her to back off, but she pipes up before I can get a word in.

"I meant to say, there's this guy, Angus, works with Rory." My breath slows to a stop. She's busy scratching her head with the benign end of her pen. "He was at the Ship, talking to that guy Eddie you thought you knew." I pause to formulate a response that won't betray me but my cheeks have dibs on most of the blood in the bank leaving insufficient funds to operate my brain.

"Who?" I cough and give my chest a pretend thump, all thoughts of bawling at her dispelled.

Distracted, she opens her drawer and rifles the contents. "Anybody seen my stapler? It's gone walkabout." I hold my breath for fear she'll lose the thread, but she picks up where she left off and keeps going. "Anyway, Gus – he asked Rory, who was the girl in the blue floaty top? I didn't see anybody else in a blue floaty top, did you?" I shake my head, pick up my pen and scribble on a paper scrap, concentrating as if I'm writing down the combination to the secret of life itself. "Did you speak to him at all?" she asks, still preoccupied with her search and recover mission. Now she's on her feet and heading for the stationary cabinet to expand the quest for the missing stapler.

Ahem, choke. Cough. Thump. Ahem.

"Never met him." Cough, choke, choke, cough. "Sorry, frog in my throat."

"Hmmm. He must have meant somebody else," Cat mutters, her eyes scanning the inside of the cupboard. "You know what men are, especially when they've had a few. No matter, I'm sure Rory said he'd be there on Saturday, along with Jo and Denny, and blah-de-blah blah."

I zoned out after *he'll be there*.

He's been a busy boy this week, popping up everywhere – in the shower, at work, in the car. Now I have an opportunity to get the lowdown and I can't let it pass. "Who is he anyway?" I say and try to make it sound casual.

"Just one of the gang," Cat mutters, still playing hunt-the-stapler. "Never married. Broke up yet again with his long-term on-off girlfriend a couple of months ago, has a toddler he dotes on. Think they thought the baby would settle them down but it's been a while now. Not sure what happened, Rory's hopeless with details."

Then Cat utters the magic words. "She's a few years older than him, you know. He must like being mothered or something." I could jump up and kiss her right here, right now, but instead I issue a detached '*Uh-huh*,' and continue to stare at my screen. Stapler located, she slams the cupboard doors shut, oblivious to the shimmering sphere of hope she's dropped in my lap.

But wait – he's way out of my league. If he walked up to me, I'd have a guaranteed one hundred per cent mental malfunction. But I could admire him from a distance, couldn't I? Just like at the Ship. It's not stalking, it's surveillance. A stake-out, if you will. Maybe Scotland Yard do training courses. I could...

"*Maggie*," Della prompts, the swing of her eyes signalling that Cat's still waiting.

"OK, you win," I tell Cat, and try to sound indifferent. "Tart me up, turn me out, I'll go." She studies me with genuine surprise and I shrug my response. "Why not," I tell her, "I enjoyed last Friday and you're right, I do need to get out more." Then I add, "and practice. No point getting overhauled on a Friday and staying in on the Saturday."

"But you sat in the same seat with your back to the wall all night," she says, confused by my about-face.

"Christ, Cat, give her a break," spits Della. "First you hassle her 'cos she won't go. Then you hassle her 'cos she will. What's your problem?"

"Nothing," Cat says, "nothing at all." And, happy to get her way, lets it go.

I allow myself an inner smile. This time I mean business so she can wave her blusher brush wherever she likes. Look out, Project Me, I'm comin' atcha full throttle.

Lordy though, am I bricking it or what?

Friday, 8th August

Cat and I set off at half past eight this morning. I half expected to come home looking like a drag queen but do you know what? I don't look too bad. Quite good, in fact. Low expectations = big woohoo when a Plan B exceeds its remit. I had to fend her off a few times, like when she got all insistent about a too-short dress and again when she vetoed the one I liked, which made the effort to cover the parts her dress refused to meet. But overall her advice was sound. Now when I inspect myself in the hall mirror, whadya know – it's changed its tune. It's not that I look twenty-five; heaven forfend; I just look like me with va-va-voom.

Brian at Blow lifted my dreary bob with shades of caramel, toffee and deep mahogany then styled it shorter and choppier with flicks and a side-swept fringe. Then he rough dried it and teased it into place with product. If you screw your eyes up tight, from a hundred yards or so I resemble Natasha Kaplinski.

Almost.

At Elements, the brow wax acted as an eye-lift. Then Catriona dragged me into Jenners make-up department where she'd booked me in for a make-over. The beautiful and gifted Paige gave me a master class in cosmetic nip-and-tuckery and before you could chant *carpe diem* her mascara wand had magicked up a spell to match any hocus pocus the Potter kid could conjure, after which Cat spent an embarrassing amount buying me just about everything Paige recommended, and then some. How much? Too much. But when I saw my reflection – wow.

She'd brushed away a trolley-load of years and a bucket-load of stress. My skin, which used to groan 'one careless owner who couldn't be arsed' now purrs 'dewy with a hint of peachy blush'. Smokey eye shadow in the socket, a bit of kohl pencil and lengthening mascara worked wonders. Nude lip gloss completed the look. Then she showed me the easy way to clean it all back off.

After that we went to L'Amuse Bouche for a four star lunch and I swear to God, the Rufus Sewell-type waiter gave me a cheeky wink which made my cheeks bloom. That said, the sun streaming through the window might have flashed in his face. Or maybe he had something in his eye. Hah, listen to the old me. Nope, far as the new me's concerned, he fancied the pants off me.

Talking yourself up really does work.

"Time to hit the shops," mumbled Cat, dabbing her mouth with her napkin. "Whose style do you admire the most?"

I pitched her my best thinking-it-over face but I already knew the answer. "Adele's."

"Adele, the singer?"

"Della, you numptie. Della from the office. But she's way younger than me."

"But her style isn't – effortless, ageless, chic – we can work with that. Come on, your capsule wardrobe awaits." And off we went again.

We fairly flew along Princes Street in search of the three little words every girl lives for – half price sale. Frasers, Next, Wallis, Warehouse – we hit the lot and my credit card skimmed through the tills so many times it developed skid lines. I bought skinny jeans and dressy tops, cargo pants and t-shirts, a tunic-style blouse, a short silky dress and black three-quarter length leggings to wear with it. Accessories – scarves, jewellery, belts. A stone coloured casual jacket. And heels, two pairs – oh, how I love those heels, a thing I could never wear when I was with Ken. Add a pair of flat black be-jewelled pumps and an oversized bag and voila – the best three hundred and seventy-five quid I've ever spent.

Fine feathers, it could be said, make fine fifty-year-olds and I'm no exception.

Cat insisted I get measured for a bra and it turns out I'm not a 38B, I'm a 34DD. I have bazookas! Once they're hoiked up into my fancy new balconette bra they look amazing.

The fact that I also purchased an item of shapewear which entombs my torso in orthopaedic beige is neither here nor there. A girl's gotta do what a girl's gotta do.

I've had more grooming than a prize pooch and it's time to unzip my cobwebby cocoon and climb out into the light.

I'm seeing Mr McQueen's niece tomorrow and if it all works out, I might earn enough to keep the refurb going without Stella catching on.

Fuddy-duddy forty-nine going on a hundred? Not Maggie McCardle. Watch out world, as of today Project Me is well and truly launched.

Friday evening, 8th August

Once the Royal Bank of Scotland, The Dome is now an uber-swanky bar, restaurant and conference centre, and the last word in class from its stained glass ceiling to the brass trim around its mahogany bar. Tonight its inner sanctum is jam-packed with hand-tailored suits and designer handbags while a pianist tinkles his way through the American songbook.

The new, prototype Maggie is waiting for Fran at a table for two with a glass of rosé, and looking smart but casual in skinny jeans with a navy two-in-one top, a stone coloured casual jacket and the bejewelled pumps. Bazookas are set to 'stun'. Clothes don't maketh the woman but they don't half make a hell of a difference and the same goes for hair and make-up. Every now and then I fluff up my layers on the sly. Do I spy a hunk in a suit at the bar making eyes at me, just like Rufus Sewell at lunchtime? *Hmmm*, maybe he's muchos myopic. Or muchos blitzed.

Hey, if I say he's lookin', then he's lookin'. Is self-delusion the best thing ever or am I kidding myself?

Hair – check.

Make-up – check.

Confidence – check.

Rating Update – by daylight: 3, by candlelight: 4.

Progress indeed.

Hey world, get a load o' me. I've developed a deliberate saunter and am practising eye contact with complete strangers, first in the street and now in the bar, unwilling – nay – unable, to wipe the painted smile off my face. And people smile back.

Result!

Ten minutes late, a harassed Fran pushes through the door wearing beige canvas slacks and a pink V-neck sweater. She almost rushes past me until I grab her arm and speak. "Fran, I'm here," I say and she does a double take.

"Bloody hell fire, I didn't recognise you. Oh, sorry, that's cheeky..." She sinks into her chair, gawping at me.

"No, it's fine, I've been busy since I last saw you. Whadyathink?" I stand up to do a twirl and she peers into my glass.

"I don't know what that pink stuff is, but I want some," she says, her eyes still trying to take me in. A waiter appears to take Fran's wine order while she wiggles her butt to the back of her chair one bum cheek at a time and settles down.

She tells me about her twins. Michael is a property developer with a growing portfolio of luxury homes to rent who's married with two kids. Richard is single, gay and the Marketing Manager of a Scottish hotel chain. Her husband works with equities, which I've never understood but I decide not to say so in case I make myself look dippier than I already am. They're in the process of building a designer house tailored to their own specifications, and she gives me the lowdown on her new home.

Me, I tell her about my two bedroomed end-terrace in Monkswood, gloss over the beginning and the end of my marriage and side-step the twenty-eight years in between.

"Are you over the break-up?" she asks. I give this some thought. I am, I say, and tell her about his divorce offer and my fears of redundancy.

"I thought you worked at the solicitors where we 'bumped' into each other."

"No, I work at Manders and Healey, the accountancy firm further along the High Street."

She sits up a little straighter. "Interesting. How long have you worked there?"

"Over thirty years, man and boy," I jest, but it feels sad, not funny. "I sat my 'O' levels and got good passes but I didn't stay on," I tell her. "I started as a typist then computers came in and our workload dropped. Now we're now called Secretarial Support and when we're not producing specialist documents, we're inputting data or scanning stuff into the files."

"What's the office like?"

"A nightmare. Our old boss retired and for some reason they've brought in an odious super-bitch to run the place."

"What's she doing to cause such distress?" And once I start, I can't stop. I tell her about Stella's self-introduction to the staff; about the escalating targets and her banishment of Renwick; her questioning the term 'bereavement syndrome' on Esme's sick note; how she twisted what Esme told her about me altering her curtains; I finish with Felicity McQueen's offer and how I'm terrified to take the work in case Stella finds out and uses it against me.

Fran looks horrified. "She doesn't have the right to dictate what you can or can't do outside of work, so long as there's no security risk."

"Hah, saying it's one thing, coping with her is another. She'd go mental. She's not a devotee of the pat-on-the-head-and-a-sugar-lump style of management, she's pitched her tent in the spare-the-rod camp and I'd rather not go there."

Fran sucks air through her teeth. "Sounds like she's got you all running scared. What about the Union?"

"Our rep's a wimp at the best of times, he's terrified of her. She does all this on the edge of the rulebook and keeps quoting 'business needs' and he just accepts it."

"I can't believe any manager still uses those tactics, they're so Dickensian," she says and picks up her glass.

"Ho ho, you haven't met Stella," I say with a wilting look, and decide it's time to change the subject for fear of killing the mood.

Two hours later we drain the last of our drinks and pull on our jackets to go home. We've already swapped phone numbers and promised to keep in touch by the time we descend the steps of the Dome and walk out onto George Street.

I scrunch up my nose in apology. "Sorry if I went on a bit about work but, oh, it felt good to get all that off my chest."

"Not at all, I found your stories fascinating and it's just so good to see you. Hopefully we'll meet again, sooner rather than later."

And at that, we hug and say our goodbyes.

On my own little tourist trek, I meander past the still-lit shop fronts of George Street, gasping at the designer price tags. Somewhere along the breeze I hear a piper playing *Highland Cathedral* and I stop, close my eyes and let the music weave around my heartstrings. The pipes always bring a lump to my throat, it's my birth right. This is my city, the place I call home, the place where things might finally be going my way.

When I turn on my heel to absorb the grandeur of the New Town's Georgian architecture, the sight of my image in a plate glass window brings me to a standstill. I stare, and the new Maggie stares back. We're sympatico, these buildings and me, the old embracing the new, still standing after all these years, the original fabric intact but refurbished and rebranded for a new era.

All is well in Maggieworld.

Tell me, does it get any better than this?

Saturday morning, 9th August

I'm not sure what I expected of Felicity McQueen but her poreless skin, platinum hair worn in a smooth chignon and snooty expression all taunted *better than you* before she'd even crossed my threshold. Now little Miss Lah-de-dah's sashayed her stick-skinny Chanel-suited butt into my hallway, one impeccably plucked brow arched in disapproval, and is turning her pitch-perfect nose up as if I've set free a particularly earthy pong.

She grants me a cool two second smile followed by a condescending sniff and proffers a lily-white hand, which I attempt to shake just as she pulls it away leaving me grasping the tips of her fingers.

"Felicity McQueen, City Interiors," she enunciates in slow, deliberate tones like a 1950s newsreader but she's not looking at me, she's running a critical eye over my hall from the carpet and up the walls. My eyes track hers, trawling for faults. Oh crap, looks like half the cast of Arachnophobia are squatting up there; it'll take a million gigawatts of cyclone technology to clear that lot and I'm sure I saw her shoulders give the daintiest of shudders. The woman is surrounded by an invisible four-foot-in-diameter exclusion zone. She clears her throat to indicate she's about to strew her precious gems of prose towards my undeserving ears and I should listen up.

"My uncle informs me your drapes are a dream," she articulates in slo-mo, "but he's no expert so I'll be the judge of that." She eyes me the way a pedigree poodle might eye a stray then swans into the living room uninvited to stand square in front of the bay window. She looks up, her cold eyes mapping my lounge curtains in a grid pattern, up, across, down, across, appraising every inch, scoring them out of a hundred. Her facial muscles twitch and flicker in an attempt to crumple her features, but all they can muster is a restrained frown. Clearly she's botoxed to the max. Or part-cryogenically frozen and it's restricting her muscle movements. She steps back and twirls a lazy finger at my coffee and cream curtain and roman blind ensemble. "And you do all this on your little domestic sewing machine?"

"Yes, I do. Our – sorry, my – second bedroom is a workroom and I have a cutting table and over locker. I'll show you if you want."

"I'm not interested in the process, just the end result," she interrupts, tilting her head to confer a wisp of a smile on me, a smile which fails to invade her cheeks therefore has no hope of making the trek to her eyes. From her attitude I can tell she thinks the conversation in her head is much more riveting than any she's likely to have with me. "I'd like to view your other window dressings." She's already drifting towards the stairs minus my say-so, with me teetering behind.

"No, go ahead. Can I say, I also made the bedspread, and the matching…"

"*Yesss*," she fizzes with a note of impatience, "I know. Uncle Herbert told me *all* about it."

His name's Herbert? I wonder if he was ever spotty.

She puts a foot on the bottom step and makes to climb but when I pull up behind her she freezes. Without turning she raises an authoritative forefinger. "I'd rather see for myself," she says, "if you don't mind." And floats up the stairs and into my bedroom. *Aaargh*! She's been here all of three minutes and already I feel like the hired help in my own home. As if the marching band in my gut isn't enough to cope with, I hear a snap in my head. A little piece of brain matter exploding. Or the rubber band that is my tether creaking under the strain.

I'm still trying to work out how to smack her and get away with it when she starts back down the stairs, brushing a shoulder with one hand as if the very air in my home is depositing dust on her smart suit jacket. I bite down on my lip till I think it might bleed.

"The standard is acceptable," she drones and comes to a deliberate stop on the second last step, making her appear loftier than she is. "I won't need you to design as such, I do my own drawings, but I understand from my Uncle you make your own paper patterns for swags and such. Ideal, you can do that for me too. Now, I suppose you'll want to know about remuneration," she says, as if payment is a dirty word.

In an attempt to quash my rising anger I take a moment and count to five. "I've compiled a chart of charges and printed it out," I say, and reach out to pick up the sheet of typed A4 I left on the hall table. "You'll see from this that I..."

"All very well," she cuts in, dismissing the offer of my chart, "but I'll pay you the same as I pay my other workers so that thing's of no interest to me. I have several women who do such work so it's up to you whether you accept my terms." She opens her bag, pulls out an A5 leaflet with rates of pay printed on it and hands it to me, but all I can think is, I wish I wasn't terminally polite. I'm working hard to be civil but much as I try, I can't gain any ground with her. It's like a game of draughts with me on the defensive and every move I make not only captures three of my markers but sets me up for the next hit. My stomach swirling with frustration fuelled by one part disappointment, one part desperation, I decide it's a bad idea to make a spot assessment, although I'm sure Frosty the Snowman would be warmer to deal with so the job's not so attractive any more.

"I'll read this over and get back to you," I say, deferring a decision until I can think straight, "but if I do this, it has to be confidential. I don't want my boss to find out."

"Not a problem, Mrs McCardle, I prefer that no one knows

of our arrangement, therefore I also require your discretion." A smile threatens to grace her lips but thinks the better of it and retreats while she awaits my response.

"Of course," I say, unsure why she wants secrecy since she's a legitimate business, all VAT registered and above board.

"For my part I'll provide the materials, delivered to you by Joy, my PA, with measurements and/or drawings of what's required and a completion date. I cannot stress strongly enough that you must meet my deadlines for delivery," she says. "I simply cannot have my customers let down. When a job's completed you'll contact Joy. She'll pick them up. After delivery and my satisfactory inspection of the finished article I'll expect you to send me an invoice and I'll send a cheque by return. Errors are not, of course, acceptable. You won't be on a payroll, you'll be sub-contracted. If you don't know how sub-contraction works, I can explain it to you." *Watch it, sister*, says the tilt of my head.

"I know how it works. But I still have some questions."

"It's all on the leaflet, please read it. My contact details are there, as are Joy's. Call or email your decision and we'll take it from there. I do have one pressing job so if you could let me know as soon-as. I'm also about to tender for a huge contract, very high profile, so I need all the machinists I can find. However, from next weekend I'll be on holiday in Naples for two weeks so be aware, you won't receive any further work or communication until I return."

"Ah, Italy – how lovely," I say in the hope of introducing some warmth to the proceedings.

Her face is a study of bemused disdain. "Not Italy, Mrs McCardle, Naples, in Florida. My uncle has a villa in the suburbs."

Open mouth, insert foot, crash.

"Now, I have a paying client to see," she coos before I can recover from this faux pas, then turns and strolls purposefully towards the door. "I'll let myself out. I'll look forward to your call." Jaws clamped tight to incarcerate my tongue, I nod.

Sure Lady, soon as hell gets booked for the winter Olympics.

She's gone. The woman could give Eva Braun a run for her money and she's goose-stepped over the mark with me. Wish I was Della. She'd have stood, arms folded, her standard sneer oozing attitude. If the woman thinks I'm working for her after *that* performance, she's got another thing coming. I have my principles, and this lady's definitely not for turning.

Wow, hold the bus, I've just caught sight of her rates and I don't have to do anything except make them up. No measuring or coming up with inventive ideas, no shopping for fabrics, no delivering or hanging and no direct dealing with customers. And if I understand her system, no direct contact with her either – this could work.

Principles be damned, there's money to be made here, and I'm just the girl to make it. So, your Highness, as long as I don't have to deal with you or your customers face to face, I think you can count me in.

But be wary of this woman, the voice in my head chimes, just be wary.

Saturday, 9th August, 8.30pm

Eleven of us met at 7 o'clock at the Ship Inn, had a drink, then straggled along Monkswood High Street to Mr Chow's Canton Emporium where we're now sitting around a huge circular table, the gorgeous Gus seated next but one on my right. Thank God Eddie M.W.K. is between us, his wife having called off with a cold. At least I don't have to look at him direct.

The downside being, I do have to look at Eddie.

Squat and with a face like a slater's nail bag, his head's a turnip in a toupee with a little tuft of sandy hair sticking up at the crown, the remainder plastered flat to his head. He's already three sheets to the wind, his phlegmy lungs whistling and wheezing like a collapsing accordion. A forty-a-day-man, judging by the nicotine-stained fingers.

But given the vista beyond him, I'm sure I'll survive.

Aha, here comes my starter.

Be honest, have you ever tried eating chicken noodle soup in a lady-like fashion? Exactly. So why the hell did I order it? I really do need to ramp up my forward planning skills.

Anyway, yet again I digress.

I'm using Winnie's tip by tapping into my secret alter-ego, a version my single self before I met Ken. She was lively and bubbly and had a good sense of humour. I've decided to call her Tallulah. Why?

Well, why not?

I believe it's called accessing my inner teenager.

I feel calm and confident in my green patterned silky dress and three-quarter length leggings, my black patent heels making me feel sexy for the first time in decades. Mark and Julie are seated to my left, then Rory and Cat, then next to them are Cat's next door neighbours who I've never met, then Joanne and Denny. Next to Denny is Gus, then Eddie, and back to me. Rory's been telling funny work stories for the last twenty minutes, everyone guffawing in the right places, the atmosphere relaxed and friendly, aided and abetted by the wine.

But my eyes, against my express instructions, keep darting to the right. It's amazing how much you can see using peripheral vision over the rim of your glass as you give a tinkly little laugh. *Ha ha ha, hee hee hee.* If I tinkle towards Eddie, I get a brilliant view of Gus's profile.

And my word, is he a fine specimen.

His eyes are topaz blue; eyelashes – long and dark; skin – olive, to bring out the colour of the eyes; teeth – straight, apart from one that's skewiff so the smile's a tad lopsided. Oh, and did I mention – he breaks out that smile a lot. An awful lot. Hubba hubba. And those hands – sensitive hands; caring hands; lay your hands...

Sorry, where was I...

His faded blue Rolling Stones t-shirt and black leather jacket give him an air of danger. He's exuding pheromones from the crown of his gypsy curls all the way down to the Johnny Walker belt buckle that bestrides my visual cut-off point.

Can't wait to cast my eyes south of the border.

Is it me or is it hot in here?

Let me give him another sneaky once-over – uh-huh, definitely a ten. Me, I'm now a whopping three point five assuming the eye of the beholder is drink-shot. So he's out of my league and I've promised myself I won't get too close in case I'm revealed for the gibbering quarter-wit that I aspire to be. But have they passed a law against window shopping yet? No, they have not. And here comes my main course.

Mmm, this lemon chicken is pure heaven.

Muchos calories.

Muchos no carus.

Suddenly Eddie twists round in his chair and focuses on me, his gaze failing to rise above my décolletage. Talking out of the side of his mouth Popeye-style, he proceeds to give me chapter and verse on How I Beat Down the Customer with lots of, 'so I told him straight, take it or leave it', and 'so then he said "Eddie, you're some banana, I'll never get the better of you"'. My face locked in the type of smile that normally necessitates a closed casket. And so far he hasn't asked my boobs one single thing about me.

A definite candidate for a custard pie in the coupon.

Now I know why Cat said he's worth the watching. Worth avoiding, more like. I've been treated to a fifteen minute monologue peppered with raspy, sooty coughs through the row of condemned buildings that masquerade as teeth, his fag breath offering an undertone of manure. Oh for a gasmask. I envision all that cold creamy custard squidged into his crumbly features, slithering down his over-gelled hairpiece and dripping down his shirt, his bottom lip dangling. But no luck, he's still prattling on, gunge-free. Will he *ever* stop yammering? Hey ho, I'll just have to self-administer some liquid anaesthetic. I raise glass to lips, take a lazy sip and turn my head towards Eddie, who at that moment bends down to pick up the knife he's knocked to the floor and *wham*.

Gus.

Our eyes connect. It only lasts for a nano-second before he slides them coyly away but not before they've fired a flaming dart at my solar plexus discharging hot embers that radiate and make my skin tingle and sting. Wow. I put my glass down and toy with the stem to work out what that was. What it meant. What to do next. Ah, of course, silly me. This is a dream. Or I'm hallucinating. Bloody hell, this wine's good, must make a note of the name.

Without warning Eddie folds forward and broadcasts a loud belch, straightens up again and, looking mighty pleased with himself, rubs his burgeoning beer belly to coax another little burp out. Dammit, I was so busy daydreaming, I didn't notice he'd stopped yakking. Cautiously I crane around. Gus has gone back to his chat with Denny on his right so our impromptu eye-lock was in all likelihood a coincidence.

Hmmph.

Eddie's resumed droning. "Steady Eddie, Ever Ready, that's what they call me, oh ho ho." I smile the smile of the afflicted. "It's like my old man used to say – Eddie son, you'll get nine hard knocks for every slap on the back in this life; never refuse the slap on the back, it's the only one that isn't guaranteed – ah ha ha." I gaze into my plate and nod as though I'm engaged in this riveting brag-fest, then pick up my drink to take another sip, swivel my eyes back and there they are again, two ink-black pupils ringed with blue, indulging in a spot of eye to eye combat. This time he rolls his eyes at Eddie, slashes a finger across his Adam's apple and mugs sympathy at me. On the slim chance that it isn't all a figment of my imagination I give him my best Lady Di smile.

No, don't hope. Don't you dare. It's a co-incidence, he's drunk. You're drunk. We're all drunk.

Not yet we're not.

"Anybody want more wine?" Eddie asks around the table, hoisting the dripping bottle out of the ice bucket. Gus glances at my glass.

"Maggie needs a refill," he prompts, and stuffs a forkful of food into his mouth.

Confused, Eddie's eyes dart around the table. "Who?"

Gus dips his head in my direction, Eddie's mauvey complexion deepening to purple when he comprehends his gaffe. "Oh. Right. Sorry. Here you go."

Lordy Lord, he knows my name.

"And stop boring her with your daft stories, Ed. Maggie, tell him to belt up," says my saviour, then grins and throws me a cheeky wink. Somewhere in the depths a Catherine wheel spins, radiating embers that spark and fizzle, heat and smoke further befuddling my Gus-infused brain.

Eddie turns to him to protest. "I was just telling her…"

"Yeah yeah, Eddie my man, I'm just yanking your chain." And he laughs, gives Eddie a matey shoulder-punch then leans right back and pitches me the tiniest of winks. "Anyway, how's the wife doin'?" Eddie picks up the ball and runs with it.

Did you spot that? He's only broken Eddie's stranglehold on me and forced the attention onto himself. Deliberately. While Eddie updates him on Mrs Eddie's condition I look around the table to see if anyone spotted our little tango but they're all too busy tucking in and chatting. I replenish my fork but my appetite's long gone so I push the food around my plate instead. A few moments later I glance to the side and yep, those boys in blue are beaming my way again. This time he gives me a warm grin and Tallulah takes over, grins back and mouths a silent *thank you* at him.

He's flirting with me! Me, on the brink of decrepitude. Me, the trainee old duffer. Me, who thought she was too old for romance.

Eddie suddenly announces he's going out for a smoke and vacates his seat, throwing me into a tailspin. It was fun flirting from behind the barrier that was Eddie but he's gone and I feel exposed and vulnerable. Now all that's between us is an empty chair and a positive charge that threatens to arc and short circuit my entire mainframe. I pick up my glass and stare at it, twirling it one way, then the other, hyper aware of the vacuum that lies between us.

For fear of spilling its contents I set my drink back on the table, smooth the tablecloth down, straighten my plate, brush a crumb off my left arm, reposition my glass again, anything to resist the magnetic force that's pulling me sideways. Do I speak? Do I wait? What if he doesn't…

"I'm sure I know you from somewhere," he cuts in, "where do you live?"

What did Winnie call it? Oh aye – *Game on.*

***

The rest of the meal passed in a haze of wine and chatter and more wine and I didn't take in a word. Gus pitched in and took Eddie's attention off me several more times, all the while winking and smirking behind Eddie's back, and I savoured every second. At half past nine Cat and Rory suggested everybody go back to their place for a house party so off we staggered while Rory and Gus went to Tesco's to chase down some back-up booze.

I'm in Cat's kitchen now with a half glass of wine in my hand and despite my best efforts, Eddie has ambushed me yet again. He's quaffed way too much wine and in the absence of his wife to put the brakes on, he's giving me an earload of How I Bested The Boss.

When Gus and Rory bustle through the kitchen door, Tesco carrier bags a-chinking, a cheer goes up. While they're busy unloading their booty, Eddie homes in on Rory to bend his ears back for a while and I relax a little. Gus gets busy opening bottles and replenishing drinks. Suddenly Eddie glances round and gives me a grubby-toothed grin, my cue to make myself scarce before he gets a chance to corner me again.

While Eddie's distracted looking for the bottle opener, I slip into Cat's lounge. Julie and Mark are chatting on one settee, the music player on low volume. I take a seat on the other settee, cross my legs, set my glass on the lamp table and join in with their conversation.

Gus pops his head round the door, his eyes settling on me for the tiniest moment until he pops it back out again. Hope sinks, another little hole appearing in the timeworn fabric of my self-esteem.

"We're off to get a drink, you coming?" asks Julie.

"No, think I'll stay put," I say, and they pull the door behind them when they leave. Seconds later the door swings open and in he strolls, beer can in hand, and my heart quickens. He makes for my settee and plops down next to me, as if it was the only available seat in the house.

"Hi, how's you?" he grins, those eyes dancing. I can't make out if it's attraction or the drink but I don't care, he's next to me, talking to me, and that's all that matters.

"Yeah, great, having a ball," I say, all upbeat and Tallulah-like.

"I see you like a drop of white."

"Prefer rosé, to be honest."

"Ah," he says with apologetic grin, "if only you'd said before we raided Tesco's happy aisle. I'm sure I saw you at the Ship last week."

I lean in. "That was my identical twin. I'll let you into a secret but you're not allowed to tell."

He leans closer. "Whassat?"

"She's Maggie the Frump. I'm the fun one. My name's Tallulah but keep it schtum. I only come out when she's had a few. *Ssshhh*, it's all hush hush," I whisper, a finger to my lips, "You'll have to sign the Official Secrets Act now." And he laughs.

Isn't alcohol the best?

"I like you," he says, those eyes tugging at my heart. "He-ll*ooh* Tallulah." And offers me his hand, which I shake. "I'm Gus, I work with Rory."

"Just Gus? No closet twin? How disappointing, you struck me as a potential super-hero at least."

"Which one?" he asks expectantly. Oops, I don't go to see those movies, don't go to see any movies these days.

Think, Tallulah, think.

"Blue Eye Man," I finally decide, booming it out voice-over style. "Damsels in distress a speciality. He'll rescue you from the party bore." And he laughs.

"I like that. I could be your Blue Eye Man." And he gives me

97

a hopeful smile. "If you have a vacancy that is."

I cannot believe this is happening. My heart is beating a path out of my chest and yet, I'm not tongue-tied or stammering.

Keep going, Tallulah.

"There may well be a vacancy but you'd need to apply in triplicate, with a superhero-style CV and references of course." Then without thinking it through I add, "And then there's the interview."

"And what form would that take?" he asks, carrying the joke a step further.

"Competency based I'd imagine," I chirrup, and he grins again. Shit, did I really say that? I did, oh God, I did. I try to think of something to say to cover my confusion and add, "or maybe a bit of role-play."

Shit shit shit. Now I've suggested role-play. As in, the plumber with the big wrench and the buxom housewife who offers to pay in kind. Gag me somebody, for God's sakes, gag me.

While I'm wondering how to climb out of the grave I've dug, he gives this some thought. "So I'd need to act all hero-like and be competent at banishing bores and rescuing said damsel?"

There he goes again, saving me, only this time from myself. "Uh-huh."

"I think I'm the chap for the job," he says, and slaps his thigh. "Maybe we should go out for a drink to discuss terms and conditions."

Did he just ask me out? Did he?

Help! Brain going into a cramp, need time to think – Yes! I'll absent myself. "I'll get back to you with the details," I say, fight or flight mode kicking in. "Sorry, I need to go, erm, do something…"

Nooo… He suggested a drink, and what did I do? I brushed him off by implying I needed to pee, that's what. And to top it off I've turned red. Thank God for HRT or I'd be in full hot flush mode by now.

I've blown it.

The beat of my heart amplified in my ear, I jump up, pick up my glass to skittle towards the door and the anonymity of the crowd in the kitchen. When I get there Cat sways towards me, wine bottle in hand, and claps the other hand on my shoulder. "D'you wan' a refill, Mags?"

"Do I ever." She pours a huge dollop into my glass, hiccups and totters away. I close my eyes and lean against the worktop for a few minutes, my heart toiling as if pumping sludge, and scold myself. It's not that I don't have a filter between tongue and brain; it's that sometimes I think the two have no synaptic connection whatsoever. But when I open my eyes he's beside me, grinning from ear to ear and hope bobs to the surface again.

"Hah! Found you," he declares. Hamming it up he checks from side to side to make sure no one's listening and whispers as if we're complicit. "Come with me, out here, for a sec." He grabs my hand and guides me along the hall and through the front door onto the step, the cool clean air tightening my face. Still holding my hand he leans back to pull the door behind us then turns to face me, smiling, and I just know he's going to kiss me.

And God knows I'm going to let him.

Somewhere in the back of my lust-struck brain I hear a drumroll. He moves in, inch by inch, centimetre by centimetre, rests his lips on mine for a moment then tugs me close, one hand stroking my neck, the other sliding around my waist. And just like that we're lip-locked in heart-stopping kisses that deepen and intensify. A firework explodes in a deep, dark place; beating blood rushes to the scene, commanding my attention; hot sparks spray and pulse, buzzing, radiating. His mouth shifts left, sketching a path across my cheek and down to my neck, his hot heavy breath singeing my skin, a rainbow of colours swirling and popping inside my eyelids, illuminating the dark within.

The man must be a drain on the national grid. People up and down the land are probably checking their fuses or phoning their supplier to report their lights flickering.

At last he pulls back, his eyes glittering.

"I meant it, Tallulah," he pants, his breath short and shallow. "I want that interview. Maybe you'd like to discuss it over a drink some time?"

I know, I'm acting like a love-struck teenager, but I don't care. That one kiss has dissolved my determination to keep my distance and God help him if he kisses me again.

I pause for the merest moment to re-assess my resolve but who am I kidding. Eddie's words echo in my brain – *never refuse the slap on the back.*

"D'you know what, Blue Eye Man?" I say. "I believe I would."

Sunday, 10th August, 10am

Six hours and thirty-seven minutes ago (give or take) he kissed me goodnight, the promise of a few drinks on Wednesday sealed in my heart. Then off I went in a taxi, all because I had some daft notion about absenting myself.

But he promised to call and that's fine by me.

When my doorbell dinged at nine o'clock this morning I leapt out of bed and bounced down the stairs. I knew it wasn't him, he has no clue where I live, but my percolating hormones tell me it's time for a walk on the wild side so he'll know soon enough.

That's the Tallulah in me. Honestly, she is *such* a bad influence.

I opened the door and Felicity McQueen's assistant Joy introduced herself. Talk about a misnomer – Joy's the most sullen creature I've ever met, which is no surprise given who she works for, but as promised, she handed over a bale of fabric and a jiffy bag and everything I needed was there.

I snipped the plastic tube open and gasped at the lightly padded oyster polyester silk embroidered with a delicate wine and apple green flower trail. When I pulled the advice note out of the cardboard tubing I gasped even louder – seven hundred pounds in all so no room for error.

The instructions requested two pairs of matching lined curtains, width-and-a-half, 220cm long, three inch header tape, with two inch, weighted hems. No tie backs, no pelmets, no fancy headings, just standard drapes. The Thursday deadline seemed a bit cheeky but hey, I figure it's a test.

Since she deluges my desk with work, I've set Office Outlook to forward a copy of Stella's emails to my Hotmail account so I can get ahead of the game at home. Plan A was to spend the day sifting and prioritising, but when the fabric arrived I devised Plan B, which is work late during the week and use today to make the curtains.

Am I clever or what?

***

Nine o'clock and I'm already watching TV in my jammies, drinking tea and nibbling on a chocolate digestive.

It took me until half past seven but I finished the curtains and texted Joy, who arranged to pick them up tomorrow night with my bill for four hundred quid.

Cat called earlier to get the lowdown on last night but she sounded more concerned than excited. "I thought you went outside for a chat, not a chat up. Are you sure about this?"

"Why wouldn't I be?"

"You're both on the rebound, that's all. *Acht*, ignore me, I'm just being over-protective."

"Yes you are – my life, my decision." And just to throw her off the scent, I added, "and I'm fairly sure he's not gonna propose so where's the harm?"

Five minutes later she was gone but she'd cast a negative net and I'm starting to feel queasy. I dial 1571 – no messages left while we were chatting. My eyes check the clock for the umpteenth time. What if he woke up this morning all sober and sensible and thought – yeah, right, as if. Or worse, was too drunk to remember. Please, Jesus, Jiminy Cricket and Nellie the elephant –prompt him. It's just a teeny-weeny phone call…

The phone shrills and my stomach jolts.

Pleading works!

"Hallo, Maggie," drones Ken. I slump. Experience tells me that the melancholy in his voice is designed to invoke both curiosity and sympathy and damned if he isn't jamming up the line.

"Make it quick, Ken. I'm waiting for an important call."

"I wondered if you've considered my offer yet. It's just that, uhm, Babs is kind of, well, pregnant." A siren goes off in my head, screaming in my ears. "Uhm, we want to get married. ASAP."

Somehow, I manage to speak. "Pregnant. As in, having-a-baby pregnant?"

"That's enough, Maggie," he scolds, and abandons the sympathy-seeking in favour of his school master approach.

"*Enough?* After the miscarriage you said, maybe best not to try again, Maggie. You're just courting misery, Maggie. Now you've been with her for five minutes and you phone to tell me she's pregnant? Like it's nothing? WHAT THE HELL ARE YOU THINKING?"

Dead air.

A vein in my temple pulses so hard it threatens to burst and spray my life's blood around the room.

"I was doing what I thought was best."

"For who?" I demand.

Kaboom… A twenty megaton chunk of puzzle detonates in my brain, the resultant fireball blasting my pathetic jigsaw into oblivion. I breathe laden air down the line, a non-verbal nuclear winter to chill his ears. He's mute, his silence reinforcing the certainty that any minute now fall-out must reign down upon his selfish head.

"You can have your divorce," I seethe, the words teeming like acid rain, "then I don't want to see or hear from you ever again. Sign the papers. Post them to me. I'll take it from there." I hang up. I hear a crash and realise it's my cup shattering against the wall.

After half an hour I'm all cried out, the blaze of fury replaced by cold, grey anger. I close my eyes and a mess of purples and blues billow like a bruise. Well, sod you, Ken, this is war, and telling you about my pension? It's so off my divorce to-do list. I worked for it. I earned it. You're getting none of it.

Deal with *that*, you loser.

***

The phone buzzes into life once more and I jump. Ken, I'd bet my life on it.

"*HELLO,*" I shout down the handset, brusque as you like.

"Hi Lullah," chimes the voice I've been praying to hear. My heart pumps pink to my cheeks, sparkle to my eyes, all my angst evaporates like a noxious mist.

"Hi yourself, Blue Eye Man."

Tallulah, are you there? C'mon girl, it's time to shine.

Wednesday, 13th August, 5.30pm

I thought tonight would never arrive but here I am, driving home, my cheeks flush with excitement.

I open my front door and a huge envelope, which was dangling from inside the letterbox, thuds to the floor with a bang. No name, no address, no stamp. I drop my keys on the hall table, sit on the stairs, pull out the paperwork and sigh. It's the quickie divorce form, completed and dated. He's already had the Justice of the Peace notarise it, although I've yet to sign on the dotted line. And, surprise surprise, he's omitted to include a cheque for the fee.

So, that's it, fini, the end.

Sad.

But timely. I'll have this lot counter-signed and posted by lunch-time tomorrow, complete with our marriage certificate and a cheque.

In fact, I've had a better idea – I'll take a long lunch, catch a bus into town, and hand the papers into the court instead of posting them. I return the forms to the envelope.

Right now I need to hit the shower.

***

What a difference an hour makes and I've had two. My taxi's almost there and I'm dressed to kill.

Oh alright, lightly daze.

He texted last night to say he was looking forward to getting together, so how thrilled am I? Ecstatic, me, over the moon.

Bunch up, Mrs Robinson, there's a new girl in town.

Tonight's just a drink and a chat so I'm decked out in my skinny jeans, pink tunic top, sucky-in pants and a smug expression. A delicious meld of anticipation steeped in a potent blend of petrified-but-excited is bubbling in the background. I had a word with myself and am resolved to saying yes to fun and no to saying no.

Me? Shit scared? Absolutely.

My taxi pulls up at the bus stop and there he is, sprinting forward to open the door. Good grief, what is the boy trying to do to me? As demi-gods go he's looking pretty spectacular in a purple t-shirt, leather jacket and those fabby faded denims that fit where they touch.

Deep breath, here goes.

"Hi Lullah," he chirps when I step out of the taxi, and I get a little whiff of beer when he pecks me on the cheek. So, even sex gods need a fly one for Dutch courage, eh? "You look great. Thought we'd have a couple in The Plough, if you're up for it." I feel my face fall.

"That's an old man's pub, they don't even play music."

"But it's my local," he protests, then thinks again. "Of course, you're right, it is a bit basic." He thinks. "I know, let's go to the Ship. I know some people there too." Another pang of disappointment. This isn't how I imagined it, not how I imagined it at all.

Hang on – I've been with him all of ten seconds and already I'm moaning. So I won't have him to myself and the Ship isn't the most salubrious gin joint in town but hey, it's a step up from the Plough and I don't care so long as I'm with him.

I smile to turn the brightness up a bit. "Sure," I say, "lead on."

Maggie to Tallulah – stand-by, girl, I'm not handling this too well.

***

A glass and a half of rosé later we're perched on stools at the end of the bar, my anxiety dissolving into the wine. I did offer to buy the next round but he said no, he'd pay since it's our first date and my ears heard, it's not going to be our only date.

He's sparkling and grinning and I haven't felt the need to call on Tallulah once. Twenty minutes ago we were chatting to a couple he knew at the bar and before that he introduced me to two guys he once went to a gig with. He's a first class charismatic people magnet and he's introduced me to everyone of them as his girlfriend. Did you catch that? His girlfriend. What an ego boost, sitting at the bar with the most divine man in the world and the age difference doesn't factor into it.

Confidence check – sky high.

Cool points – a bazillion.

Suddenly my mobile beeps into life with its tinny rendition of Black Sabbath's Paranoid. I pull it just far enough out of my bag to read the screen and panic when I see it's Mum. I slide the phone open and press it to my ear. "Hi, what's wrong?" He gives me a puzzled look.

"I need to take this," I mouth, twist away from him and cup a hand over my free ear to block out the sounds of the pub.

"*Nothing, deary,*" she says in a gruff voice, "*I just wondered how you're getting on.*"

It takes a few seconds to find my voice. "Sorry?"

"*With your date,*" she rasps, "*has he taken you somewhere nice?*" Oh God, she's in Time-Out Mode and for the first time, by telephone. His right ear is way too close to my left, to which the mobile is currently clamped, so I swap it to my other ear and try to focus.

"I'll get back to you on that," I say in a breezy kind of a way, hoping she'll pick up the vibe, but she's not backing off. "Oooh, *I'll get back to you on that,*" she taunts, mimicking me in full voice, "what are you like? So tell me, what are you wearing?" Everything she says is a question and all require an answer. I glance round to check if he's cottoned on and his eyes telex another enquiry so I beam him a bear-with-me smile and turn away again, my skin prickling.

"Just the usual, Mum. I'll let you know tomorrow."

"No, I want to know now," she protests, and mentally stamps a dainty size four. "Aw, c'mon, is it the chiffony thing? Is it?"

In a clear case of saved by the bell, I hear an electronic chime in the background. "Drat, somebody's at the door," she hisses, "hang on 'til I get rid of them."

"NO, Mum," I get in before she takes the phone from her ear, "hang up and go see who it is. I'll call you tomorrow, I promise." There's a weighty pause.

"Hmmph. Be like that." And she hangs up.

I do love my mum, but there are times...

***

Suddenly it's closing time and I don't want it to end. What if he wants me to go back to his? Or worse, doesn't? What if he puts me in a taxi and says 'bye Lullah' and that's the end of it? Even scarier, what if he expects *s-e-x*? I've had neither hanky nor panky for yonks. Well, excluding Gregor but, thanks to the amnesiac effect of alcohol, he doesn't count.

Oh dear, I did vow to say no to saying no, though, didn't I?

"Fancy another glass of wine?" he asks.

"Sure," I answer, relieved our parting's delayed, "where's open?"

He tugs a set of keys from his inside pocket and jangles them mid-air. "My place, it's five minutes' walk from here." I pause for a full millisecond. Safe and sensible or spontaneous?

"Sounds great," I chirp and off we trot through the pub door and out onto the street hand in hand.

I'm sorry you've had a wasted night waiting in the wings, Tallulah. You can go home now, girl, I'll take it from here.

"Wow, this is…compact," I say.

"Yeah, and cheap. Only one bedroom, if you can call it that, and a shower room. Grab a pew." He throws his keys onto the window ledge, switches on the TV and loads an R Kelly CD into the DVD player. "I'll get you that drink."

"Don't open any on my account. I've had plenty already."

"But I bought something special for you," he says.

I nod in the direction of the loo as he heads for the kitchen to do the honours. "Can I…"

"Sure, go ahead."

On the way back I sneak a peek into the bedroom. There's not a boy toy in sight, not even a laptop. No plants, no rugs, only a Heart of Midlothian supporters' scarf pinned across the wall above his bed. The flat has no curtains, only blinds, and no mirrors save for the full length one in the shower room.

Poor Gus, divorce can be hard on some men.

I reclaim my end of the sofa and he lopes out of the kitchen with two glasses – rosé for me, white for him, and hands me mine.

"See? I remembered – again," he says and sits down beside me on the settee. He's tantalisingly close. So close I can smell him and it's making me giddy.

"Here's to you, Tallulah," he toasts, eyes fixed on mine, and we chink glasses.

"Here's to you, Blue Eye Man." Lust is a many splendored thing and I think I've hit the mother lode. I lower my lids, raise my glass, savour.

"So," he burrs, extending an arm across the back of the settee, "tell me what went wrong with your Happy Ever After."

I shrug. "I was married, now I'm not. What about you?"

"Ah, the lovely Raquel. That's Rachel to you," he says, and my heart cowers to hear her name on his lips. "We'd split up, only got back together because she found out she was pregnant.

She's walked away so many times over the years, we were apart more than together, so this time when she asked if I'd be the one to leave, I did. End of."

I run a thumb around my glass, mopping up drizzles of condensation. "Why didn't you try to sort it?"

"Didn't want to go back to all that fighting and aggro. She's a hard one to please, is Rachel. No, so long as I get to see the wee chap every fortnight, it's fine. But let's not go into all that, Lullah, it's such a downer. Let's talk about tonight. I've had a great time." Oh Holy Mother of God, there he goes with the eyes again, he might as well connect me to the mains. He leans in a bit closer, so close that I can almost taste him.

"Me too," I say, and smile. A warm hand tucks around my thigh just above the knee. Even through the fabric of my jeans, a network of nerves and sensors pick up the DC charge. My glow evolves into a slow burn so explosive, I'm terrified I might burst into flames.

"Sorry," he says and pulls his hand away, "didn't mean to sexually harass you."

This is it, the moment.

"It's only harassment if it's not welcome," I pant, almost under my breath. We both stall, waiting to see who'll make the first move.

He does.

With the tip of his tongue he moistens his lips, then gently brushes them across mine before he pulls back slightly and licks them again, tasting me. He turns, sets his glass on the side table, lifts mine out of my hand and stands it next to his. One hand on the back of my neck, he cups my ear with the other and traces a path across my cheek with his thumb. Then he pulls me in closer and lowers his lips onto mine, his tongue gently probing.

And for the second time in less than a week I'm hooked up to the national grid.

Friday evening, 15ᵗʰ August

"Look at you," exclaims Winnie, pulling the passenger door shut. She twists in her seat, the better to scrutinise my new look. "I know you said you'd made changes but wow, you look so different." She looks around to check her bearings and feigns suspicion. "You *are* the woman previously known as Maggie McCardle, yes?"

I put the car into gear and take off. "I am. And it didn't even cost that much, maybe five hundred quid all in, along with a butt-load of HRT and being wooed by a young stud. A dawdle."

She gasps and slaps me on the arm. "Oi, I thought you just had a snog with this schoolboy of yours."

"I did but I'll tell you this much – me likey. Me want more. Me seeing him tomorrow night. Now stop grilling me, you're getting nothing else."

Ten minutes later we're at the door of Vendange. A pair of bouncers stand guard at the entrance, Monkswood mobsters in Mafioso-black suits with white shirts, slim black ties and mirrored shades when the sun's long gone. Heavies in the literal sense, one grunts permission to enter and steps aside but since his semi-sumo frame fills the doorway, we're obliged to squidge around him to get in.

"Wow, this new décor's the dog's bollocks," says Winnie, surveying the bar. "Very snazzy. I don't see a dance floor but look – they've extended it at the back to make a dining area – it's huge." The place is packed, people swarming four deep at the bar. The hum of voices and wafts of hot butter, herbs and sizzling steak infuse my senses, pulling me in. My eyes soak up the reclaimed timber floor; the rich cream and gold walls; the fairy lights garlanded around the gilt not-tonight-Josephine mirror that hangs above the Napoleonic fireplace. Electric candelabra in antique gold dangle on chains from plaster ceiling roses and the walls are littered with what look like reproduction old masters, but the faces are those of modern-day celebrities. Fascinated, I turn to check out the rest of the room and gasp when my eyes reach the curtains – my curtains, hanging on brushed gold poles with ornate finials on each end and held back by sparkling gold cords.

"I made those curtains for Felicity McQueen," I tell her, excitement bubbling in the pit of my stomach.

Winnie stares at them. "Wow," she declares, "and that material must've cost a few bob, it's stunning."

"It was seven hundred quid, the receipt was in the bag. Let's get a seat in the middle of the room so I can admire my handiwork." I make a bee-line for the only vacant table I can see. Winnie gets in the first round – soft for me – and we settle down to catch up. Suddenly someone calls out her name and we both jerk our heads up.

"Oh my God, Steve," she says, "I haven't seen you in years." He smiles and runs a hand through his short, dark hair. "Me and my mates thought we'd check the place out and have a pint. They're over at the bar. God, Winnie, you haven't changed a bit." His dark brown eyes are shining and when I look at Winnie, her eyes are shining too.

"By the way, this is Maggie – Maggie, this is Steve." We nod hello. "Maggie made those curtains," she says, "she didn't know they were for this place until tonight. Aren't they brilliant?"

"Aye, very nice," he says, without looking at them at all, but what do I care?

Checking confidence: yep, off the scale.

Steve decides to sit down for a chat so to give them a bit of space, I join the scramble at the bar for another drink.

112

As soon as I get back at the table a shorter bloke with a mass of tight curls lurches towards us, his drunken grin bordering on a leer. His eyes are a little too lively for my liking, setting off alarm bells in my head.

"And who is this gorgeous babe I see before me?" he burbles, speaking to no one in particular. His head bobbing like a float on the water he grabs for my hand and slops his mollusc lips across the back of it.

The biggest halfwit in the room and he has to pick on me.

"This is Winnie's pal, Maggie," says Steve and casts him a look of wafer thin patience. "This is my buddy, Billy."

I give him a diluted smile and pull my hand away.

"I fancy you," he slurs and leans in, the whites of his eyes shot red, his features slack with the booze. "I fancy you a lot. I think you'd like it if I gave you a wee kiss."

I wouldn't.

"Oh, no, it's Friday," I say and make a sarcastic face. "Don't do kisses on a Friday." In a futile attempt to create a barrier I lean back and raise my hands but he blanks the rebuff and lurches at me, almost knocking me off my chair.

"Billy, leave her alone, you're a bloody nightmare," scolds Steve, and stands up to tug him away by the collar. "Sorry about this, honest to God, the devil's in him when he's had a few." Steve's eyes fire his friend a warning shot but Billy-boy's in crazy mode and it's obvious he's not accustomed to people saying no. His vision being less twenty-twenty and more forty per cent proof, it's unclear how many Maggie's he can see but his failed attempts to focus on me suggest it's more than one. My stomach pitches. This guy has no boundaries, way too much energy and he's one drink away from a breach of the peace.

Still tagging me with his eyes he elbows Winnie, and hard. "I fancy a bit of a cuddle with your mate."

Not of the fool-suffering persuasion, she shoots him a look sharp enough to cut him in two. "I think what you fancy is a

113

bit of knee to go with that elbow," she threatens, but he's too busy trying to focus through the alcoholic haze to pick up on it.

I'm spooked.

At any moment he might drop to his knees and dry hump my leg and I can see from the irritation on Winnie's face that she's had enough of him too. She leans across the table and taps my arm. "I'm feeling the heat but you look a bit chilly."

Heart thudding in my throat, I shiver my shoulders. "I'm *frrreeee*-zing."

She nods and sends me a semi-wink. "Comin' to the loo?" I judder a series of animated nods. "Back in a mo," she tells Steve, and jumps up, with me scooting after her leaving Billy boy to gape bleary-eyed at our retreat.

"I've always fancied Steve," she says when we tumble into the ladies toilets. "Don't see a wedding band but that doesn't mean he's single. Do I give him the glad eye or not? I don't want to make a prat of myself."

"You an' me both, kiddo, but it's the other way round for me. Billy's freakin' me out and I'm not interested. Where does Steve live?"

"About ten minutes' walk from my place."

"Brilliant. Offer him a lift home with us, then when I drop you off, invite him up for coffee. See if he takes the bait."

"That'd be great, so long as you don't mind. And I know I'm safe with him."

"Ah but the question is, will he be safe with you?"

She giggles.

When we get back to the bar Billy's disappeared and last orders have been called. But Steve's still there, at the table, waiting.

I stop dead.

He hasn't spotted me but I can see him, Johnny Davidson, sitting at a table in the restaurant area at the back of the bar. A young, pretty blonde is beside him with another young couple sitting opposite, plates of leftover food and empty glasses

114

littering the table. He takes out his wallet and drops some banknotes into the dish containing the bill at which point the girl reaches up, wraps her arms around his neck and kisses him on the cheek. He looks uncomfortable at her display of affection but she ignores this and puts her head on his shoulder.

So, he's still emotionally unavailable.

Some things never change, John.

Winnie gives me the nod – Steve's accepted her offer.

The barman hoves into view, a brace of dirty glasses in each hand. "C'mon now folks, finish your drinks," he hollers, "we don't do bed and breakfast." Although paunchy and balding, the long dark sideburns and almost-handlebar moustache give him an air of barbershop, the illusion assisted by his collarless shirt, waistcoat and watch chain.

"Stevie, my man, how's tricks?" he says, and slaps Steve on the shoulder.

"Aye, fine, Fred. You?"

"Uh-huh, great. What do you think of the place then? Re-opened yesterday."

"It's cracking, must've cost you dear though."

"Aye, it was a bloody cringer when I got the bill, but to be honest, I'm well chuffed."

"Actually, this lady here made your curtains. Meet Maggie – Maggie, this is Fred, the owner."

Fred swings around and glowers at me. "So you're the rip-off merchant. You should be embarrassed to come in here, lady, you're a damned disgrace."

My heart starts pounding like a blacksmith's hammer. "S-sorry, I don't understand, I thought they went well with the décor."

"Aye and so they bloodywell should, the price you charged," he booms. "Nearly broke the bloody bank. You've a cheek coming in here at all, but then to brag about it…" He shakes his head and, too angry to risk another word, storms off with two handfuls of dirty glasses leaving me shaking.

"Sorry, he is *not* getting away with that," Winnie decrees, and turns to Steve. "Scuse me while I go paper the walls with your pal." Before I can stop her she leaps off her stool and stomps after him. "Hoi, Fred," she shouts, "You've no right to speak to my pal like that and I think you're due her an apology." His face flushed red he turns on his heel to face her down.

"Do you know how much your pal here charged for those bloody curtains?" he hisses, his face now turning purple. "Two thousand pounds a pair, four thousand quid all in, a flaming fortune."

What?

She wouldn't have.

She couldn't have.

Fred strides up to me and puts his face right up to mine, so close I'm forced to lean back to avoid his garlic-breath. "I realise the flame-proofing cost extra and it was a rush job," he says, "but two thousand quid a pair? Daylight bloody robbery. She told me how she'd already signed your contract and you wouldn't even consider a discount. I don't want you in here again. In fact, you're barred." He storms away muttering, "… bloody show off, comin' in here crowing about the bloody curtains."

She did.

"Fred," I call out and jump off my seat to walk towards him on jelly legs, but he stops dead to round on me. I turn the colour of milk, take a shaky step back and say it slow to get it right. "S-she didn't sign any contract with me. I'm an office worker who s-sews curtains at home in my spare time." He glares, the doubt on his face obvious. "I promise you, it's true. She sourced the fabric, not me. I saw the receipt, it was thirty-five pounds a metre including the lining, twenty metres in total, and it was already flame-proofed when I got it. All in all, around seven hundred quid. She's paying me two hundred quid a pair to make them – her rates, not mine. I'll show you the cheque when she sends it if you want. I'm so sorry she did that,

I wish now I'd never got involved with the woman."

"I suppose it makes sense," he says, calming down now. "Why admit it was you if you'd fleeced me? But you can see where I'm coming from."

"Absolutely, and excuse the pun but I'll not be lining her pockets again. Am I still barred?"

He grunts and shrugs. "Suppose not, I need all the punters I can get."

"Listen, we should go and let you get cleared up," I offer, and the three of us turn file out of the door towards my car, blood still buzzing in my ears.

On the way home I try to sound cool, collected, in control but underneath I'm blazing mad. When I pull up outside Winnie's house I say a tactful no when she invites me in to join them. I can't think about anything other than those curtains and the news that she had the cheek to charge a small fortune for them and blame it on me.

Stupid, stupid me.

But the bigger shock is that someone – anyone – was impressed enough with my handiwork to actually pay it.

Saturday, 16th August, 1pm

"Maggie, I've been waiting for you, come away in. I've got a wee problem," Mum says as I walk in her front door. "My furniture arrived this morning but one of the – those fancy things on the front – is missing, come and see." I follow behind her along the hall to her bedroom and sure enough there's an unvarnished patch on one of the bedside cabinets where a moulding should be.

"I asked the delivery men to take it back but they said they just deliver and unpack, contact the shop." She screws her face up and goes into her *helpless pensioner* routine. "Could you call your friend, John?"

To be clear, he's not my friend.

"I can't see the numbers on this phone (she can) and you're so much better at these things than me." (I'm not.)

My inner child scowls. I could do without this, especially after spotting him with that slip of a girl last night. Mum thrusts the receipt under my nose, one finger pointing at the shop's telephone number, but to me it just looks like the shitty end of the stick. "I mean to say," she raves on, "it's a diabolical liberty. Ridiculous if you ask me. The delivery men should've taken it back, don't you think? *Hmmm?*"

"Don't worry," I sigh, already wearied by her attempts to recruit me to the cause, "I'm on your side." In a half-hearted attempt to show willing, I rifle my bag for my ready-readers and there, in a dark corner, I spy four foil-covered chunks of compensation that I'd forgotten about.

Hallelujah, I'm packing chocolate.

I sit down, pick up the phone, punch in the number and wait while it rings.

"Vickers and Innes, Sarah speaking."

"Hi, my mum had her new furniture delivered this morning but a moulding's missing. Can you help?"

"Certainly. If you could tell me the name of the salesman…"

Here we go…

"John Davidson."

"Putting you through now."

"No! Wait – can't you deal with…" Too late. The sound of Vivaldi wafts across my eardrum.

The line clicks, then clicks again. "John Davidson, can I help you?"

I take a breath. "John, it's Maggie, Maggie Baxter."

"Maggie, hi! What can I do for you?"

"My mum's bedroom furniture arrived this morning and a moulding's missing from one of the cabinets. The delivery guys refused to take it back." There's a moment of silence while Mum jumps around waving both hands in front of me, trying to relay what she wants me to say via some form of semaphore.

"Strange," he says, "they're not supposed to deliver imperfect goods, they should've put it back in the van."

"Meaning what?" I ask, an edge to my voice.

Cool it, buster, this isn't some story I invented as an excuse to phone you.

He picks up on the chill. "Nothing, nothing, I just meant I'll look into that. I assume she wants a replacement." The less heed I pay to Mum's tick-tack signals the more frantic they become, and she's fast approaching fever pitch.

Sidebar: Remember to check she's on top of her meds.

I'm so distracted by her non-verbal gesturing, it takes me a moment to digest what he's said. "Erm, a replacement, yes."

"No problem, but because it's been delivered I need to process a return first. I'd offer to pick it up myself but my car's off the road until next week. It's a discontinued line so we need to move fast. Could you pop it into your boot and return it to the showroom tomorrow?"

Mum appears to be threatening a spasm. "Fine. I'll bring it in around 2 o'clock."

"See you then," he says, and hangs up.

"What did he say?" she asks, her brows knitted over those beady eyes.

"I've to take it back tomorrow."

She pokes a finger at me. "You make sure he deals with it personally. Tell him, I've got a photogenic memory, and the one in the showroom had all its bits. The cheek o' him, selling me duff furniture, indeed."

"I will," I say, although I intend to do nothing of the kind and she heads for the kitchen to put the kettle on.

Oh lucky me, I get to face him yet again.

With any luck this'll be the last time.

Saturday evening, 16th August, 8pm

At the entrance to Mr Chow's I take a moment to close my eyes and say a silent prayer. *Please Venus, St Valentine and Match.com, let this be a great night. I don't expect him to be a keeper; I just want to make a good memory. To keep me warm in my twilight years. Cheers.*

Oh, and, *PS – don't let me dribble food down my frock. Muchos gracias.*

There, that should cover it.

I bought this tribal-print maxi dress thinking, I love it but when would I ever wear it? Yet here I stand, poised on the brink in that same garment, uplifted and demi-cleaved thanks to thirty quid's worth of military grade, weaponised, boob-boosting technology. Hair – flicked to perfection. Denim jacket – collar up, cuffs back. Make-up – full-combat. Gold toe-post sandals and a little bag slung across my torso complete my chilled-out-chic. At least, that's what I was aiming for. The words mutton and lamb spring to mind.

Or should that be, lamb and slaughter?

He's texted so I know he's in there, waiting. I smooth down my dress, fluff up my hair and run my tongue round my lips. No Tallulah tonight, just me, flying solo, minus the net.

This is it, girl. Chin up, chest out, *shhhowtime…*

Mouth dry, hands trembling, my every cell is on high alert. I draw in a full breath, slap on a smile, breeze through the entrance and *ffwhmph*! A fusion of chatter and laughter assaults my senses. Warm air wafts over me, chiming cutlery and oriental muzak providing percussion to the babble while waiters

121

scurry up and down the aisles, the tables garnished with wine buckets and steaming plates of fragrant food.

I can do this. I'm cool, I'm calm, I'm laid back.

Ah, here he comes, snaking his way through the tables, smiling. Good God, the Jack Daniels t-shirt, the black leather jacket, those faded denims, are more than my heart can take.

Somebody, pass the smelling salts.

"Wow, you look great," he says, those eyes taking in every inch of me and I get a whoosh of panic. It's too much, isn't it? The long dress, the flicky hair, the make-up. Too Liz McDonald. Wait – his eyes are like glitterballs.

"Erm…don't sound so surprised."

He shifts into sombre mode, places a hand in the small of my back, and with a sweep of his arm waves me towards the walkway. "I apologise, my lady. Your table awaits." A giggle escapes as I sashay up the aisle in front of him. True, at this moment he has an unfettered view of my nether wallop which, due to the bot-enhancing effects of cellulite, is normally in danger of skimming the deck. However, thanks to the gravity-defying powers of spandex, if my toosh could talk it would say (drumroll) 'but tonight Matthew, I'm going to be – Beyonce!' (canned applause).

God bless Lycra, the eighth wonder of the world.

The other diners are deep in conversation, oblivious to the momentous event that's taking place before their very eyes. 'Yes, that's right, I'm with *him*' I want to cluck at the womenfolk when I arrive at our table to take my seat, my escort dancing attendance on me. I spot that he's already started a bottle of White Zinfandel, his glass half full of the rich pink liquid.

Well, well, he remembered.

He sits.

"D'you want some rosé?" he asks, and raises the bottle.

"Sure," I say, confidence climbing, and he swirls a generous dollop into my glass. "Just the one though. It gets me too drunk too fast." He pauses to study me for a moment, tips in another splodge and sets the bottle back on the table.

"Is that a fact. Maybe I should order myself a Chateau Neuf du Pepsi, and you can quaff the rest of the Zinfandel."

"Tut tut, what are you like? If I did get sozzled, would I be safe with you?"

"Of course," says he, followed by a loaded silence. *But I don't want to be safe* I'd like to murmur below my breath so that only he can hear, but I don't.

Damn, I missed my cue.

Half an hour, a starter and a glass of wine later, our main meals have arrived – Cantonese pork with Chinese vegetables for me; kung po beef for him – and thanks to the wine I'm starting to relax.

"I lost a bet because of you tonight," he says and I glance up at him.

"You did?"

"I told my mate Mick how I, err – let's say over-imbibed on Wednesday so I thought I'd failed the interview. Thought you wouldn't turn up tonight. He bet me a fiver I was wrong." What, *he* feels insecure about *me*? Suddenly I've got the urge to scrape back my chair, hitch up my dress, climb over the table and sexually assault him.

Instead, I smile.

"Aaaww, you wee soul, thinking I'd stand you up." Unsure of what to say next, I stare at my plate.

He speaks first.

"So, I told you my relationship woes but you didn't share yours, although I did hear a rumour about you at work yesterday." My eyes widen. Surely Cat didn't tell Rory about Gregor?

"A rumour? About me? God, I hope it's true." I rest my glass against my lips and wait while the blue of his eyes deepens.

"Rory tells me you've decided to get divorced." Yikes, Rory, that's more damning than the Gregor story. I'd planned to keep that quiet in case he thinks it's because he's on the scene, vaults the table Olympic-style and legs it up the High Street and away.

"His idea, not mine," I say, quick as a flash. "I don't much care either way, although all the best folk are divorced or on the road to it. It's virtually de rigueur these days."

"*Hmmm*, not so sure. That's why I've never tied the knot, it's too risky. What went wrong?" I weigh up my options – the moany-faced truth or the short snappy version.

"He had an affair so I put him on the naughty step. Permanently."

"Aaah. You must miss him."

I don't want to treat it too lightly but if I come over all angry-ex-wife it might put him off, so I go for the post-marital analysis option.

"At first I did. Took me a while but I've picked up the pieces and I want to have fun. On the upside, I lost a pile of weight and got the house to myself so it wasn't all bad."

"You were *fat*?" he says, the shock darting his eyes into focus.

"I can-NOT believe you used the F-word. Not fat, Rubenesque. I comfort ate before the split, didn't eat properly after it."

He nods. Another pause. "I need to ask one more question."

"Okay."

"I don't get why you gave me another chance after my behaviour on Wednesday. I'd drank more than enough in the pub but could I leave it there? No, Gussy has to guzzle even more so he invites the lady back to his and starts uncorking vintage 2012. You must think I'm a complete boozer-loser."

"Don't be daft," I tell him, "it was a great night, we had fun."

He spends a few moments rearranging the food on his plate before he looks up. "So, why give me a chance in the first place?" Oh no no no, you're fishing without a permit, pal. "You looked great last Saturday," he angles on, "and I know Eddie had his eye on you but…"

"*EDDIE?*" Eek, too loud, and amplified by a momentary lull in the commotion, which recedes to a hush leaving only the

124

sound of the muzak plinking in the background. I stiffen. Forks, spoons and chopsticks are suspended mid-air; mouths hang open, unissued words dangling on the tips of tongues. Every eye is upon me, a hundred halogen spotlights toasting my cheeks puce.

I squeeze my eyes shut and wait. Long seconds later a tiny drone buds and grows, grows and matures, matures and expands until a ripe roll of gossip unfurls across the room, complete with steel against plates, and normal service is resumed.

Breathe, Maggie, breathe.

A finger strokes the back of my hand, jerking my eyes open. His face is flush with charmed concern. "You okay?" A moment passes between us, an AC bolt across the table, and I smile from the inside out. Warm fingers curl around mine making my heart spin on its axis. There he is again, looking out for me. Taking care of me.

"*Eddie?*" I repeat somewhat quieter this time, as if I doubt my own ears and need to hear the name spoken aloud to confirm how ridiculous it sounds. "He's the last person I'd be interested in and anyway, he's married. I'd *never* do that to another woman, especially after having it done to me. Whatever made you think he was an option?"

"He told me, here, before we left. I assumed he was bruising your eardrums so I ran some interference, but he made out you'd given him the green light. Gave me the wire to back off."

I giggle so hard into my napkin, a fresh tear rolls down my cheek. "Oh Gawd, Gus, that's priceless." I blot my lashes with the edge of my finger. "Wait 'til I tell Cat, she'll wet herself." We revert to re-arranging the food on our plates with our free hands, my fingers content in his reassuring grip.

"You didn't answer my question," he says, and goes all serious again. "There must be other applicants for the job so why give me a second chance? I'm not even sure why you gave me one in the first place."

Unable to think of a wittier retort I say, "I'm gonna take the fifth amendment." And he can see this line of questioning isn't going anywhere.

"Well, that's your constitutional right, lady," he drones in a pseudo-American drawl that's more Dublin than Dallas. He lifts my hand, kisses it old-style, lays it back on the table and with a friendly pat on the knuckles, lets it go. Shucks, I was enjoying that. "Your criteria must be seriously low if you chose me," he murmurs into his plate. Brilliant, another fishing expedition and me still squirming on the hook.

"FYI, my criteria is exceptionally high and you asked me out, not the other way around. That's how it works. You Tarzan, me Jane."

From where, I ask, comes all this juvenile chatter? Is it a free extra that comes with the electric lust-fest? A one-night-only special offer being fed down via some cosmic link that I've somehow tapped into? Not that I think my repartee is particularly funny and I so don't want to come off as a menopausal bimbo but dammit, I can't seem to stop.

He cocks his head. "You're barking."

I try to think of something smart to say.

I fail.

By way of a stopper to prevent further nonsense leaking from my mouth I stuff another fork-load of food into it and send him a careless shrug. But when I twist in my chair to cross my legs, the tips of my toes brush across the shin of his jeans and my heart stills. His fork, bearing several slivers of unspecified meat and a mysterious clump of vegetation, hangs partway between plate and mouth, those eyes urgent as if I'm brandishing a hand grenade, one finger straining at the pin.

"Sorry," I say.

"Don't be."

Lord above, it's a wonder we haven't set off the smoke alarms.

There's a lull while we push the food around our plates but there's not a lot of eating going on.

"Are you tiddly yet?" he probes, dangling that fork over his plate by the handle.

"Not yet."

He smiles his lazy smile, tops up my drink and issues a cheeky grin that hugs me tight around the sternum. "Shame. I'm much more attractive when you're tiddly. And the more you dwink, the more attwactive I become." He gives my glass a tiny shove, shoots me a grin and takes a gulp from his own while my blood tries to break the speed limit with no regard at all for my physical safety. I missed my cue before, I won't miss it again.

"I think you're just fine either way," I say, quiet and low. He stops dead and swings his eyes up to give me The Look. You know, the one that says, right. That'll be a yes. It's a go-er. Ding ding, round two.

That look.

He snaps the silence. "Maybe you didn't turn up tonight after all," he says. "Maybe you're a figment of my imagination."

Another delicious pause.

"Maybe I am."

He takes a moment. "But you can't be," he says and I feel a little squirm in my chest.

"Why?"

He stares at his plate and I get the feeling he's screening the words, selecting, editing, making sure they fit, before he slowly lifts his eyes to meet mine. "Because I can feel you drawing me in from here. You're my magnetic north."

Sod smoke alarms, we're going for the sprinklers.

His eyes weaving a spell around my heart, he reaches across the table and takes my hand in his again. The warmth of fingers intertwining and the damp heat of his palm pulses tremors up my arm and across my chest. Neither of us moves; neither speaks.

What seems like an eon later, he checks his watch. "It's only five past nine."

"Uh-huh."

"I could ask for the bill."

"Good idea."

He signals the waiter. "Then we can…"

"Sure." A brief pause. "Can what?"

"Back to mine?"

"Great."

"OK."

So we do.

But not before I hit the toilets, rip off my wonder-nix and swap them for the scanties secreted in my bag.

Ever the Girl Scout, dib, dib, dib.

Sunday, 17th August, 2am

He's cradling me so close, his face buried in my hair, our bodies swapping heat and perspiration in the dim. My mind is alternating between rewind and replay so that I can relive the last few hours over and over again. I can't believe how deftly he took off my clothes and undressed himself at the same time while he kissed my neck, my shoulders, my lips. It was almost choreographed.

And I'm pleased to report, he's twice the man Gregor was.

His heart is a metronome, tapping out a slow steady rhythm; syncopating. My heart is holding back, matching his pace; synchronising, time marching to every beat. For, as much as it would be fabulous to lie here wrapped around his sleeping body all night, I'll look like Methuselah by morning. Hell, the transformation's already underway, and he cannot see me like that. Winnie's voice echoes through the caverns of my brain – *leave them wanting more.* Oh God, please let him want more. Plan A – sneak into the bathroom, get dressed, leave him a carefully crafted note and call a taxi.

I extricate myself from his arms and slither out from under the covers to gather up my clothes, which are strewn across the hallowed ground that is his bedroom floor. I know jacket and handbag were abandoned in the living room, so in the semi-dark I track down dress, sandals and the back-up briefs-to-match-the-bra.

Drat, my beloved boob-enhancer is missing in action. It must be in the bed, under the duvet, I'll never find it in this murky light. My eyes probe around the shadows and squint at the floor again. Nope, no trace. Damn, if I leave the thing behind, he'll think it's a ploy so I can come back for it and I'd prefer that he didn't inspect this particular piece of equipment too closely.

Think, woman, think.

Tah-dah – Plan B. I evaluate the duvet all muddled up around his sprawled form and work out a sequence. Little by little I lift what's left of it off my side of the bed but my missing wonder-garment's nowhere to be seen. I lower the coverlet as if it were impregnated with gelignite and any sudden movement might set it off. Why oh why did I let him slip the thing off me? The mood I was in, I'd have chucked it on the floor pole-dancer style but oh no, he had to ping it open and let it slide romantically down my arms to fall into the bedding and let's face it, I was too lust-glazed by then to make a note of where it landed. I tiptoe round to his side of the bed, check he's safely asleep then raise the other edge of the duvet off the mattress a centimetre at a time. Result! My missing apparatus is poking out from under the duvet, dangling over the bed end. I link a finger through the strap and give it a gentle tug but somehow it's anchored.

He stirs.

I stall, let go, shrink onto the carpet and hold my breath. A snuffle, a snort and he rolls over, dragging both duvet and bra with him.

Bugger.

Nose pressed to the carpet, I wait for his breathing to deepen before I bob up and risk raising the duvet again. Oh Holy Moses, there it is, hanging off his foot, one strap twisted around his big toe, the remainder swinging back and forth.

I need a new plan.

This isn't any old bra. This bra is a feat of suspension engineering rivalled only by the Forth Road Bridge. I'm certain the sweatshop who built the thing designed it for me personally, to hoick my wobbly mammaries off my midriff and up into firm, perky bozombas. The contraption is a double D dream and I want it back.

C'mon, brain, work.

Suddenly he grunts, stirs and makes to turn over again. The instant he draws his foot up under the duvet I take hold, yank the thing free, throw myself on the carpet commando-style and wait.

He sniffles; he snuggles; he snores.

Phew, that was close.

MI5 would not be impressed and anyway, I'm sure you're supposed to undergo the de-briefing after the recovery mission, and not before.

Oooh, a *déjà vu* moment. Here I am, on all fours, on a bedroom floor, praying a man I've done the deed with doesn't wake up and see me in all my naked glory. Yes folks, I'm a middle-aged hussy who no longer gives a toss, so farewell Mary Poppins, you were no fun at all. Ken would be appalled.

Well, fuck you, Ken. See? I feel even better this time.

This is where a spot of *been there, done that* is a bonus. No mirrors = higher self-esteem. Since the only mirror in the house is in the shower room, I'll dress in the living room. I'm really getting the hang of the forward planning thing, don't you think?

Five minutes and a few practice runs later, my farewell note says a simple 'thanks for a brilliant time' and signed with only one kiss. No *see you later*; no *call me*; no pressure. Then the cab firm tell me the car will be a further ten minutes.

That's ten precious minutes, six hundred glorious seconds more, that I can spend worshipping at his altar.

I sneak into the bedroom to gaze upon him while he snorts into the pillow. Chinks of incandescence from the streetlights outside seep around the edges of the closed blinds and strike the wall above his head, illuminating the inky blue-black of the night. Every fibre of me is besotted with this man – his hair, his smile, his oh-so-blue eyes. Even his darkening five o'clock shadow is endearing to me. Every day he tunnels a bit deeper and part of me is starting to pray. I reach out to push a rogue curl from his forehead. If I can keep his interest going without coming on too strong, it might last that tiny bit longer. Just a few more dates before I shuffle solo into my dotage.

An idea pings into my head. A spot of auto-suggestion might be the thing, since sleep is similar to hypnosis. I could speak directly to his sub-conscious, tell him how much he wants to see me again. My integrity picks this moment to raise a finger of moral objection and much as I want to, I can't dismiss it. So instead of taking advantage of his pliant state, I voice what I'm terrified to tell him face to face. "Gus," I whisper at his tousled head, "I absolutely adore you." And in that instant, that precious moment when I lay bare my sacred soul before him, he responds to the song of my heart as only a man can, and punctuates the night with a turbo-charged fart.

**

Lust is sexually transmitted.

The delicious deed intensifies the feeling ten-fold and the more of him you get, the more of him you want. I didn't sleep a wink; in fact, I might never sleep again. He's in my mental eye line all the time. Hot breath, static-charged kisses, electric fingertips and… Oh, enough already, my hormones are fizzing.

It took me over an hour to prepare for my trek to the furniture shop. My eyes were still bright with the feel-good factor but the bedhead and lack of sleep took a bit of disguising. I refuse to face John Davidson feeling dowdy today so I'm wearing my new cargo pants, a dusky pink t-shirt and a dressy, edge to edge cardi teamed with metallic bronze flatties and bag. My make-up is applied to perfection and my hair flicked back up to its pre-Gus glory.

Butterflies flutter in my chest when I push through the revolving door and stride towards the back of the shop where the salesmen are all standing in a circle chatting. And there he is, my nemesis.

Deep breath, here goes.

"Hi," I chirp and his eyes pop at the new improved me – a confidence booster and my starter for ten.

"Maggie, hi, how are you?"

"Yeah, good," I tell him, and swagger a bit more than intended. Oops, need to dial it down a notch. I take a calming breath. "Thanks for helping me with this, John, the cabinet's in the boot. If somebody could lift it in for me?"

"I'll do it," he offers, and I stride along beside him towards the revolving door and out into the car park.

Be still my beating stomach, it's all going well.

"Ah," he says when I open the boot, "seems Quality Control have made a booboo. I'll order up a replacement on an urgent docket and have it sent direct to the shop. You can collect it, if you like. It's quicker than waiting for a home delivery."

"Thanks, John, that'd be great," I hear a voice say but it doesn't sound like me, it sounds like some sassy, self-assured woman who's in control of her life.

"Why don't you give me your mum's phone number," he says, "I'll call her when it arrives."

What, and have her attempt to bulldoze you into the Five-O party plan again?

"No," I say quick as a flash, "I'd rather you called me instead."

Damn, that came across as an invitation. I should've said send her a letter, but I didn't and it's out now.

He breaks into a smile. "Sure, gimme your contact number and I'll do that." Cringing, I rummage through my bag, locate an old receipt and a pen, give him my number and he pockets it and staggers off towards the revolving door, the cabinet in his arms, me trailing along behind.

It's amazing the difference three weeks can make. This is not the easy-osey Maggie of old, ho no. New Maggie bites back.

133

And since Rory 's night out at Mr Chow's, she hasn't called on Tallulah, not even once.

Beep beep – a text is announced. Excited, I slide my mobile out of my bag, read Gus's name on the screen and blush up pink. John looks up from his form-filling. "Do you need a minute to reply to that?" he offers.

"S'OK, I'll get it later," I say, like hey, it's no big deal, while I fight the urge to do cartwheels up the aisle. Understand, Johnny m'laddo – I'm not some trainee old duffer, and I'm not your sixteen-year-old Mogs any more either. I'm kick-arse confident and getting texts from a hunky man.

I am refurbished, rebranded, relaunched, and having a ball.

As soon as the paperwork's done I voice my thanks, sashay through the revolving door, and once out of his eye line, scramble the mobile out of my bag to devour every word of the text.

> 'Hey wherdyu go? I knew you were a mirage. Wanna b my imaginary pal Weds nite 4 a drink? Gus x'

Well, whadya know – absenting yourself works. Thumbs working like Billy-oh, I start to key in a witty response but think again.

He can wait.

Confidence check: yep, blasting through the mesosphere and about to go into orbit.

Boy, do I owe Winnie a ginormous drink.

Wednesday, 20th August

The barmaid apart, I'm the only female in the Plough and a tad over-dressed for the venue in skinny jeans and an oversized shirt, my gold wedge sandals Velcroed to the beer-spattered floor. At least, I hope it's beer. Balanced on a high-backed stool at the bar sipping brandy and ginger ale, I'm surrounded by a horde of wanabee-drunks but I might as well be on my own for all the attention I'm getting.

I sensed the chill when we met at the bus stop an hour ago, which activated Panic Mode, Level 3. Then he suggested we come to The Pub That Time Forgot but this time he turned tetchy when I gave him my 'really?' look. That ratched me up to Level 5 so I agreed – one drink if we could move on. We traipsed along the High Street in silence – Level 7. Now we're on drink number two and he's spent all his time talking to his mate about football.

"Meet Mick," said he of the frozen face when we arrived, but he didn't tell the man my name. A sun-leathered Australian in his forties, Mick had already enjoyed one too many and it wasn't yet eight o'clock.

The drumbeat in my gut racks me up to Level 8.

Not exactly a dream date.

This place isn't so much a pub as a communal attitude. My nose detects more than a hint of un-deodorised male, every last one of them drunk and competing for airspace, yattering and yelling at ear-splitting pitch like Wall Street in the movies, the din hammering through the fragile shell of my heart.

One old derelict, his face battered by decades of chips and

booze, perks up in his chair and starts warbling a toothless version of *I'll take you home again, Kathleen.* The voice of a twenty-something buck at the far end of the bar struts above the din. "Hey, Jimmy, that's ma woman's name. You givin' her one?" His comrades erupt into boozy bellows, little boys acting big, but Jimmy's not fazed; not fazed at all. He shakes his wrinkled head and offers them his gums.

"Ah *ssson*," comes his slurred response, "think yerself lucky I'm no. She'd not get better in Heaven than what ah've got…" And points a bony finger at his crotch. In a split second Kathleen's paramour mutates from wise guy to Incredible Hulk; through blue air he lunges at the old man but his crew tug him back and huckle him into the Gents. Unaware or unafraid of how close he came to a beating Jimmy cackles, throws back his last mouthful of beer, closes his eyes and folds into unconsciousness, a wound-down clockwork clown, the empty glass juddering in his gnarled claw until it stills in his lap.

I sit back to consider the ceiling while my inner child lies curled in a corner heaving bloody great sobs. Part of her wants to throw a hissy fit; the rest of her is wounded and needs a hug. I glance to my left and sigh.

He's still talking to Mick.

I swill the brandy around in my glass and study the ice cubes, each a tiny iceberg to my sinking Titanic. Ken used to do a similar thing, I remember. He'd leave me sitting in a room full of strangers and ride off on his hobby horse. He never included me in those conversations either. But that was thoughtlessness, not rejection. I knew he'd come back.

I knew where I stood.

So here's the thing. I'm sitting here in limbo, po-faced and with blood on my lip through biting my tongue. Played with fire, got burnt, get over it. What would he care if I got up and left? I rehearse my exit speech over and over in my mind, adjusting the attitude until it conveys exactly the right tone. All I need do is act cheerful, hang my bag on my shoulder, and with a squeeze of his arm say, listen, it's been fun but I've got stuff to do so I think I'll make tracks...

"Wanna drink?" Mick calls out in his Aussie drawl, catching me off-guard. My gaze flips from Mick to Gus.

For the first time tonight, his eyes click on mine. "Mick's offering you a drink, Talullah."

"*Talullah?*" scoffs Mick, and lets out a low whistle. "That's one hell of a moniker for a Scots gal."

I glance at Gus but he's taken to chugging down the dregs of his pint. "That's n-not my name," I stammer, "it's k-kind of a joke."

Gus wipes his mouth with the back of his hand. "Nah, it's Lullah for short, isn't it, Lullah?"

Hurt morphs into anger; anger I'd prefer to hide and can't help but show. "Actually, the name's Maggie," I fume through gritted teeth. I watch Mick's face pick up on the change in barometric pressure. Realising he helped light the blue touch paper, he mouths me a guilty '*sorry*' and retires to the safety of a chat with the bloke on his other side.

At that moment the barmaid thuds another pint onto the bar in front of Gus, dumps a glass in front of me containing what is clearly a double, and without a word walks away giving the impression she'd rather climb the north face of a pile of ironing than serve out the rest of her shift. He heaves glass to mouth, again leaving a fresh rim of creamy foam on his top lip to be wipered off by his tongue before he leans over and drops a mechanical kiss on my forehead.

"You don't look too happy," he says, innocent as you like.

And here I have a choice – make a point or make a joke.

"Don't tell me the Botox has worn off already," I jest, but fail to smile and I can see he's got the message.

"Let's finish this and go," he offers.

I nod, but my anxiety is still stuck at Level 5.

"Sorry Lullah, wasn't ignoring you." He was ignoring me and I'd love to tell him so, but damned if a combination of brandy, replacement hormones and the smell of his skin aren't messing with my head. He gifts me a full on, high powered smile. "Me and Mick had stuff to talk about, you know?"

"Aye, Hibs and Hearts; I heard."

Lip petted, he grabs my hand and gives it a squeeze. "Does my Lullah forgive me?"

What I'd like is to be carefree, laid back and cool. "*Of course*" Tallulah might say, because she's not needy, not needy at all, and maybe they'd laugh and move on. But I'm not Tallulah and he switched off the power and left me out in the cold. Now he switches it back on and I'm supposed to pretend, like it never happened?

"Dunno," I say, and stare at my glass. "Depends on whether I'm speaking to Dr Jekyll or Mr Hyde." But when I look up into those eyes, a fair sized chunk of my resolve melts.

He grimaces. "Sorry, had a rotten day. Took a wee while for that first pint to do the trick, that's all, it won't happen again." This time he beams me the full one hundred and fifty watts complete with crinkles around the eyes.

God, I'm such a misery guts, maybe I do need to lighten up.

I take a slug of my drink and swallow it down. "It'd better not," I say, like I could ever be the boss of him and he smirks, leans in for a perfunctory kiss and licks his lips.

"*Mmm*, brandy, delicious. You're a little firecracker when you get going."

"You bet your life," I say, and try to sound determined, but it's a sham and from the smirk on his face, he knows it.

"I won't suggest another one here, then." My eyes issue a warning although I can't help but supplement it with a giveaway grin.

Something still doesn't sit right but I'll figure it out later.

"Bar Vendange?" he suggests.

"About time," I say, and raise my glass.

Panic Mode – suspended pending further developments.

Maybe now the date can begin.

Friday, 22nd August

Aaargh, I've slept in, I'll never make it into Monkswood to meet Gus at eight.

This two-day-hangover is the work of the devil. I came to yesterday morning in my own bed and with the mother of all headaches – no man-sweat or after-shave, just me and the impression I'd been jolted with a defibrillator. For my sins, the booze had declared a biochemical Jihad on my entrails while a tiny Roger Taylor pounded We Will Rock You against my inner skull. The bass beat's subsided, but it's day two and he's still tapping at the cymbals.

Not so much a case of me hitting the bottle as the bottle hitting me.

Thanks to the Molotov cocktail I threw down my throat, I don't remember anything after we left the pub so I must've caught a taxi home on my own.

Now, where's the fun in that?

I crawled into work yesterday morning at half past nine with the attention span of a woman in a coma. I pieced the night together thanks to various flashbacks, such as when he suggested we share a bottle of house red and I forgot about the brandies I'd downed in The Plough. After that I danced up to the bar in yahoo mode and bought us a couple of jiggers of his favourite Johnny Walker Black, which turned into Armageddon in a glass. The chatter became louder and more loud, the room swayed and then nothing. A haar descends and it's blank.

Turns out I'm a bit of a wild child when I've had a few.

As the day ticked on, the alcoholic pick 'n mix fermented

into liquid dynamite and downgraded me from peely wally to green about the gills, complete with full-blown cramps. Oh how Della laughed.

Ha flaming ha, she's another joker for the hit list.

I managed to sustain life until half past three then skulked home to bed, where I stayed until the alarm went off this morning. I had no clue if I'd ever see him again. Then I opened my diary and alongside a red wine splodge he'd written – *Another date with Gorgeous Gus, Vendange at 8* across Friday's page.

Bugger, now he knows my secret name for him. Oh cursèd booze, I never intended to share that little snippet. I tell you, truth serum and alcohol have a lot in common. A hefty dose of either will lower your inhibitions until you blather like a toddler, although I'm not sure you'd get a shot at the karaoke with the serum, and let's face it, if you snorkel enough booze you won't have time to remember singing your socks off, you'll be too busy throwing up into them. You might have no memory of the destination but oh, how you'll enjoy the journey. Yep, a good suck at the sauce bottle trumps a shot of sodium pentothal any day.

Until the next morning.

My only saving grace is that, judging by his drunken scrawl, I wasn't the only paralytic person in the room.

I drove home tonight in a full scale monsoon, water slewing across the windscreen. As soon as I was indoors I threw off my shoes, pulled on a pair of slipper socks, lay down for a disco nap and – well, you know the rest.

I stare into the fireplace mirror and the lovechild of Dracula and the bride of Chucky stares back. Prison pallor; hair matted over one eye; mascara reduced to full stops and commas peppered around the eyes and trailing down the cheeks. The only plus is that I have a reflection at all. Angelina Jolie, rest easy. Fifty in a fortnight? More like ninety and counting.

Hang on, I feel a bit better.

Maybe I *can* do this.

I could call him, say I worked late so I'll meet him at nine, which would give me time to eat and tart myself up. It'll take a lot of work to salvage something from the wreckage, but it's doable. Excitement building, I jump up, grab the handset and key in his mobile number.

"Hi Tallulah," he yells above a hubbub of men shouting and the sound of booming laughter in the background. I get an image of him straining to hear, the mobile clamped to one ear, his hand held over the other, the only thing missing being a base beat in the background.

Ah.

My tenner says he's in the Plough.

"Sorry, I must've got it wrong," I say, "I thought we were getting together tonight." Somewhere in the backdrop a female laughs, a real throaty, earthy chuckle, and my heart freezes.

I'm thinking, another woman.

I'm hoping, the barmaid.

"Correct, we are. I came straight from work to the Plough for a pint. Didn't want to drive home in the rain so I stayed and bought a couple of filled rolls. You still coming out to play?"

"To be honest I worked on a bit, then I had a scary toilet episode so, had a bit of a lie down."

Aaargh, there I go again, posting classified information.

"Aw, *Lu-llah*," he coos, "and I was so looking forward to us partying. Now I'll have to party on my own and I've got the wee man tomorrow so I won't see you this weekend."

"I don't mean I can't come," I jabber, "what I mean is, I'm fine but I'll be a bit late. I can be there for nine, no problem. I'd rather not drink, but I can have a Coke."

Silence.

"Gus? You there?"

There's a lull while I try to tune out the clamour around him. "But you can't come out to play if you're not well, and let's face it, it's a rotten night. No, stay where you are. It's fine. I'll see you another time."

My end of the seesaw hits rock bottom with a thud.

My head heard *it's fine,* but my heart picked up a flat *no.* As disappointments go, this rates a big fat eight. To my horror he invokes the dreaded throw-away stock phrase no woman wants to hear, the classic accompaniment to a serving of cold shoulder. He utters the words, "I'll phone you."

Ye Gods, what've I done?

"I'm fine, honest," I yammer, sweat beading on my top lip. My ears pick up Mick's Aussie tones through the dial-a-mob din. "You want anuvver, mate?" The penny drops with a heart-shattering clang.

My Plan B needs a Plan B.

The line goes muffled and Gus says something I can't catch before the racket comes back into focus. "You still there?" he asks and I wait for a cacophony of drunken guffaws to pass before I respond.

"Uh-huh."

"You shouldn't be out with a dicky tum. It's pouring, you don't want to get soaked."

"S'OK, my skin's waterproof." I have no idea why I'm still trying to batter down the door since it's closed, for tonight at least.

"Like I said, busy day tomorrow and I'm going for a pint with my old man this Sunday. Don't worry," says he, the parent reassuring the child that Santa will come if only they'll comply and get back into bed and out of their way, "stay put and I'll see you soon."

"But—"

"You should rest," he cuts in, "can't have my Lullah getting any worse, now can I?" There's an awkward moment where I sense him mentally check his watch before he adds the addendum, "For your own good. Don't want you to think I'm bumping you for the boys."

The subtext being, he *is* bumping me for the boys since he'll have a better night quaffing pints in the Plough than sitting in Vendange with a teetotal me.

My heart sinks into my purple patterned slipper socks. I hate these friggin' socks. They make my legs look like friggin' totem poles. So why in God's name do I wear the friggin' things, eh? Why?

"Better go, Lullah. Away and get into bed, take care of you. Text you later. Byeeee."

"OK," I mumble, but it's not. "Text me later, then." And *click* – he's gone.

And there it is.

No date tonight. No definite dates for the foreseeable, not even an IOU, just a clichéd *I'll phone you*.

Why did I say I was ill? Why not say 'I'm running late' and leave it there?

I realise now that there's a smugness to being a wife. Forget the Mills and Boon notions of your youth – married, you feel fireproof and buffered from the struggles of singledom. Sometimes marriage is about the stuff you *don't* have to do. No more bachelor breath, smelly smalls and cringing through his favourite jazz album while making out it's the biz. You know each other and it's gone beyond making the effort, hiding the habits. The trick is to ensure you choose to love him enough not to want to leave the safety of your trench, and hope that your man chooses to do the same. For some women the terrain between Mrs and Ms can be a bleak no-man's-land, booby-trapped with land mines and barbed wire. So here I am, picking my way on tiptoe, getting nowhere fast.

And it's a nightmare.

***

I've lain on the bed staring at the ceiling for the entire four hours since he hung up. The world's at a party and I'm not invited. A hard rain is lashing against the window, my mind a blur of worry fused with anger laced with humiliation. Wish I could merge into the paintwork; become part of the building; cease to be as a separate entity. There's nothing but a cleft, a fissure, where the whole of my heart used to be. My mobile's on the bedside table but did he phone? Did he text?

Welcome to The Pits.

I don't remember dating being this difficult. Is this some kind of karmic pay-back for diddling Ken? Maybe if I'd taken control, said I couldn't go and left it there; absented myself and left him wanting more. But oh no, not me, and the result is, I spooked him and he was in such a rush to hang up that he didn't get time to ask if I needed anything. Like, food. Or medicine. Or that pistol to shoot myself with.

After I've blasted Stella, of course.

I sigh, turn over and stare at the wall. The bricks and mortar creak and groan as the building cools down for the night, the muffle of canned laughter from next door's bedroom television seeping through the wallpaper.

Beep beep.

I burrow under the pillow and moan. Now I really am a twenty-first century girl; he's probably dumping me by text.

Or…

I jump up, switch on the lamp, grab the phone and read.

'Weather crap. Company crap. Beer good. Wish you were here, xoxo'

It's a postcard from the Plough. Wary of appearing too keen, I work out a response and thumb in:

'Still in quarantine, put a towel on my deck chair for next time ;-)'

A gut-churning thirty seconds stagger by before the reply comes zinging through cyberspace.

'Lounger at poolside bar reserved for Weds. Will call to arrange. Miss you, xoxoooo'

I lunge into the bathroom to run a hot bath and while it's

busy filling, skip downstairs to put on the kettle, switch on the oven and take a lasagne out of the freezer.

I know I said I'd play it for laughs but that was before he pocketed my heart.

But hey, are things on the up or what?

Wednesday, 27th August, 5.30pm

I lock the front door, hurl my keys at the hall table, drag my butt into the living room and collapse onto the sofa. What a day – letters, minutes, reports, and as usual Stella wanted everything ten minutes ago.

Since she's neither called me back nor sent out a cheque in response to the three voicemails I left, I check my mobile for missed calls or texts from Joy but there are none.

I pick up the house phone and dial 1471. Someone called half an hour ago. I check the number against my contacts list and nope, it's not City Interiors, and I know it's not Gus's number; in fact it's not in my phone book at all. I dial 1571 to check whether they left a voicemail, which they didn't, but instead find a message left at 10.20am this morning.

"This is Felicity McQueen," says she, and my ear frosts over. "I believe you've spoken to the owner of Bar Vendange."

Uh-oh...

"It seems you've broken confidentiality and apprised him of production costs, including the price of the fabric," she continues. "You have therefore violated our verbal contract, Mrs McCardle, and since your actions have obliged me to offer him a discount equal to your fee, I'm passing the cost on to you. Accordingly, you will receive no payment. Good day." *Click,* and an electronic voice chimes 'end of messages'. My blood burns. She overcharges him, lies, gets caught and I'm hit with the bill? Ho no, you're not getting away with conning *me*, sister. My hands are shaking so much I can hardly punch in her number but when I do it rings way beyond where the machine

146

should pick up. Switched off, I decide, in anticipation of the scud missile I'm itching to launch down the line.

Well that's fine by me your majesty, but as a Grade A Class 1 User-in-Chief, consider yourself added to my hit list and you'll be pleased to know, as befits your superior status, you go straight to the front of the queue.

***

Two hours later I've shaved my legs, French manicured my nails and painted my toenails a fetching shade of hot, hot pink.

As those Girl Scouts would say, Be Prepared.

I've also put a bottle of rosé on ice and some cans in the fridge.

There's those Scouts again.

And I changed the sheets.

Dib Dib Dib.

The Ice Queen will *not* ruin my night.

Ratta-tatt-tatt-tatt! The force applied to the door-knocker almost fires me off my seat. I take a second to smooth down my clothes and give myself the once-over before I breeze out and open the door.

My heart gasps.

He's beyond gorgeous in faded denims, white V-necked t-shirt and leather jacket, and for good measure he's topped it all off with that smile. Yep, I've bagged myself a beaut.

"Come away in," I say, as chilled as I can manage, but he hangs back on the doorstep.

"Actually, I've got a cab waiting." Ah, so he has, parked across the street, engine running.

"I was going to invite you in to see the place. When you texted that you'd pick me up, I assumed in your car. I had thought we could go down the coast to Dunbar."

"But I've told Mick we'll meet him for a drink in Fred's."

This isn't how it played out in my head at all. I'd planned to play the hostess, ask him in, offer him a drink and he'd say sure, love to, kick off his shoes and make himself at home. And maybe his car would be parked outside my door all night while I introduced him to the delights of my lovely sleigh bed.

See how lust can take reality captive?

"You ready?" he asks, bringing me back to the now. He flashes those baby blues and my heart hums like a spinning top.

"Sure," I say, and beam him a smile I've hauled all the way up from my toes, "let me get my jacket." And I run up the stairs while he lingers on the doorstep.

So what if he doesn't come in. All that matters is, I get to spend time with him and taxis are expensive to keep waiting, aren't they? He can come round another night.

Or maybe, later tonight? *Tee hee hee…*

***

As soon as we climbed into the taxi he grabbed my hand and held it all the way to Monkswood High Street. It's still proper tingling.

Vendange is quiet with only a few tables occupied and a couple of pint-drinkers loitering at the bar. Me, I'm sipping my usual rosé and Gus is elbowing a pint of lager, while Mick has still to make an appearance. Fred's nowhere to be seen, praise God, not that I give a damn about any dictum issued by the Ice Queen.

"Don't think I said before but I made those curtains," I tell him, in an overt bid to impress, and he flicks his eyes over them.

His mouth curves up at the corners, "So, I've got a clever girlfriend."

"Not that clever," I tell him. "The interior designer gave me the job then charged the owner a whacking great mark-up and refused to pay me for the work."

"Did she, now. Never mind, you'll sort it out."

"I'm not so sure; she left a cheeky message on my phone, barred me from talking to him. She's lied to both of us and diddled me in the process." I notice his gaze, fixed in the middle distance, staring at nothing at all. I click my tongue and offer his arm a couple of gentle pokes. "*Hello-oh*, prod prod, you still awake?"

He turns and blinks, the flimsiest of smiles crossing his lips. "Sorry, it's – well, we're out to have a nice night, Lullah, so let's not go there."

"Go where?"

"You know. Venting anger, letting off steam. Not tonight. It's such a buzzkill."

Ouch.

My lips move but in my confusion nothing comes out so I swallow and try again. He shakes his head and tuts at himself. "I'm sorry," he says, and gives my knee a gentle squeeze, "but I can see you're upset. Don't want you getting even more upset, do I? You can tell me all about it another time. Let's have a few drinks and enjoy ourselves, yeah?"

"Sure," I croak, my stomach beating ten to the dozen, but he's distracted by an incoming text and has already opened his phone to read it. I heave a sigh. Maybe he's right. Things were swimming along nicely and now I've gone and darkened the mood.

"Text from Mick, Lullah, says he can't make it. Back in a mo." He snaps his phone shut, pockets it and heads for the Gents, giving me time to work out how to prevent my foot from going any further down my own throat.

Hmmph. This is why I needed Tallulah.

She was all about the good times and she'd never pester him with her problems. But she was a one-night-only gig and no matter what I do I can't summon her up again, which is a nightmare since the real me is cocking it up big style. He has his own problems. Work's a bitch and he's still getting over the separation. No, if this thing keeps going I'll tell him about it all somewhere down the line.

I almost jump out of my skin when Fred appears out of nowhere.

"Oooh, you startled me," I say, not sure whether to be on the defensive, but he grins and I breathe a bit easier.

"Sorry, I was in my office, saw you on the CCTV, wanted a word. I phoned that bloody McQueen woman."

"Aye, she left a hoity-toity rant on my house phone."

"You're honoured, she's yet to call me."

"She didn't speak to you?"

"Nope. She refuses to return my calls so I emailed her. Four times. She finally emailed back this morning saying, if I'd gone elsewhere it would've cost me even more so her bill stands. Cheeky cow."

"She told me she gave you a four hundred pound discount and she's keeping my fee to cover it."

"Hah," he scoffs, "I got zilch. She's threatened to call in the lawyers if I don't cough up. I can't afford a legal fight. Her uncle's some hotshot estate agent and bloodywell minted. I think we've both lost out Mrs…"

"It's Maggie."

"Maggie. Sorry about that, I didn't think she'd do you over as well." He glances behind me and I instinctively whip round to see Gus walking towards us, curiosity scrawled across his face.

"Angus my boy," chirps Fred and spreads his arms as if to welcome the prodigal son back to the fold, "are you with Maggie?"

"I am that, Fred my man, she's my girlfriend. I didn't know you two were acquainted." My heart sinks. He's already forgotten that I'd made the curtains and he didn't tell me he was on back-clapping terms with the owner.

"Let's just say we have a mutual enemy," says Fred, and I laugh. Gus laughs too but I can see he's still not sure. "Hang onto this one, Maggie, he's a great guy, and you take care of her m'lad. I'm away back to sort out the order for the brewery." And he claps Gus on the shoulder a few times before he strolls off towards the office door. Now there's a turn-up for the books – Gus, rattled because I was chatting to another man.

"Same again?" he suggests and I nod. He crosses to the bar and waits to be served, my eyes locked on his rear view and believe you me, it stands up to the scrutiny.

And he's with me.

A glass in each hand he saunters back, places our drinks on the table and drops sideways into his seat. "It's your birthday the weekend after next, isn't it?"

"Yup," I say, disappointed he bought me white instead of rosé but thrilled he remembered my special day. "Why d'you ask?"

"It should've been my weekend for the wee man but I spoke to my ex, arranged a swap so I can take you out for your birthday."

"That's fantastic," I yelp, my cheeks flush. He takes my hand and moulds it into his and what do you know, it's a perfect fit. All this time I've been worrying about, does he care, will it last, will he remember and all this time he's been making plans on the quiet.

"Only one drawback," he says, and I press 'hold' on the inner rejoicing. "I'm taking my boy now from this Friday after work 'til Sunday evening so once again I won't see you for the whole weekend. But I'll see you during the week, Lullah."

My shoulders slump. "I suppose," I say, and mug pathos at him.

He pulls me closer and brushes his lips across my cheek. Sweet mother of Jesus, I'm tingling all over – naughty, naughty boy. He puts his mouth to my ear and I close my eyes at the warmth of his lips and his soft breath on my neck. How can I resist this man? How can I refuse him? I wish I had the strength to say, not here, there's a time and a place, but the wine has joined forces with my hormones again and my resolve is all but gone.

I gradually open my eyes to see a gap-toothed drunk with a two day growth and a forehead that's way too low gurning at us from his standpoint at the bar, grinding his pelvis in an all too familiar mime.

"Gus, pleeease, stop, we're behaving like visual Viagra," I plead in his ear, and Gus's eyes follow my gaze. He winces comically and nuzzles my neck again for effect. "It-is-not-funny," I protest through sniggers, and attempt to shove him away, but in my alcohol-engaged state it is funny; hysterical, in fact. I giggle and give him another push to fend off further attack but his fingers continue to caress the back of my neck, keeping my system on high alert.

I get a flashback to my panic when Steve's pal spooked me in this very bar, oh, less than a fortnight ago. And now here's Gus, molesting me in the self-same place while I giggle like a schoolgirl and make only partial protest. "C'mon, jack it in," I plead with a bit more gusto, "any moment now he's gonna come over and offer to pitch in with a threesome."

He pulls away. "Sorry," he grins, and raises both hands as if I'm staging a hold up, "but all bets are off once we get to my place."

"You could always come to mine," I suggest hopefully. "I've put some cans in the fridge." He looks cornered for a second, then lets out a long, exasperated breath.

"But Lullah, we've got a rush job on at work; need to start at half seven in the morning so I need to be where my car is. You don't start 'til nine, you'll have more time than me to get organised." I make a sad face. "Aw, come on," he pleads, "I live two minutes up the street and you live a ten minute taxi ride away." His face alters from a plea to a lust-laden grin. "Not sure I can wait that long to get my hands on you." Lord above, when he does that thing with his eyes I can't seem to say no, and he knows it.

Drug of choice, thy name is Angus.

"What are you like?" I say and giggle.

He sits up a bit straighter, clears his throat and tugs at the lapels of his jacket. "You're right, I shouldn't seduce you in public, so there's only one thing for it."

"Which is..."

"Bop you over the head and drag you by the hair to my place, of course." I consider the alternative, which is to go home alone and I know that's not an option I'm prepared to take. Dammit, the man's got my heart in a headlock.

Lord help me Jesus, here I go again.

Friday, 29th August, 9am

Uncle Pete ambles through the double doors and saunters towards my desk, glasses at the end of his nose and the weight of the world on his shoulders.

"'Morning, lass."

"'Morning, Pete, how's you?"

He hitches his trousers up by the belt, hangs a hip off the edge of my desk and pats his spherical paunch. "*Acht*, I've got a wee touch o' pregnancy this morning. I see you're all on your lonesome."

"Not for much longer. Della will be here soon, she's a late starter."

A finger tugs his glasses a fraction further from his brows, the better to deliver his best hackneyed look. "She's no late starter, that one," he says, and smirks. I grin. "The buzz from smokers' corner is, Stella's inundated you with work again. You look tired, you losing weight or were you out on the randan last night?"

"I'm on the Stella Diet – all work, no lunch."

He drops his eyes to the floor, shakes his head and sighs. "Tell me about it, I used to spend my days surfing the Figleaves site but since she arrived…anyway, don't shoot the delivery boy but she wants to see you in her office, *afore ye even sit doon*," he says, caricaturing her harsh tone. My shoulders slump.

"I've no idea what it's about, lass, she doesn't tell anything," he adds, giving me a paternal pat on the shoulder. "All I know is, she's pacing the floor in there. I'm nothing more than a human Stella-gram."

154

I straighten up and sigh. "Got any silver bullets?"

Amused, he tugs an earlobe. "I suspect she's more your wooden stake type of a gal. If you need to, come and see me when she's spat you out," he says, "I've got a new supply of consolation Kit Kats you might be interested in. I'll leave you to it." He slips off the desk, rams his hands deep into his pockets and, humming to himself, walks off, his pot belly pointed towards the main section.

"Thanks Pete," I tell the back of his head and he raises a hand in salute. I rise, take what I hope is a calming breath, and head through the double doors, my heart hammering in my ear. I imagine the calm in the corridor is how Hiroshima felt in the seconds before the shock wave. At least the auditors have moved out of the training room, so they won't hear whatever's about to go down.

I knock twice and crane my head around her half-open door and oh, but she looks exhausted. The regulation black dress and crimson lipstick have joined forces to drain the life from her face, the dark of her eyes accentuated by the undead pallor of her complexion.

In contrast to her usual custom she stands and takes a few steps towards me, a welcoming hand extended to usher me towards the legendary hot seat, and I can't help but take a step back. "Hiya, Maggie, come away in. Shut the door and sit down. How're you doin'?" Whoa, hang on – Stella being nice? She's never nice to anybody. Ever. And she never chews anyone out without broadcasting it along the corridor so why close the door?

"Pete said you wanted to see me?"

"Aye. Sit down for a minute." Still on her feet she lowers her chin, one hand splayed on her hip, the heel of the other massaging her brow while she rootles the back of her brain for the right words.

"Ah've missed a pre-meetin' meetin' in Glasgow to speak to you this mornin'," she says, and straightens up, "but no matter,

I'll head for the main meetin' straight after this." She leans both hands on the desk and scours the wall behind me with her eyes, as if praying the answer to her problem, were it secretly scrawled by the Gods in invisible ink, might spontaneously reveal itself right there, just above my head. "A wee problem's come up, it's nothin' really. I made a wee mistake when I was sendin' you stuff last night, emailed some things I shouldn't have. I'm assumin' you've not switched on your computer yet so when you do, can you open your Outlook Express so I can recall them?"

Stella, asking, not telling. I swallow hard. If I say I've set my computer to forward copies of her emails to my Hotmail account, she'll throw a fit.

"Sure, no problem, I can delete the lot if you want and you can resend those I should've had."

"*NO!*" she hollers, then as quick as she bares her fangs she retracts them. Palms pressed, she takes a calming breath. "Sorry, I meant, no," she says. "Unless I do a recall, they'll still be on your computer somewhere, and they're highly confidential. If by chance you do open somethin' you think you shouldn't have, do me a favour. Don't read it, just delete it. Then delete everythin' in your recycle bin, okey doke?"

"Sure," I say and stand to leave. "If that's all, I'll go to my desk and get right to it."

Stella, on her back foot? No strutting or gnashing of teeth? No bawling or bullying?

This must be big.

I can't wait to tear along the corridor and get back to my desk. The computer takes a dog's age to load up but when it does, I log onto Outlook and up pops her usual batch of directives. My eyes roam the screen to single out any headings of interest but nothing jumps out in the moments before they disappear in one block from my inbox. Then it strikes me.

It's not confidential, it's incriminating.

And she's sent it to me.

156

***

Keys jingling, I barge through my front door, drop my bag on the floor, make straight for the laptop and flick it on. Sod food, curiosity is providing my brain with all the sustenance it needs.

Why oh why does this machine take so long to fire up? While I'm waiting I text Winnie to invite her over for a Saturday night drink. She replies that she's seeing Steve on Saturday, can I do Sunday at seven instead and I say yes.

The instant my laptop finishes loading the phone rings. I check the caller display. It's that number again, the one that didn't leave a message yesterday. Sod it, I decide, and ignore it.

Wait – it might be Cat from her holiday hotel. I pick up.

"Hello?"

"Maggie."

Hmmph. "John. Hello."

"I've got your mum's cabinet here. When can I drop it off?"

I sit up. "*You're* gonna deliver it? *Personally?*"

"Why not? I thought it might be a nice gesture from the firm after everything that's happened. How's about Tuesday afternoon?"

"Uhm, okay, fine."

"Great. I'll be there around four."

An empty silence. "Well, bye then," I say, desperate to get picking through those emails.

"Right, sure. Bye, Maggie."

A double click later and my inbox opens. There they are, a whole page of emails waiting for me. I click on the first and dart my eyes right to scatter the floaters. It's a health and safety notice to all staff. The next – a general reminder of the rules on smoke breaks; the third – an update on the repair of a computer glitch, again addressed to all staff. I'm beginning to wonder if I've got the wrong end of the stick when I open the fourth and gasp.

Addressed to screen name andypandy007, she's carving him a new one. What does she mean when she says, if the powers that be find out she'll lose her job? And she's making it clear, if the law get involved she's not going down with him.

Who the hell is andypandy007?

If only I understood.

Hang on – Stella said emails, plural.

I need to keep reading.

I open the fifth email and my spine stiffens. It's her reply to a message from James Baldwin, District Director for Central Scotland. I scroll down and read his original email first, in which he said his diary would be free for a few hours on Friday afternoon, could they hook up. Geezus, that was today. I scroll up to her reply. She says she'll tell staff here she has some meeting or other in Glasgow and see him at the Grand Union Hotel on Clydeside.

They're having an affair.

He's married, so is she. He's also her line manager, which makes it against the rules. Forbidden. A major no-no.

And I was worried about a one night stand with geeky Gregor.

Frustration is burning a hole in me. I'm too frightened to confront her, and I can't tell anyone else, especially anyone in authority. In truth, I don't know anyone in authority. They're all based in Glasgow and we only ever see them being guided past our desks, gawping at us like day trippers at the zoo. For all I know andypandy007 is James Baldwin's boss, hell it could be Baldwin himself, and who knows how many senior management the two of them are buddying up to.

There's nowhere to go.

Unless – *Fran*! I ferret through the pocket of my handbag, locate the napkin she wrote her number on and pick up the phone.

"Fran, it's Maggie."

"How weird, I was just about to call you," she says. "I want to see you again, the sooner the better."

"And I'd like your professional opinion on something, if that's okay."

"Sure, I need your help too. I'm not going home this weekend so we could do Sunday lunch."

"Sure," I say. "How's about you come to mine and I'll cook. Say, three o'clock? I want to show you something on my laptop."

"Text me your address and I'll see you at three."

I put the phone down and head for the fridge but instead of foraging for food, I pull out a fresh bottle of rosé, unscrew the top and pour myself a huge glass. I have only two options – one, stay sober and sensible, or two, get unapologetically, mind-numbingly, head-down-the-toilet drunk.

I plump for option two – much easier than tracking down a size twelve straightjacket at this hour on a Friday.

Buckle up, folks, it's set to be a long, long night.

Sunday, 31st August, 2.30pm

"I just *love* your co-ordinated curtains and blinds," Fran says, staring in awe at my bay windows. "Did you make them?" She hands me her coat and a bottle of pre-chilled Chenin Blanc and settles down to admire my drapes from the vantage point of the sofa.

"Aye, and the cushion covers and bed throws and every other blessed thing," I say with a weary roll of the eyes.

"I take it you use paper patterns."

"I don't. I get ideas from magazines or off the TV and design my own templates out of tissue paper. I assume you brought the wine to have with lunch, fancy a glass now?"

"Just the one, I'm driving," she says. "You have some, though."

"Thanks, but lack of sleep means I can't risk even a sip or I might nod off mid-sentence and dip my nose in the bolognese." Teeth clenched to suppress a yawn, I head for the kitchen to fetch a solitary wine glass.

"Do you have photographs of your handiwork?" she shouts from the living room, "I'm looking for ideas for the new house."

"Sure," I tell her when I arrive back from the kitchen, "I take a picture of every finished job." And I pass a half-full goblet into her hand. I nod at the laptop on the end of the dining table. "They're all in a folder on the PC," I tell her. She licks her lips, dons a pair of half-moon glasses and pulls up a dining chair while I click on the folder, which springs open to reveal neat rows of jpeg icons. Eyes scanning the screen she clicks the mouse, opening pictures of swags and tails, mediaeval pennants,

160

goblet, pencil and triple pleated headings, lined and draped voiles and puddled curtains alongside Roman blinds in all styles, fabrics and finishes; it's every window I've ever dressed, apart from my Vendange creations.

"I like a challenge," I say and shrug a shoulder, an apology for the sheer number of photographs. "I get bored doing the same old styles."

"I can see that," Fran says. "This is like curtain-porn to me. Can I email the folder to myself so I can study it later? And I've left my mobile in the car, can I use your house phone? I need to make a quick call."

"Of course, go for it," I say and give her the handset. She punches in a number while I head for the kitchen to dish up the spaghetti. Maybe she'll ask if she can use one of my curtain ideas for her new house, I think. Maybe I'll even get the job of making them up.

"How did you get on with the designer woman, what was her name again?" she asks, sucking the leg of her specs when I return to set the plates on the table.

"You mean Felicity McQueen? I did one job for her, in double quickie time mark you, and she refused to pay me."

"Why?" She bumps her chair closer to the table. I tell her all about Felicity and her money-making scam while we swirl hot spaghetti into spirals with our forks.

"I'm sure you could take it further," she suggests, wiping tomato sauce off her lips with her napkin, "you should see a lawyer."

"It was a verbal contract, Fran. Anyway, I'm off the legal profession big time. No, I'm writing it off as a lesson in life. Remember – Felicity McQueen, City Interiors – make a pact with yourself to brandish your barge pole if you ever come across her. I won't make curtains for cash ever again. I'm sticking to friends and family, at least they appreciate what I do."

"Well you might want to rethink that someday," she says,

still scoffing her pasta. "So, what did you want my input on."

"It's Stella."

"Your boss."

"Yup. She's Goebbels, Himmler and Hess all rolled into one and the way she *treats* people. I thought she had a fridge motor where her heart should be but turns out she's bonking the District Director."

Fran looks at me, her eyes steady. "How do you know?"

"She sent me emails by mistake then had to ask me not to read them but I did. They were forwarded to my Hotmail address."

"Show me."

I swing the laptop round and bring the incriminating evidence onto the screen. She turns it to face her and, fork stilled in her hand, and reads them one at a time, before pushing her plate away and sitting back.

"I'm not surprised you wanted my help," she says, elbow on the table, fingers tapping her top lip. "I'll need to think about it. Leave it with me and I'll get back to you."

"Sure," I tell her. "You were the only person I could talk to. If I tell somebody at work and they grass me up, she'll devour me whole just for forwarding her emails home. I do it to try to keep up with the workload. Is that a security breach? I don't know."

"Maggie," she says, her eyebrow hitched the merest fraction, "I cannot stress this enough…" I get the feeling I've overstepped an undefined line. "…you must keep those emails hidden and don't tell a soul, understand?"

I swallow. "Sure."

"Now, tell me how your mum is," she says, and pushes the laptop away.

"Fine," I reply, my gut twisting. I know a change of topic when I hear one.

Fifteen minutes later and the temperature's taken a nose-dive. Oh, we've chatted about the weather, the X-Factor,

162

anything except those emails, and all the time I've sensed her edging her way towards the door. Finally she babbles an excuse, gives me a hug and, without saying if or when she'll get in touch, scoots hell for leather up the path and away.

If my legs were long enough I'd kick my own backside. She expected to have lunch and a curtain chat, not be pestered for a professional consultation on her day off.

So, you thought you'd thumb a free ride on the good ship Fran, eh? Well look what you did, Maggie, just look what you did.

Sunday, 31st August, 5.30pm

The TV is buzzing, the volume low. The leftover lunch is congealing on the table alongside Fran's empty glass and the remains of the bottle, now tepid and undrinkable. I'm curled up on the sofa, the velour throw cosying my shoulders. Head heavy, eyes drowsy, I'm in a dreamy state, my mind swaying to the rhythm of the clock on the wall. The big hand ticks forward, counting off the lazy minutes, pulling me down into the warmth, deeper and deeper, drifting, drifting...

Ratta-tatt-tatt...

I jump to my feet and meet myself head-on in the fireplace mirror. Puffy-eyed and flush of cheek, the evidence of an interrupted sleep is there, folded into the pink creases on my face. When I reach the door and peer through the peephole Ken bobs into view, his ill-omened face distorted through the lens. Scobie's words echo in my ears – *"I assure you, he is entitled..."* I shudder.

I brace myself, open the door and step sideways to let him in. He's scruffy, a two day growth on his chin, and on a Sunday he still smells of old books. He's never worked Sundays so this is off-normal. His face registers my crumpled clothes and sleep-lined features but he doesn't broach the subject, his business being, as standard, of much higher grade importance than anything that might affect me.

And he's failed to notice the new-improved Maggie.

"We need to talk," he says, which in Ken-speak means he needs to talk and I need to listen, and perches himself bang in the middle of the three-seater, a man primed like a coiled

164

spring.

He makes his first mistake.

He grabs the remote to click off the TV then chucks it to one side without so much as a glance. A seething ball of anger flares in my chest, not only because he's so casually taken charge of the remote, but also because he thinks he can walk in and resume his role as king o' the castle. *My* castle. Eyes vacant, he's staring at the pattern on the rug but if I asked him to describe it, I bet he couldn't. Instinct says this isn't about my pension or he'd just come out with it. No, he needs something and I don't know what it is but he needs it from me.

Breathe, Maggie, breathe...

He interlocks his fingers, his face taut. I make to sit on the two-seater to wait for the skid of stylus on vinyl followed by several tracks of classic Ken but in my drowsy state miscalculate, land heavily and let out an involuntary grunt.

Squidging myself square, I cough a few times to clear my throat. "What's the problem?" I croak, still trying to marshal my weary brain cells. He narrows his eyes and studies me for a few seconds before making a start on his scripted speech.

"Look. Here's our dilemma." My stomach flips.

Our dilemma?

He clasps and unclasps his hands, stares at his feet and sighs the sigh of a man resigned. "I'm in trouble."

Did you spot that? No *nice to see you* or *how are you* or *how's it going.*

"So – now you need my *help*?"

He steps out of his forced melancholy, raises his threadbare head and shoots me an end-of-tether look. "I've got no choice but to come to you. Babs and me, well, we're not getting along."

"Shame. What about the baby?"

He looks at his feet rather than look me in the eye. "No baby," says he, and hunches his shoulders, "false alarm. But listen, Maggie..."

*Whirr, click click, PING…*mistake number 2.

"Aaah, I see. Did she concoct a baby to manipulate you or did you fabricate it to manipulate me?"

I watch him waver, that muscle in his cheek twitching, but rather than go off-script to strike back, he ploughs on. "That's not it at all," he says, his face hangdog, and polishes one palm with the other. "I'm here because I've got myself into a tight spot. With the law. And money." He sighs and does his best to look downhearted. "Bought a fifteenth century book off a bloke about a month ago, something called the Liber Sextus, said he inherited it from a relative in America but had no idea of it's worth and needed to sell it quick. I couldn't check its value with a dealer, they might've gazumped me on the sale, so I checked the internet. Lowest estimate said quarter of a million." He gives me a sheepish look. "So I offered to buy it."

My jaw drops. "Geezus, how much?"

He stares into space as if checking his mind for a way to dilute what he's about to say. "Fifteen grand." I gasp. "I was gonna replace the covers, repair the spine…" he gets in, before I can recover enough to say a word, "…but I don't know much about books that age so I thought, better double check first in case I devalue it. I took it up to the National Library in Edinburgh on Friday. Turns out it's stolen. The Police arrested me and confiscated it as evidence. I might as well have chucked the money up to the birds 'cos it's gone."

To help decode the underlying text, I think it through out loud, counting off the points on my fingers. "So…without checking it was kosher you bought a book you thought was worth a fortune…shortly before you asked me for a quickie divorce…then you speeded things up by not claiming what you were due from the house…aaah, I get it. You couldn't wait to diddle me out of my legal half of the profit so you jumped the gun. You didn't tell me you had that kind of money, where the hell did you get fifteen grand?"

A shadow flits over his eyes and expands to darken his face.

Then comes his downfall, proof positive of his fatal flaw and his third blunder of the day. He goes for gold and talks down to the one person he hopes can pull him from the wreckage.

"You can cut the attitude, madam. I'm telling you I've made an error of judgement and all you're thinking about is yourself. I didn't have that kind of capital lying around so I borrowed it from the business and I need to put it back before my uncle realises. He's decided to sell up and I needed all the profit from the book to buy him out. I've got big plans, Maggie, I want to pay off Stewart, take it down to a two-man outfit, make some decent money. Babs doesn't have a bean so she couldn't help even if she wanted to."

"And you think I can loan you the funds to replace it? Pah! Where, I ask, would I get fifteen thousand pounds' worth of ready cash?"

"Not loan, Maggie, give. I figure I'm due at least twice that from the house alone. I only want what's owed to me and the balance would give me a start on buying the business. You've always kept a few bob stashed away so don't kid a kidder. I'm giving you fair warning – if you can't come up with the readies then I'm seeing a lawyer, tomorrow, to stop the divorce before I lose out on what I'm entitled to." At this he leans forward and makes what I pray is an empty threat. "And I think maybe I should move back in, let's say, next Saturday?" And with a sneer adds, "You know the drill, to protect my investment, etcetera etcetera."

I'm still reeling when I'm struck by a sudden bolt of clarity.

"Babs is throwing you out, isn't she? First sign of trouble, she pulls the bung and you head for the nearest lifeboat – me." And there it is, the old bottom line. Knowing the game's up, he drops his head, one hand spanning his balding brow, and grunts.

That's one to the power of Me.

"Honest to God, Ken, you make Jack the Ripper look like the archangel Gabriel. Thirty thousand quid? I don't have that kind of money either. Do you even remember how big a day next Saturday is for me?" He jerks up his head, lowers his brows.

He has no clue.

He's gazing at the window, trying to work it out, his face lighting up when his eyes snag on the dirty wine glass and half empty bottle on the table.

"I don't like your tone," he snarls, acting the big I am. He scowls me up and down. "I know what this is – the swollen face, the dishevelled clothes, the bloody-minded behaviour. You're *drunk*. I'm appalled, Maggie, drinking during the day, at home, on your own. You never drank when you were with me." I open my mouth to put him straight but before I can form a coherent sentence he beats me to the draw. "I heard you were associating with some Champagne Charlie, a useless tosser by all accounts. It's obvious he's introduced you to this alcoholic lifestyle. Not my Maggie, I thought, not her, but it seems I was wrong. Why should I walk away from what I'm due so you can party it all away?"

Man oh man, that was below the belt. I knew he'd stoop low but this is off the register. Did he always insult my intelligence? Be this blatant in his manipulations? I'd have to say no, although this is quintessential Ken – shifting the focus, taking the high moral ground, putting me down to win points. Only these days he doesn't feel the need to be subtle and conceal his finagling behind a veil. Or maybe it's me who's thrown away my soft-focus lens. But now, since he doesn't require to keep me sweet, when I refuse to go along with his plans he thinks he can whip out the Bully Boy Book of Tactics.

Well, not on my watch.

Face blazing, I scramble to my feet. "You don't have the right to disapprove of me, mister high-and-mighty who buggered off with a slapper and didn't give me a second thought. And don't presume to judge Gus either, you don't have the moral authority. You might be right; maybe he is a useless tosser but from what you've just told me you make a much better one."

Wow. All this is coming out of me, Maggie McCardle, one time wallflower, now she-devil-in-a-strop. It is; it's all me.

I'm giving him what for.

He slumps his shoulders and changes the set of his face to contrition, a prelude to yet another U-turn. "I'm sorry, Maggie, really. I didn't want to leave you at all, you forced the issue by finding out about Babs. I was trying to end it with her at the time. It was only a fling, you know? Something and nothing. I never meant to hurt you. I wish we could go back to where we were but we can't. If we could just come to some arrangement about the house..."

Dear God, he actually thinks I'm buying into this reverse guilt-trip.

I laugh, not your usual run-of-the-mill laughter but fall-on-the-floor, open-jawed mirth complete with snot and tears, and by the set of his face he is not amused.

"So it was all my fault to blame?" I say when I regain the power of speech, and shake my head at the brass neck of the man. "You were half packed before you even came home that night, and desperate to throw the marriage away for a second time when you thought you'd stumbled into a fortune. Well the papers are filed with the court, Ken, and I can't wait for you to be rubber-stamped out of my life."

But deep down I'm not so sure. Is it truly official without benefit of money-grabbing, back-stabbing, cadaver-stripping lawyers? And so far he's failed to stake a claim to my pension. Simon Scobie's words echo through my head for the second time in half an hour... '*it is his right...*'

Ken chooses this juncture to ramble a bit further up the sympathy trail and softens his face. "But Maggie..." Molten anger solidifies grey in my gut.

"Don't you dare," I glower and make a face; the kind of face that says, you're not listening, pal; as usual, you're too busy making sure you get your own way.

Well two can play at that game and guess who learned from the master?

He blinks as if to reboot his vision but I know he can never conjure up the old me, the one he could talk circles around.

He clicks his tongue and changes gear yet again then, with all the theatre he can muster, jumps up off the couch and glowers with such hatred in his eyes that I take a step back. "It's not over 'til it's over," he growls and storms out, slamming the front door with such force that he almost shakes the foundations.

I pause to listen. In the back of my mind I hear ticking but it's not a stopwatch, it's a legal time bomb. If he does consult a lawyer, if he stops the divorce, they'll put him straight about my pension. I lift my eyes and issue a petition to the heavens – *how much more can my sanity take?*

As if en route for Damascus, I'm graced by my most vivid Pivotal Moment of them all. Sometimes the decision to scrap a cherished chunk of jigsaw, the piece you'd rather pluck your own eyes out than see squandered on your traitorous ex, is the choice that sets you free. In the name of dignity and integrity I close my eyes, breathe deep and take a minute to accept what I've been dodging all along.

He is entitled.

I'll sell the house, move in with Mum, give him his thirty pieces of silver and start again.

Desperate tears spill down my cheeks, tears of hurt and loss and resignation, but they're also tears of relief.

And the last salt tears I'll ever shed over Ken McCardle.

Sunday, 31ˢᵗ August, 7.30pm

"Aw, c'mon, I hate to drink alone." Winnie's on the three-seater, both legs curled beneath her, her glass held high as the golden liquid bubbles from the bottle in my hand.

"Nope, signed a twenty-four hour pledge this morning."

"I'm offended," she mocks. "This is the best sparkling perry our local ethnic minority superstore had, don't you know, Monkswood Moet it is, cost me a whole two pounds forty nine AND it came ready-chilled. Better than yon fancy pants gut-rot you've got on the table, which probably tastes like warm cat's pee 'cos *somebody* should've put it in the fridge..."

I snigger, hug my coffee cup and take up residence on the two-seater opposite. "How's it going with Steve?"

She affects a silent movie swoon. "What can I say, dahlink? He's got that sexy I-can-take-you-or-leave-you thing going on, but I know he'd rather take me. A little bit of me's always fancied him and methinks you already know which bit. He's helping me release my hidden tart."

"Hussy. He only wants to bonk your brains out."

She looks positively put-upon. "Again? Oh well, if he must, he must..."

I roll my eyes and grin. "*Tsk, tsk*, isn't this what the tat mags call an overshare?"

"No, Maggie, it's what they call a do-before-you-die thing."

"How do you mean?"

"Living, Maggie, living." I gape at her for the full five seconds it takes to assimilate this basic, core ethos before it hits me. That's exactly what I'm *not* doing – living. Oh, I'm going

171

through the motions; existing between phone calls; hoping, praying, pleading even, but not living. She realises something's happened and drops the act. "You okay?"

I shrug a response, but I know my face betrays me. "I'm just working through a few problems, that's all."

"Gus-type problems?"

"Amongst other stuff."

She blinks and raises a sardonic eyebrow. "And how is little boy blue, what's he doing to upset you?"

"Acting the bloke, basically. He's gone all one-of-the-boys on me. My super-hero's turned into the invisible man, I haven't seen him since last Wednesday. Between him, Stella and the curtain fiasco, I'm exhausted. Then Ken wheeled up an hour ago, demanded thirty grand, which I don't have so divorce halted because, why should he walk away from what he's owed?"

The shock is stamped across her face. "Away you go…"

"Yup. After a bit of prodding on my part he admitted he wanted the quickie divorce because he thought he'd struck the deal of the century and he didn't want me claiming my half. But it went belly-up. Now that he's got himself into financial and maybe even legal strife, Babs has had enough and is pushing him towards the door."

"Holy moly. She probably thought he was minted, him working for his uncle and all. What about the baby?"

I shake my head. "Never was a baby."

Winnie goes to speak but thinks the better of it and raises her hands to fend off any further revelations. "Don't tell me any more or I'll be forced to kill him. Change of subject – tell me what's happening with Gus."

I take a deep breath and sigh. "I thought he was the solution, "turns out he's the problem. Seven dwarves to choose from and I had to pick Grumpy."

"I think you need to make some decisions, girly, for instance *is doormat my default?*" My eyes mist and threaten to bubble tears.

"I am *NOT* a doormat, I'm just out of practice. I'm trying my best…" Mortified, she jumps up, shifts from her couch to mine and drapes an arm around my shoulders.

"Sorry, Maggie – sorry, I didn't realise…" I close my eyes to stem the flow but tears are already streaming down my cheeks.

"S'OK, I'm a woman on the edge, that's all. Gus is behaving like I'm Typhoid Mary, Ken is channelling the Plymouth Brethren and I'm parenting a pre-pubescent pensioner – *help*. You taught me how to break the ice but this is a whole different game of twister and I've tied myself up in knots."

She considers for a moment. "So Gus is blowing hot and cold, jerking you around." I lower my chin and nod through fresh tears. "Men, honest to God, he clearly doesn't know which side his baguette's buttered on. I'd try the *treat 'em mean, keep 'em keen* approach if I was you."

"You mean mess him around deliberately?"

She scoffs. "God, you really are out of whack with the whole dating thing. It's just a strategy, like the alter-ego thing, or when men rate themselves a nine out of ten, then seek out a five to make sure they won't get rejected." Her words hit me hard – did he see me as a five? And then I realise – it's a higher score than I'd awarded myself.

"You need to work out what you want and how to get it," she goes on. "You're giving him a God complex, so demote him. Make him think you've gone off the boil, scare the bejesus out of him."

My eyes issue a sideways scowl. "I see. So the plan is – dump him? Are you mad?"

"Ye Gods, you've got it bad. I didn't say that, I meant give him a taste of your own sweet and sour. Put a price on your head, he'll be your slave forever. Men are just overgrown kids, they need rules and boundaries and the occasional verbal slap. Look – the heart wants what the heart wants therefore you can't walk away. But you can work out a ploy or two, change your approach." The raised inflection at the end of her sermon is begging a response.

"You mean, play games. I hate games."

"What you're doing now isn't working, is it?"

A break-through hot flush is making me clammy but my head is crystal clear. I'd assumed if I jogged alongside, the situation might take care of itself but it didn't, it slithered into a deep, dark hole. Now that Winnie's hammered a tiny crack in the wall at the end of the tunnel I can see the twinkle of light and the more she talks the brighter it glows. And it dawns on me, I contributed to the breakdown of my marriage too. Took it for granted. Didn't put in any maintenance.

There's another angle.

"I haven't done much to further feminism, have I?" She elevates an eyebrow and smiles. "I was offered promotion, you know, a few years ago. Turned it down, figured I didn't want to cope with more responsibility *and* running the house since Ken was so busy at the workshop. Our marriage ended up with him as driver-slash-navigator and me as his passenger. What the hell was I thinking?"

She tilts her head and smiles. "Stop beating yourself up, woman. Ken should've given you your place so it's not all your fault. But this was your life, Maggie, you should never have let him dilute your power like that." Winnie gives my shoulder a friendly pat. "Hey, you'll be fine," she says in a hushed voice and nudges me with her elbow, "but I think you've fulfilled your quota where halfwits are concerned for this lifetime. It's high time you converted one of them to the cause. Your duty to the sisterhood, in fact. Turn him around, you can do it."

I sigh. "I'll give it a bash. What've I got to lose?" She swigs a mouthful of wine, glancing at her watch over the crescent rim of her glass.

"Oh no, just when I've had a breakthrough," I moan, "d'you have to go?"

"Not at all," she says, the goblet still resting on her bottom lip, "I was only working out how much time I've got versus how much wine's left in the bottle. I'll have to go in half an hour so better put the kettle on, Polly, since you're on the wagon." She parts her lips, tilts her head, drains the rest of her wine and presents me with the empty glass and an elfin look.

"A hint is a hint is a hint," I chirp, then pick up the bottle and unscrew the top. "More tea, vicar?"

Sunday, 31st August, 9.30pm

I've been working on a replacement Plan B since Winnie left, trying to figure out where on God's earth I can lay my hands on thirty thousand pounds without selling the house, and how to keep Cat from finding out.

The phone rings and pulls me back into the room. Ken, to have another pop at me, I'd put money on it.

I pick up and say a nervous "Hello?"

"Well hellooo, Maggie," sings a disembodied voice.

"Oh my God, Cat! You must be psychotic, I was just thinking about you."

"The cheek o' you, calling *me* psychotic. How's tricks?"

"So much more expensive than they used to be, my sweet. Tell me about the holiday."

"I cannot tell you how brilliant it was," she enthuses, "except for the last few days. Got a bug of some sort. Kept throwing up my pina coladas."

"Tut tut, that's you all over – such a wastrel."

She chuckles. "Never mind, all better now. Oh, but we had such a great holiday and to prove it I've brought home just over four and a half million photos for you to pore over one at a time, with personal narrative."

"*Aoww*. Suddenly not feeling so well, Cat, *aoww aoww*. Might have to take the week off, maybe the rest of the month. In fact, not sure if I'll ever be back…"

"Listen, if Della's sitting through them, so are you. And I'm her team leader so she's sitting through them. What are mates for, eh?"

"Torturing?" I suggest and she tuts.

"So, what news from the war zone?" My brain stalls. If I tell her what Ken's been up to she might call him, go ballistic and make things worse.

Not to mention what she'll say to me.

Don't mention the emails either, whispers a voice in my head, *remember Fran.*

"Hmmm, let me think… I won the lottery, only 1.4 million, mind you, not one of those huge wins, so it won't change my life. Brad's left Angelina for me but the paparazzos haven't caught on yet. He's been pestering the life out of me to go to LA and move in with him but I'm not budgin'. Honestly, he might've checked with me first."

"Yeah, who wants an ex-sex symbol trailing a tag-team of kids behind him, right?"

"Exactly. Such a shame, and he used to be so shaggable too. Oh, and I've been promoted to Chief Exec so the first thing I did was sack you in your absence. And…yep, I think that's it."

"In yer dreams, sunshine," she scoffs. "Anyway, I was so relieved to hear you didn't take up with that loser, Gus."

"…what?"

"You remember – Gus   from Rory 's office. Well, wait 'til you hear this. Rory and me, we popped into Tesco on the way home to pick up a few things, bumped into his ex, Rachel." I tense. "She was rushing around with a trolley, trying to get home before he dropped the wee one off. Told me he's desperate to get back with her, always pestering, pestering. Even relented and said he'd take their son for the whole weekend to let her go to York for a couple of days with her sis, which is a major coup considering he never takes him overnight." Gus? My Gus? So where was he all those nights he said he was with his boy?

"She asked if he'd take the baby for the weekend ages ago but he kept saying no 'til she said don't bother, she'd get her mum to do it, and he knew he'd lost that one. Her attitude surprised me, I'd always thought she was head-over-heels with him.

Anyway, think you had a narrow escape there, lady." She's revelling in the gossip, unaware her words are shredding my heart into teeny, tiny slivers.

"Maggie? You still there?"

"Yes, I'm, trying to process," I say, but the pulsing in my gut is distracting me. "Sorry, Cat, I just…" And then it happens; my voice cracks.

"*Nooo,*" she cries, "tell me you didn't…"

"He said…he'd swapped…weekends…so he could take me out…on my birthday," I stammer through the sobs.

"Aw *noooo*, I assumed it was just a couple of dates. I didn't realise you were still seeing him."

I'm knee-deep in betrayals, but this is the boldest of the batch. "What else, Cat? Tell me what she said."

"You sure about this?"

"Oh for Gawd's sakes!"

"Sorry, had to ask. She blames it on his ego, says it needs feeding at regular intervals. Says it's all about the chase with him, likes to flaunt his pulling power in front of his mates." A bell goes off in my head but it's not an alarm, it's the ring of truth. So that's why he took me to the Plough and the Ship. Why we always sat at the bar. The victor parading his spoils in front of The Boys, eh? All that fishing for compliments. I close my eyes and sigh.

"Sorry, Maggie, I did say he was worth the watching."

"I thought you meant Eddie, not Gus."

"Christ no, Mags, you could blister-pack Eddie's patter and prescribe it to insomniacs. Of course I meant Gus. Look, I'm gonna come over."

"No, I need time to figure this out. He's due to call me anytime now."

"Okay, but promise me you're not gonna do anything daft."

"Don't worry, you don't have to put me on suicide watch. Not over a man. I'll see you tomorrow – you *and* your four million photos."

"Yeah, well, maybe I'll spare you that pleasure 'til the end of the week. You know where I am." *Click* – and she's gone, leaving me hurtling towards the gates of hell.

Monday, 1st September, just after midnight

Never did get that call.

Alone in the gloom, all I can hear is the beat of my heart toiling above the sound of the wind whapping the rafters. My life has all the appeal of a ghost town. A solitary tin can rattles up the street outside, a depressing echo to the tumbleweeds in my mind. Four words, that's all, just four tiny, devastating words run through my mind for the umpteenth time since Cat hung up.

Gus is a liar.

The thought that I might never see him again fires a slingshot through my soul. I'd be able to think straight if one of his stray sparks hadn't hit me that night at the Ship and ignited a bonfire. Tears gather on my lashes, sobs rise in my throat.

I thought he was Maggie-heaven, but this is Maggie-hell.

My legs shift one way, then the other. I plump the pillow, knead it down, pull up the covers, push them off, turn, toss, turn again. Since I started this stupid project my world has been like the night bus – full of users, chancers, wasters and halfwits, and all with their own agenda. Me, I'm just collateral damage to the likes of Gus or Ken or Felicity friggin' McQueen. I check my self-esteem for proof of life but can find no pulse. Oh how I yearn for my solitary but comfortable rut, why did I ever poke my head above its parapet?

Untethered, time trudges on, its progress glowing neon in the night – 1:00, 1:36, 2:12, 2:47. If I don't drop off soon I'll sleep through the alarm and be shattered all day. I count sheep, do breathing exercises, but still sleep refuses to come, held at bay by the helplessness and the hurt. There's a black hole in my heart and I fear my sanity might fold into it. I could slap myself for letting this bauble of a man take a wrecking ball to my life. He should come with a warning – Beware! This person is addictive and may seriously damage your mental health. Lust is a form of dementia – only the clinically crazy would inflict this on themselves.

My head's a snarl-up of sobs and worries and bargains with God. My heart, the heart he's so carelessly crushed, is hunting for a lifeline, desperate to protest his innocence. It's possible he did want her back until he met you, it says. What if she didn't know about you after all? You've only been on the scene a couple of weeks, what if she'd assumed the situation hadn't changed, it suggests.

Is that really *what you think?* the walls seem to jeer. I pull the covers up to block my ears, but they pump up the volume. *If that's true, why didn't he tell her about you? And why didn't he text last night? Where was he? Who was he with?* I shake my head to dismiss the negative thoughts but here they come again, sounding stronger. *'He hasn't phoned you since that first call, so why would he start now?'*

Shuttup shuttup shuttup…

Before long I'm straying into no-man's land, the territory between asleep and awake, consciousness dissolving into a mash of imaginings. Breath deepens, my mind slipping in and out of focus. In my state of drowsy confusion I trip into weird, crazy dreams, people running around and shouting and I've no idea why before I'm slammed conscious, soaked to the skin, and for the briefest of moments the discomfort distracts me and I forget.

Until I remember.

I glance at the clock: 6:15.

Damn.

Aware of first light seeping through the blinds I peel off my soggy nightshirt, cast it to the floor and curl down to catch the remaining hour. Soon I'm sliding into semi-consciousness again, reality giving way to fluid thoughts; a dream state where time speeds up, the movie in my head on fast forward. I'm in a runaway dodgem car. My heart thuds as it zigzags and pitches, the wind whipping at my hair. It's dark, so dark I can't see my hands but I can feel the steering wheel. My foot finds the brake pedal and pumps like fury but the brakes don't work; the lights don't work either and there's nothing to protect me. I'm grappling at the wheel, trying to take control, but it comes off in my hand and now there's nothing to hold onto and no seat belt to secure me. In a frenzy of fear I open my mouth to scream but nothing comes out. The car is careering on, twisting and snaking, throwing me side to side, skimming through bushes and branches that flail and thrash at my face, my neck, my right arm. I'm aware of a faint buzzing in the distance which is moving closer, growing and surging, a thousand bluebottles droning in my ears, increasing in volume while the car speeds on. Blood pelting, I slide down in my seat, arms raised to shield my face as the chaos engulfs me and...

Wham.

I jerk awake, sweat beading on my face, my chest, all around my hairline, gasped into consciousness by an animal yowling in the dark.

Oh.

It was me, wailing. Damp, anxious breath funnels up and out of my trembling body, tears streaming from my eyes, some ear-bound, some soaking the pillow. It was a dream, just a horrible dream, but oh, it seemed so real.

Curled up on my side I close my eyes and issue a silent rebuke to the universe. *Aren't you supposed to take the jokers out before you deal someone a hand?* I let out a pitiful moan, then another before I can send off a further invective. *Why were you never there for me? I asked you, I pleaded with you...*

I freeze.

In the dim at the end of the bed, a shadow lingers. I strain to look but I'm paralysed, my heart thumping against my ribs. Every part of me is primed, adrenalin pumping through my veins. I'm aware of it moving to the side of the bed behind me, but no matter how much I struggle I can't turn around. *"Go away,"* I want to screech, *"don't touch me,"* but it's impossible; my lips are moving but my voice is mute. It moves closer and yet closer, but still I can't move, terror crushing my chest, constricting my breath, my nails digging crescent cuts into the palms of my hands. To my horror it closes in on me from behind and I feel the weight of it huddling against my back.

Then the strangest thing happens.

Like an attentive lover on a cold, cold night it wraps itself around me, it's head on my shoulder nuzzling my neck, but it's not scary, not scary at all. I relax, close my eyes and let it envelop me, its warmth and affection swathing me in a serenity so blissful that I can't help but give myself to the embrace. My sixth sense tells me this is no intruder, nor is it a hot flush or a night sweat. No, this is intense love suffusing my soul, salving my tortured psyche. It's shelter and protection, it's emotional sanctuary, it's safety and security, and I'm scared to breathe for fear of breaking the spell. Am I dying? Maybe, but I don't care if it feels this good. Somewhere above me I hear the lazy tinkling of bells, the sound of wind chimes on a balmy day, and a soft voice whispers in my ear. *'Everything's going to be all right; I love you; I'm here for you; trust me; have faith…'* and I'm lifted, raised out of my sorrow to a place somewhere close to seventh heaven.

Just when I think it might never end it eases its grip and little by little pulls away, the intensity of its warmth receding. Eyes still closed, I hear myself murmur, "Please don't go…" although instinct tells me its purpose is fulfilled. A moment at a time I slide into reality, my eyes drifting open, and take a slow, deep breath before I glance around the empty room.

Wow.

The warmth is still there, calming and uplifting my very soul. Perhaps it was an angel from the Claptrap Cavalry finally answering my calls. Or maybe it was a Pivotal Moment.

If so, it was a true blue, straight up, one hundred per cent holy roller.

On second thoughts, Pivotal Moments don't mend wounds or soothe jangled nerves, they're far more likely to open them up and force you to look closer; to question; to confront. No missing chunk of jigsaw was exposed. I experienced no revelation; no insight or enforced acceptance and no subsequent change of view. Nothing's resolved. Nothing's different from when I went to bed.

Except for me.

I feel stronger and more positive than I have since – well, since ever. The problems are still there and so are the people who caused them but I'm sure now that I can rise above it.

Nothing can faze me. Nothing can stop me. Nada. Zip. Zilch.

The alarm clock buzzes: 7:15am.

After I've showered and dressed, I make for the stairs but amble to a stop in front of the hall mirror, the one I never did get around to dumping. The Maggie who gazes back has lost the haunted look, her features calm.

Three rapid knocks to the front door cut through my thoughts.

"Recorded Delivery," chaffs the postman. He hands me an envelope and his e-board, which I sign. After I close the door I sit on the stairs and stare at it for the longest time before I prise open the flap, slide out the contents and read. Something inside me blooms. Sod dignity; to hell with integrity. It really is going to be alright and I've got it in writing.

It's my divorce certificate.

Monday, 1st September, 9am

I spill through the double doors, bursting to tell the girls my divorce news. But the first thing I see is Cat, a hand on each hip and a scowl on her face.

"At last. Get in here and back me up," she says. "I've been telling Della about that numpty Gus."

"Well, good morning to you too," I say, drape my jacket over the back of my chair and sit down. Della and I exchange uneasy glances. See? This is why I can't tell Cat about Ken's blackmail, or why I'm selling the house, or Stella's affair. God only knows how she kept Gregorgate to herself. My eyes issue a stop but she ignores it and speeds through the red light.

"Well, I'm only saying. He's been at it big style, telling you porkies. I caught him out, and if you're too blind to see it…"

I cannot allow her to take a blowtorch to my cosmic calm so it looks like I've got a fight on my hands, and my guess is it's the first of a few on the subject if I don't put a stop to her. "*I* don't know that for sure," I say as evenly as I can, "*I* haven't spoken to him yet."

She throws me a look, one of those *yeah, right* snarls. "Get real, Maggie, of *course* he was," she says, and ratches it up another decibel. Here we go, another power play from Cat. I can read the look in her eye. *I'll have nothing but contempt for you if you don't side with me*, it warns.

"Honest to God, Maggie, I'm just waiting for the *plunk*."

"What *plunk*?"

"You know, when the penny drops. *Plunk…* You heard what Rachel said, how can you say you don't know for sure, how can you, I *told* you..."

Dammit, she's gone sonic.

"Cat, that's enough! This is not a tea-time topic – my life, my business." She pulls her head back at the vigour of my tone but her phone rings before she can respond. She raises a hand to put me on hold while she picks up. On any other day I'd get that familiar swirl of anger, an anger that has no voice and nowhere to go, but not today. No, today I can deal with it.

Today I have the Claptrap Cavalry in my court.

While Cat deals with the caller, I turn my attention to Della. The scorn on her face says, *first time in ages I come in early and it's all 'pistols at dawn'.*

"You're a bit previous," I say and tap my watch.

"Got a lift in," she whispers, a girlish gleam on her face, something you don't often see in young Della. I lower my voice so Cat can't hear.

"Got a new boyfriend, have we?"

A shameless smile. "Might be."

I look round but Cat's still chattering. I turn back to Della. "The fair-haired auditor, by any chance?"

Della huddles behind the safety of her screen. "Aye, but I'll tell you later. For Chrissakes, don't tell her nibs, not sure I could cope with the kind o' grief she's givin' you. What the hell is she on anyway?"

I roll my eyes and sigh. "Whatever it is, she's exceeded the stated dose. If only I knew where her 'off' switch was." And Della smothers a snigger with her hand.

Then it hits me.

She has an 'off' switch, everybody does, all I have to do is find the courage to flip it. I slow my breath and try to achieve a state of flow. Della registers the grit on my face and takes cover behind her monitor. Once I'm sure I'm in the zone I stand, stride over, pluck the phone out of Cat's hand and set it back on its base, cutting her call dead.

"Erm, what do you think you're doing?"

"We need to talk," I say, my resolve telling my stomach to stay firm. "We can do it in the training room or we can do it in the loos, your choice. Now, Cat, right away." Her eyes flick to Della, who's trying to hide behind her monitor.

No back up there, Cat.

"Oh. Are you alright?"

"No, Cat, I'm not. Right, I'll decide. It's the loos then. Come on, let's go." She glances at Della again, her face begging for a clue, but Della's keeping her head down.

"You check the cubicles on that side are empty, I'll check this side," I instruct when we get there and for the first time in living memory she does as she's told. "Now, sit on that loo lid and pay attention." Again she complies, all the while trying to read my face. "Cat, I'm gonna say this with love so listen up. You're bullying me and it has to stop."

She's horror-struck. "But I just…"

"I know, you just thought you were helping, and I've appreciated your input over the last year but it's time to step back. You've put me in a state of siege. Every time I try to do something for myself you take over. And if I don't comply, you get bigger and uglier until I back down."

She looks me up and down. "No I don't," she spits, seething now. "How dare you. I was trying to help. When I think of all I've done for you and this is the thanks I get…" This is classic Cat, pumping up the volume, shoving, bullying. Unlike Ken, she doesn't do U-turns and I'm not sure she has a reverse gear. She much prefers to jam her foot to the throttle and ram everything in her path.

My stomach should be squirming like snakes in a too-small bucket, but I can't afford that luxury. I let the moment rest, slow it down. "Think about it. I told you about Project Me and in a handclap you'd cast yourself as my fairy Catmother. Then you decided I was going to Rory's do at the Ship two days later. When I tried to get you to back off you ridiculed me."

"Pah. You're talking rubbish," she scowls, her voice rising in defiance.

I give her a sideways glance. "And here you are, doing it again," I tell her.

"I hope you're finished."

"Not nearly. I got bullied into going to the Ship then you decided where I was sitting and with who. You never used to be like this, Cat, I used to tell you everything. Can't any more, though, you're a nightmare." She makes to argue but I get in first and keep going.

"Then you got the bit between your teeth about a makeover the day before Rory's work's outing to Mr Chow's. You arranged my time off, decided what I was having done and by who and when I protested, you didn't listen. You played the best friend card and even insisted on paying so you could have it all your own way. And when you can't bludgeon me into submission, you try to enlist Della's help. I'm sick of it."

I watch and wait to let her take all this in before she sinks back down onto the toilet seat, her face wearing my words like weals. "And now this thing with Gus. You've been baying for his blood since before I got here this morning. If it was up to you we'd form a lynch mob, batter down his door and hang him from the nearest tree. You're making me feel stupid because I fell for him but we don't choose who we fall in love with, Cat. Stop blindsiding me in front of Della to get me to do what you want. You've only got Rachel's version of events, I need to speak to *him*. This is *my* life, Cat, and you're not my keeper." She goes quiet while she processes what I've said, then I watch her turn pink.

"Oh Gawd," she cries, and crumples, hands on top of her head. "I thought it was for your own good. I thought you needed... Oh, I'm so mortified."

"Listen, Cat, I value your opinion but I need to make my own decisions." I run a hand through my hair and sigh. "Giving Project Me until my birthday was pushing it at best. I need to move at my own pace. It's my project, mine to control."

188

Embarrassed, she throws her hands over her eyes and wails. "I'm such an idiot."

"It's fine. Just be my team leader at work and my friend outside. And friends let friends do their own thing, don't they?"

"Sure. Just slap me around if I step out of line. Deal?"

"Deal," I say, and give her a hug. "C'mon, let's go see Della. I need to tell you both my news." And we exit the loos and head back to the section.

Refurbish, rebrand, relaunch? It's all child's play compared to regaining control of your life. But do you know what? I can do this, I know I can.

Just as soon as I work out how.

***

"Gus. Hi." I swap the phone over to my other ear, the better to keep stirring the pasta on the stove. "Sorry, meant to text you earlier. How's things?"

"Yeh, fine." I pick up a tinge of impatience in his voice. "I've phoned twice already, where were you?"

Oh, sure. Like I should be hanging here, on a hook, waiting for you to call.

"Out," I say. "What can I do for you?" I realise I'm coming over a tad brisker than intended.

"Oh. Wanted to say, left my mobile at home last night, couldn't text you."

"No worries, I was a bit tied up anyway, and you explained all that in your text today."

The text I chose not to reply to.

There's a telling pause which allows me to give the metal spoon a couple of swift whaps against the pot rim before I clang the lid back on. "Gus. You still there?"

"Yeah, yeah, still here. So, you got my text, then?"

"Sure I did, at lunch time, yeah? Sorry, it's been one of those days. Busy, busy."

"Right. I see. So, I take it we're still on for Wednesday?" This time I detect a definite shift in his tone, in fact I could swear I heard him step onto his back foot. In my head I toss an imaginary coin to decide which way to play it.

Tails – you lose.

"Not sure yet, to be honest a lot's happened since I last saw you. Listen, my pasta's done, I need to go. I'll get back to you." And now I can almost hear his brain trying to manage this singular shift of attitude.

"Look, I can tell something's wrong. Let's have a talk." I jerk my head up. He's never wanted to talk. It's set up camp already, that germ of doubt I've planted in his brain; now all it has to do is take root; multiply; tunnel. I hang back and let the silence stretch a bit.

"Well, since you've brought it up…"

"Aw nooo," he drones, "I blew it, didn't I? You're gonna bump me. The old heave-ho. I'm dumped."

Thrown by how easy it is to rattle him, I'm shocked at what I say next. "Sorry. I've been thinking and this isn't for me. I feel like an emotional pit-stop you haul into every so often to get your ego re-inflated before you zoom off again. I think I want better."

"Aw, Lullah, that's not it at all. *Acht*, this is my fault, I've not been paying you enough attention."

"There's more to it than that, Gus. We're not suited. All I wanted was a bit of fun but this isn't my idea of a good time."

"But I thought… Look, don't do this, Lullah. Meet me on Wednesday and we'll talk."

I allow an unspoken 'no' to hang on the line. "Maybe. I'll think about it and get back to you," I tell him. "I've got a lot on this week. Text you tomorrow, yeah?"

"Sure, anything you say."

"Have fun, Gus."

"Sure, Lullah, sure, see you later. And can I say…" But rather than hear him out I hit the red button and cut him off, the same way he once did with me. Touché, Gus. Now all I have to do is figure what I want out of this and how to get it.

Yeh, like, that's going to be easy.

Tuesday, 2nd September

John jumps off his chair when I waltz into Mum's living room, her trotting behind me in a fluster, him looking like he's swallowed his tongue. I delayed getting here to avoid him but here he is again to rub my nose in it.

Well not this time, mister; today I think you'll find I'm even more self-assured, confident and fit to face my demons so think on, Johnny m'laddo, just think on.

Sugar daddy, indeed.

"Hi," I chirp, ignoring him, and launch my jacket and bag at the settee. I turn to Mum. "So, the cabinet..."

"Unpacked it an hour ago," he butts in, answering for her. "Your mum wanted me to wait 'til you got here to check it over." I catch her cast me the evil eye; that advisory look that mothers employ that says, do not face me up in front of him up, Lady, or you'll have me to contend with.

"He wanted you to have a look before he left," she explains, in a small, small voice, "in case it isn't right." The hair on my neck bristles. This is how she behaves when cornered; she either brazens it out or acts the little girl. Twisting her fingers in a theatrical display of innocence, she turns her gaze back to John. "She does everything for me, you know..."

And he smiles, patience personified.

I don't do everything for her and she's capable of handling this herself.

I point towards the hall. "Is it in the...?" He nods. "Let's have a dekko, then." And I take off towards her bedroom, the two of them behind me.

"I'll put the kettle on," calls Mum and takes a detour into the kitchen. I reach her bedroom door and there it is, dusted down and in its rightful place by the bed, a perfect match for its twin.

"That's great, John," I say and keep my smile polite, my manner business-like. "Thanks for delivering it." I turn to leave the room but he's standing in the doorway, blocking my exit.

I gesture at the door. "Shall we…?"

His hands in his trouser pockets, he looks a touch bashful. "Can we talk first?"

I glance into the hallway behind him but there's no sign of Mum, so I utter a bewildered, "Sure."

"It's just, I've been trying to talk to you for a while now. I wanted to do it at the shop but it wasn't ideal."

A chill tingles up my spine. "Has the cabinet been taken off special offer? Ah, we owe more money. Wait there and I'll get Mum to write you a cheque."

I make for the door again but he stands steadfast, yanks his hands out of his pockets and spreads his arms to corral me. "No, nothing like that. I, well, *ahem!*" He clears his throat into his closed hand. "*Ahe-ahem.*"

He's nervous. Why is he nervous?

He treats the side of his lip to a liberal chewing and looks like he might apologise for what he's about to say. "Dunno where to start, really. *Ahem! Cough, choke, ahem.* Sorry, frog in my throat." And he gives his chest a little thump, his face turning purple.

I smile, taken back to when Cat first mentioned Gus and I came over all awkward and flustered. I coughed and choked, just at the sound of his name. Poor John, I must have looked like he does now – *ahem, cough, choke, ahem…*

Uh-oh…

He can't look me in the eye, in fact, he's busy tugging at the skin around his nails.

"*Ahem,*" he croaks again, and gives his breastbone one last tap.

"I'll fetch you some water," I say and make to leave the room again, aware my voice has gone all high-pitched and wobbly.

"No, no, I'm fine. I need to – *ahem* – talk to you. I – *ahem*. Can we sit down?" He motions me towards the wicker chair, all the while craning at the door for any sign of my mother making an impromptu entrance.

"Of course," I tell him, wishing to hell she would. Where in God's name is the woman anyway? Holed up in the kitchen leaving me to cope with Johnny-boy, that's where. Hands clasped, he perches on the end of her single bed and stares at his knees. Thrown for a second by the tiniest of tremors I edge a step back and sink into the chair.

"I've tried to call a few times but I can never catch you in," he says at last.

"So *that's* the number that keeps coming up on my house phone. You should've left a message. I could've called you back if it was to arrange delivery."

His voice deepens. "It wasn't about the cabinet."

"Oh."

His eyes wander the room. Now I have a weird feeling in the pit of my chest. Or my heart. Or my stomach.

Well, *something's* squirming.

He looks uncomfortable. "I was so chuffed when you came into the shop with your mum the other week. I always had a thing for you, you know. Still do." Now, that's a proper pivotal moment right there, but this time the power's draining away, conducted across the room, and I'm floundering like a trout in a net. How many of these dratted revelations can a girl cope with in one lifetime?

Farewell my karmic calm, hello shedloads of stress.

"YOU had a thing for ME? When exactly?" The drum in my gut is gathering momentum; swelling, throbbing, reverberating until it's pounding like a fridge-sized speaker in the back of a Mini Metro.

"Back in the day," he says, and returns to appraising the

knees of his trousers.

He looks up. "If I'm honest, I was so shy. I'd never really asked anybody out before that."

I stare at him while I process this bolt from the blue. "What, never?"

He gives me a tart look. "I was only seventeen, for God's sake, and a slow starter."

"Eighteen," I correct, "you were eighteen."

"Seventeen, eighteen, no difference. I still hid behind the bike. I'd been on odd dates but they just kind of happened. I'd never gone out more than twice with the same girl."

"But I always thought of you as laid back. Joe Cool."

"The James Dean swagger worked then," he says with a bashful grin.

Well, well, so Johnny used an alter-ego too.

"This is beyond ironic."

He lowers his brows. "How so?"

"Because I had a crush on you too."

His face is blank but I can see the processor behind his eyes has gone into overdrive. "You're kidding." I shake my head. "But you flirted with my mates, never with me."

"I was trying, in my immature, teenage way, to get your attention." I let out a half laugh. "Aw, John, talk about star-crossed. But that was thirty-odd years ago, we can never pick it up again."

He looks stung. "Why not?"

"We're different people now. Plus, I'm – well, it's complicated. And you're seeing somebody, so it's a no-go."

"Me?" he says, surprised. "I'm not seeing anybody."

"I saw you, John," I scowl, annoyed by his denial. "In Vendange the other week. Young. Blonde. Draped around your neck." Oops, that sounded jealous. Didn't mean to sound jealous. Or threatened. Or even interested.

He guffaws and shakes his head. "That was Christie, my youngest. She's at Edinburgh Uni studying medicine. She finally dumped her bozo of a boyfriend but she was upset so I took her out for a meal."

Ah.

There's an awkward moment where I think I might expire with embarrassment. "So who were the other couple?"

"My eldest, Kayleigh, and her boyfriend. She's at the Art College. The girls were born fourteen months apart so they're thick as thieves, share a bedroom in a flat in Marchmont." Two eyes the colour of putty twinkle at me in amusement. "You thought she was my girlfriend. I'm flattered, although I'm not sure she'd find it quite so complimentary."

Oh dear. This is a whole new game with a different set of balls. In the hope of recovering at least some credibility I say, "It was an obvious assumption. She was, frankly, hanging off your neck and you looked, sort of, uncomfortable. I just thought you were behaving, kind of, how you always did."

He pulls his head back. "And how was I, kind of, always?"

"Uhm…emotionally unavailable?"

He shakes his head and forces a laugh. "No" he says. "I was never that. But I was shy and terrified you'd reject me. You were my Mogs, the girl with the captivating eyes."

Captivating? I thought they were standard issue, common as muck, much like my 'O' type blood.

Aaah, now I get it… It's like Winnie said, the sweet-and-sour effect. Until two minutes ago he *was* interested because he thought I didn't give a toss. Then I came over as jealous and threatened and probably turned his view of me on its head.

And I'm so not. Jealous. Or threatened.

You know I'm not, don't you? No. I mean, yes. I mean, no, I'm not. I shift in my chair. He's had a glimpse of me, the real me, barbs and all. A full-on blush floods my cheeks.

Where is my flaming mother with that tea?

"And I don't have someone, in fact I don't have anyone," he adds, hauling me out of my thoughts.

"But *I* do," I inform him, which isn't as set in stone as I make it sound, although I'm not telling John that. I can't let him know I'm too scared to even think about Gus because every time I do...*aoww*, there it is again, that squirm in the gut.

"So that's that," he says, "after all these years, it's the thumbs down."

"Sorry, but it's way too late. And I'm not pleased that you used my mum to get to me, that's so not on." He gives me a baffled look but then I see the truth of it register on his face.

He nods. "You're right, of course. I think it's time I went." He stands to take his leave. "Sorry if I made you uncomfortable. I had to give it a shot."

"Sure. And, err, thanks for the compliment."

"You know my number if you change your mind."

Now, why did he have to go and say that?

The sensation is like someone drawing a fingernail across my heart. "I do, thanks." He nods again and walks out of the door. I hear him, in the hallway, saying his goodbyes to Mum, and seconds later the front door clicks shut behind him.

All too late, my mother appears at the bedroom door. "Well?" she asks, her face full of expectation.

I give her a look. "What do you mean, 'well'?"

"Oh nothing, it's – he wanted to wait, that's all. So I let him." She sussed he had an agenda. She thought if she gave us some space...

I cradle my face. "Oh, Mum, I'm such an idiot. He's not what I thought he was at all. He held up a mirror and I know he looks into it and hopes for the sixteen year old me. If only I was still that girl. Instead, here I am, trying to make fifty years worth of life look like a lot less and making a fool of myself." Lord knows, I don't want to blub but I already feel the sting of tears.

A sign of tolerance stretched, Mum blinks from side to side and sighs. "Oh, for crying out loud, he's not that young boy either, *and* he knows it. Take a peek in my mirror. I look at you and wish I was staring at fifty. We were all line-free in our teens and correct me if I'm wrong, but you were never one o' yon femmie fatals."

Cheers, Mum.

"Truth be told, you were immature and a bit of a scatterbrain," she goes on. "You're older and wiser now. You're healthy, you're earning, you've got pals and a few good years left in you. At your age your dad and I lived like siblings. I had no job, no money of my own and no prospect of a second chance. I had to accept my lot – you don't." I watch her turn to storm towards the kitchen but she comes to a halt at the bedroom door and swings round to deal me a scathing postscript. "Life, work, men – modern girls have all the power, Maggie. Some of them know how to wield it, others just hope for the best. Buck up, stop hoping and start wielding." And she turns and struts out of the room.

I touch a hand to my mouth while the dots connect. What do you do when you've lost your power? You claw it back, that's what. *What were you thinking* I whisper out loud, knowing full well that I didn't think, I blundered on, blanked the signs, and ignored my gut.

Still riding her high horse, Mum pops her head back into the room. "So d'you want that tea or not?" And I nod.

While she busies herself in the kitchen I pull my mobile out of my bag, take a moment to consider what to say and with both thumbs, key in a text. I need to be careful how I word it to manage his expectations but it needs done and done now.

One step, that's all, one more step and I'm there.

Wednesday, 3rd September

His smile is weak, his eyes sad. My gut feels the sting of a tiny flare – a stray cinder and probably not the last of them – but starved of his oxygen, it'll soon die. It's as if I'm seeing him for the first time and my mind, which would usually be clouded by a combination of emotional starvation and lust, is crystal clear.

"I'm glad you texted, Lullah. And I'm glad we've met here, at Fred's, *our* place." I sip my coffee, put down my cup, turn to stare at the eyes that once dominated my every waking moment and – zilch. No sparks, no goose bumps, nothing.

"Talk to me," he pleads.

Deep sigh, here goes. "About what?"

"About us; why're you pulling the eject lever?"

His face tells the story; it's his turn to feel wrong-footed and my turn to call the shots. "I'm sorry but there is no 'us', Gus, we've had three wonderful weeks but the firework has fizzled."

His ego still hoping for a leg-up he leans shoulder to shoulder with me. "I thought I was your Blue Eye Man. You know I care about you."

Despite how therapeutic it would be to give him his character, I decide not to whine about how he threw me scraps, gave me less than the crumbs off his table, put me through the mincer. "C'mon, Gus, it was just a bit of fun," I say and try to make it sound light-hearted. "And why not? You're single and so am I but you're not the man for me."

"How come? What did I do?"

"That's the whole point, you didn't do anything."

His smile fades and along with it, the light behind his eyes.

"Hoi, that's a bit much, I'm not that bad."

My solar plexus opts to give me the tiniest of twangs, a reminder of the anxious nights he caused, the self-doubt he bred. Again, I could put him straight; berate him for making me feel so insecure; but for a second time I elect to hold my tongue.

Instead I laugh and shake my head. "I thought you'd be relieved to get me off your back. It's a simple case of lust versus love; alcohol versus oestrogen. The latter lasts, the former – well, you know." His brows drop, a sure sign he has no clue what I'm on about, so I elucidate. "What I thought was an inferno turned out to be a single flame and so easily snuffed out. We were both playing at happy couples. Now it's time to call it a day."

He takes a swig of his pint, licks the foam off his lips and gives this some consideration. "But I didn't do anything wrong," he petitions, "I was just doing my thing and I invited you along for the ride. I thought we were having fun."

Ladies, when a guy isn't playing the game, this is the difference between you dumping him and him dumping you – it serves to refocus his attention and you get to redistribute the insecurity he's fostered in you for God knows how long. It also redistributes your power back to you. Unless there's another woman, of course, in which case you're snookered.

And trust me, there is another woman.

"It's not your fault, Gus, it's mine," I tell him. "I'd built up a full-blown relationship in my head but I'd constructed it on rubble, it had to fall down. Let's face it, you are the anti-Ken – bright, funny, outgoing – I needed that." I give him a nudge. "Of course, you being a looker helped." Grateful for my deliberate shot in the arm to his self-worth, his smile makes its customary appearance. "The problem's mine," I go on, and watch him warm further to my argument, "you kept telling me who you were and I refused to listen. I tailor-made a persona for you that suited my needs and the problem came when you couldn't wear it 'cos it didn't fit." Another smile wends its way across the table before he places his hand over mine and gives it a squeeze.

Not even a static crackle.

"Is it my moods?" he asks, the blue of his eyes transparent. "I'll put my hands up and say I get a bit tetchy sometimes. Don't mean anything by it."

"No, I've had a busy week, that's all. You name it, I've had it – pivotal moments, visitations, interventions…"

Okay, so I made up the bit about interventions but it pushes the point home.

"Bloody hell – sounds a bit heavy. And it's all down to me?"

"Honestly? No." He looks crestfallen. The news that my world no longer orbits his has to be a further blow so I decide to give him a booster shot. "But I need to say, thanks."

"For what?"

"For the fun; for enticing me out of my doldrums, for helping me to move on. I'd still be fighting to keep the curtains closed if it wasn't for you. You'll meet somebody else in no time."

He picks up his empty beer glass and stares into it. "Funny you should say that, Rachel texted earlier, wants to talk, says she wants to try again. Maybe I'll give it a go now. Dunno what changed her mind, I really thought it was over this time."

And there she is, the lying, scheming cow, clawing to get her power back, game-playing in a league way beyond Winnie and her good-natured sweet and sour ploys. I know what changed her mind – me, and as soon as he told her about us, she started plotting. He's always loved her, always will to some degree, and she's not about to let that go. They've probably been in this on-again, off-again dance for years. How many other hopefuls have been drawn into their emotional two-step?

And the crazy thing is, he doesn't have a clue.

"Need a refill, you want another coffee?"

"No thanks," I say, my voice firm, and offer up a silent thank you for my mother's counsel. "Better go. I have a life to plan. Keep in touch?"

"Sure," he says and grins, but I know I'll never hear from him, nor he from me. "Maybe I should call it," he says, and studies his watch, a last-ditch attempt at humour. "T.O.D. 8.37pm."

I rise and give him my warmest smile.

"Bon voyagey, Maggie…?"

"McCardle. It's Maggie McCardle. Bye Gus." I turn to head for the door and keep going, determined not to look back because I'm certain that as soon as I'm ten feet from the table he'll flip open his phone and call her, or Mick, or anybody who'll give him a fix of attention.

Truth is, lust is like counterfeit money. It feels good in your pocket but try to bank it and it's worthless. I needed somewhere safe to place my hope for the future and there he was, a haven from the past, the poster boy who could never hurt me or reject me or let me down. But he was a trick of the light. He glittered and with no evidence to the contrary I classed him gold. I thought he was Land's End to John O' Groats and everything in between; Banksy, spray-painting his imprint a mile high across my soul; Mr Monopoly, not just a player but the whole game. I thought he was everything.

But he wasn't, he was just a bloke.

Once I'd worked out who the real Gus was, the rest came easy and the decision to call a halt reinstated my karmic calm. They're the warp and weft, him and Rachel, woven together into the same piece of flawed fabric. Now he's gone and I'm left with a new look, no single friends and a five foot ten inch hole in my life.

Not ideal, given that the Project Me deadline is three days away.

And yet that calm, still voice keeps echoing in my brain – *everything will be alright; trust me; have faith.*

I have no choice now; I have to believe it and keep going.

Thursday, 4th September, 9am

I find a space on the street, park and run in the main door, clocking in a minute after the half past nine flexi-deadline. I leap up the stairs two at a time and sprint along the Corridor of Power, the momentum thrusting me through the double doors.

I stop dead.

The entire staff are assembled in a semi-circle facing the door, some standing, some sitting, all gawping.

"Pleased you could make it," says a voice to my right. "We were just about to start."

I turn and gasp. Fran is to the right of the doors alongside four suited men in shiny shoes. No hint of a smile nor flicker of recognition in her eyes, only cold, grey steel. Power-dressed in a purple suite, cream blouse and clumpy heels, she's acting all head honcho and it's clear she's the lead speaker. Uncle Pete's there too, standing at the end of the row, and they all look grim. Me, I've taken root to the carpet, my outer calm concealing inner turmoil. I dart my eyes around the room and do a quick check.

Yep, this is where I work.

Uh-huh, that's Fran Henderson.

Nope, I've no idea what's going on.

Fran lowers her chin and telegraphs me a look that says, we'll speak later, then raises her brows. "If you could find yourself a seat, please," her curt tone emphasising the arm's length she intends to keep between us.

Something's not right.

I spot Cat seated on the front edge of my desk and Della

next to her, beckoning me. My feet blank the 'run' signals my brain is issuing and shuffle me over to join them.

"You might've warned me, guys," I whisper, "what in the name of hell's goin' on?"

Cat bumps Della up the desk a bit, gestures at me to sit on the corner and whispers out of the side of her mouth. "Not sure yet."

At last, Fran clasps her hands in front of her and addresses the staff. "Good morning everyone, my name's Fran Armstrong." So *that's* her married name. I sneak a glance at Cat and Della but it's plain they have no clue this is the Fran I told them about. "I run a company called Armstrong Solutions," she continues. "I know there's a lot of speculation going on so to avoid the office tom toms sending out misinformation, we've decided to talk to you direct." I hear a gasp from the congregation while she pauses to let this sink in. "My company were called in a few weeks ago to carry out a fraud investigation under the guise of an audit and our inspection is now concluded."

Shit, she's working with management. I showed her Stella's emails and gave her all the gossip, hell I even did my psycho-boss impersonation in the Dome. If Fran's told Stella, she'll chew me out then fire me for breaching confidentiality.

Where is Stella anyway?

His specs astride his head, Uncle Pete scuffs his feet on the carpet and looks distracted, as if he's off somewhere compiling his grocery list which, knowing Pete, is more likely than you'd think.

She's speaking again.

"To my right is Detective Chief Inspector Alec Nevis of Lothian and Borders Police," she goes on, shifting her weight from one foot to the other, "and to my left, Detective Constables Firth and McLean of Monkswood CID. They have a team of officers setting up camp in the training room. They'll want to interview all of you at some point today." Mutters spread through the crowd like a virus, so she raises her voice accordingly. "We've uncovered a major breach of staff regulations," she goes on, "specifically a personal relationship involving two members of staff, one of them the other's line manager."

Oh God, no – not that I care about Stella or Baldwin, but I do care what my colleagues think of me. My stomach skelters to the floor, panic creeping up my neck. I can't believe Fran sat there, in my own home, at my own computer, took it all in and didn't put me straight.

So much for the Old Pals Act of 1974.

An inverted scream echoes through my very soul at this blatant betrayal of trust. If she exposes me as the informer, no one will speak to me ever again.

I'm almost hyper-ventilating while Fran strides on. "However, there is a bigger issue. Head Office knew funds from this office were being siphoned off. They had an idea how and by who but they needed proof, which is where we came in." At this moment her eyes catch mine and issue a pointed look, sending my stomach into free-fall. "It transpires that the man you know as Gregor McAndrew was working with an accomplice to embezzle funds from the company, but we can't say anything more until the police interview her today."

Gregor?

The words tug my brain into focus and when I put them together with the looks Fran's sending me, it doesn't take long to work it out. Oh Geezus, they think I'm his partner in crime. Bonnie to his Clyde. Somehow, some way, he implicated me that night and I'm to be his scapegoat. This is so much worse than being outed as a management mole. The room shrinks around me, the sudden shockwave lifting me to my feet.

"It's not true!" I scream. Every eye in the room swivels to stare at me. I clamp a hand to my brow and try to breathe, but all the air's been punched out of me. I'm shaking and vibrating; the room revolving, spinning; whirling me dizzy; I hear a collective groan, then a mass '*aaah*', and the next thing I know my legs buckle and it all goes black.

***

Why is Cat talking to me through a metal tube? I try to focus but the scene's a blur. When I come to I recognise the First Aid Room, and realise I'm flat out on the bed. Fran is sitting on the bed end, and I catch yet another flicker in her eyes. My stomach reels. A second later Cat's face comes swimming into view above me through a riot of red spiralled curls.

"Maggie, are you alright?"

"What happened?" I croak and try to sit up. Then I remember the twist of cold steel in my back and fall down again.

"You went a funny colour and keeled over," says Cat and turns to an agitated Fran. "I'm a trained first-aider, Mrs Armstrong, I'll take it from here."

Not one to be dismissed, Fran's face fails to mask her frustration. "I'll be back Maggie," she says, her voice still firm, "so don't go anywhere. The police want to interview you but make sure you speak to me before they do."

Unable to look at her scheming face, I give her a reluctant nod and bite my lip to avoid saying something I might regret. But all I can think is, she's a liar, she's a traitor, and I'm in deep, deep doodoo.

As soon as the door clicks shut, Cat sits on the bed and starts talking. "Maggie, you're not gonna believe this. Turns out Gregor McAndrew was really Andrew McGregor, a con man and Stella's brother. Can you believe it? He's committed jiggery-pokery, embezzled a fortune out of the place. Before Stella came here she was in charge of Human Resources in the Glasgow office. Seems she fudged his application and rubber-stamped his documents to get him the job. She maybe thought if he was in a smaller office, like Monkswood, nobody would notice him. Then she requested a transfer here and next thing you know, they've nicked off with the dosh. He must've been terrified of you, Maggie, if you'd told anybody about your one night stand Stella might've been forced to move him out of Finance before he could transfer the money. No wonder he was so nervous around you."

Two pieces of puzzle click into place. "I'd bet that's why she picked on me too, all that piling on the work and the crap about the curtains. She didn't hate me, she was frightened of me. Tell me the truth, Cat – I'm their fall-guy. They cloned my access card and used it to get to the dosh, didn't they?"

She laughs so hard I think she might swallow her tongue. "Newsflash – you don't have that level of authority, dimwit. They probably intended to use somebody as a stooge but he'd quaffed a few too many that Friday night. And there you were, drunk as a puggie, and opportunity tapped him on the shoulder so he stepped out of character and into your taxi."

"Erm, that makes sense. And I kind of knew about Stella and Baldwin. Tell you later?"

She launches me a zinger of a look. "You'd better," she says. "Anyway, Stella's down at the cop shop right now giving her version of events. The police frog-marched her off the premises at half past eight this morning. Seems he's buggered off and left his sis to carry the can. Rumour has it he's known to the police, plays the fool when he's on a job so nobody suspects him, hence the Gregor character. Word is he works alone, but this time he needed Stella to help him get a foot in the door. And he lied – he doesn't live with his mother. That was all part of the ruse. Looks like we've all been played."

"So my secret's still safe?"

"As far as I know."

I give her a guilty look. "D'you know who Fran Armstrong is?"

She lolls her head sideways. "Aye, she told me when you were out cold. You were at school together."

"There's more to it than that, but before I tell you, I need to speak to Fran. Then we'll talk."

"Uh-huh. But you'll lie there 'til I say you can get up and no more fainting fits. Deal?"

"Deal," I say, "now, go fetch me Fran."

***

"Okay, Fran, tell me the truth. Am I sacked?"

Fran lets out an explosive laugh. "Why would you be sacked?" she asks.

"Because I breached confidentiality when I told you all that stuff about Stella and showed you those emails. You glowered at me out there, I thought I was for the chop."

She laughs again. "No, of course not. If it wasn't for you we'd never have figured it out. I wasn't glowering, I was giving you the wire, trying to make sure you didn't give yourself away."

"So I'm not in schtuck?"

"Nope. I emailed you yesterday afternoon to give you the heads up and asked you not to let on that we knew each other before the announcement. Did you not read it?"

"I went home early."

"Ah, *that's* why you were so shocked to see me. You might be asked to give evidence, mainly to confirm you forwarded the emails to your home PC and that they're the real deal."

"No problem. I'll forward them to you later."

"No need," she says. "I did that on Sunday when you went to the loo. I was worried you'd panic and delete them. I'm sorry, but I had to catch the culprit and it was the only way to prove she was involved."

"Wish you'd said something."

"Confiding in you wasn't an option until we'd worked it out. That's why I asked you to keep it to yourself. It was a huge job, accessing everybody's work emails, but up 'til then we'd found nothing incriminating. Those emails gave the game away and are the mainstay of our evidence. I came on Sunday to ask you some questions about Stella but there was no need after you let me read them. Thank God you forwarded them to your Hotmail address. Saved us weeks of work and the firm a lorry-load of money."

"I don't care so long as she's out of our hair. So, a new manager to come, eh?"

"Cat didn't get time to tell you about Mr Cosgrove's announcement." I stare at her. "A multi-national outfit called B4 Accounting has bought over the whole company, kit and caboodle. Frank Cosgrove is their CEO. Manders and Healey needed us to plug the money drain before the handover. After we carted you off he announced the closure of this office, the Glasgow office, and the relocation of your work to their Midlands operation. All phone lines and mail were redirected there as of this morning. A team are coming in tomorrow to uninstall the computers, so you've not to come in until mid-day. Over the next week you'll all be employed parcelling up client files to send them on. Your final date of employment is in a month, although the office will be closed down after next weekend."

"No," I cry out, "I need my job, I only have one salary coming in and I'd go nuts if I wasn't working."

"But it's compulsory redundancy, Maggie. Or in your case, compulsory early retirement since your fiftieth is in two days. Given your length of service and the fact that this company had one of the few final salary pension schemes left in the UK, it'll be worth your while." She checks her watch. "Listen, I want to make a suggestion but I need to dash up to my Edinburgh office right now. Can I come back and see you this afternoon?"

"Sure." I say and shrug my shoulders.

"Great, see you in a few hours." And she disappears out of the door leaving me with my head reeling.

Eleventh hour divorces? Declarations of love? Gold clad exit packages?

What the hell is going on?

You tell me, I'm flummoxed.

Thursday, 4th September, 3pm

"I thought I'd never get back to you," pants a red-faced Fran when she leads me into Stella's office, her laptop in one hand, handbag in the other. She drops the handbag on the floor, the laptop on the desk, unzips her jacket and shrugs it off. "It's been one of those days. Coffee?"

While she hangs up her coat, I glance around the room and shudder.

"No thanks, I think I'd choke on it here."

"She's gone, forever, you can breathe easy. Sit, Maggie, sit." I claim the hot seat and wriggle myself comfortable while Fran pulls Stella's chair out and sits on it, wheeling it back so she can cross her legs.

Elbows on the arm rests, she stretches her neck and relaxes back. "How do you feel now that it's all out in the open?"

I break out a grin and perform a little salsa in my seat. "Hey, if you're happy, then I'm delighted. It's weird, though, sitting in her office without the terror. I can't believe Gregor or Andrew or whatever he's called is her brother; worse, that they were in cahoots."

I see her gauge me with her eyes. "Can I confide in you?" I nod. "She wasn't. In cahoots. I spoke with the police an hour ago. He was just out of prison for embezzlement, asked her for a fresh start, promised he wouldn't let her down. Have you heard of Disclosure Scotland?"

"Sure, the company pay a fee to establish whether you have a criminal history before they employ you."

"She fudged his to get him through the door, took a chance

and had him posted here to Monkswood where she thought he'd be out of temptation's way doing admin. Then, with no reason not to, on day one old Gibson put him in Finance and she was mortified. She knew his M.O. so the writing was on the wall when she heard he was dressing down and behaving like the local loser. She applied for the manager's job to keep an eye on him, knew she'd be out on her ear, maybe even get herself in trouble, if he got up to his old tricks. After faking his personnel documents she couldn't tell anyone that they were related and that suited his plans just fine. I understand everyone thinks he smartened himself up after she arrived, but that's his normal way of dressing. He was dropping the geeky image before she saw him and realised what he was up to." Another corner of jigsaw slithers into place.

"So she's not in trouble?"

"Oh, she's in trouble alright, she forged official documents and had an affair with her line manager – beyond naughty. She knew funds were going walkies and she did nothing. That's why she was so uptight all the time, I'd put money on it. Baldwin didn't know they were related either. Thank God he didn't take her into his confidence regarding the 'audit'. The Police will contact the Procurator Fiscal to determine what they can charge her with, and she lost her job on the spot. So did Baldwin, for breaching staff rules and neither will get a penny in redundancy."

"Why did you want to see me?"

She pauses to take a breath. "Don't be mad at me." I tilt my head and wait; for what her face tells me is likely to be another bombshell. "I told my son Richard about your experience with City Interiors."

"Oh. And?"

"A few months ago his company agreed to let him convert two of their smaller venues into themed hotels, low budget mind you, to see whether he could turn them into profit rather than see them sold, and she'd tendered for the work. If the format's successful, they'll expand it to cover a few other venues."

"That must be the big contract she told me about."

She's trying hard to be serious but a smile breaks through. "He *was* leaning towards hiring her but he's walked away. Says he won't work with somebody who has such poor business ethics. He wasn't sure she understood him and his ideas anyway – thinks she's too much of a diva. Then he was shocked at the production cost versus the final invoice at Vendange and he doesn't want to be ripped off. You did him a favour by telling me. He's so grateful."

"So, I gossiped her out of a job," I say, delighted. "How satisfying, this was almost worth her not paying me."

"Aye, but now Richard's back to square one." She bites her bottom lip and tries her best to look shamefaced. "So I showed him your portfolio."

For a moment I'm speechless, until I work out the implication. "Oh. I see. But those are just one-off, odd pairs of curtains I made for friends."

She leans forward. "But – he – loved – them – Maggie," she says without so much as a blink, each word a slow staccato to ensure the message gets hammered through. "Then he went to Vendange to see your handiwork for himself. He wants to know how you'd feel about working with him, says he'll give you first dibs. He has an eye for interior design and plans to do a lot of it himself, but he's strapped for time, needs somebody who can research ideas, suggest soft furnishings then convert them into the finished article. He'd almost given up on finding someone like you."

I feel a surge of panic. "Fran, I can't cope with that much work. Plus, I'd be trapped in the house, on my own. It's a great time filler when I'm bored but on this scale? I couldn't, I'd go nuts."

"But you wouldn't need to do any of the sewing yourself," she says. "You could advertise for homeworkers, like she did. All you'd do is work with him on the designs, source the materials, hang the finished product and submit your invoice. No start-up costs. No sewing; no premises; no rent. You'd sub-contract the work out so no pay-as-you-earn or bookwork. You could take a two day course in running a small venture at the Business Gateway."

"I know, but Felicity McQueen's already threatened me with legal action and that was just for blabbing to the owner of Vendange. I can well imagine how she'd react if I started up for myself and poached her work. She'd make my life a misery."

Fran thinks long and hard before she speaks again. "Here's the thing," she says in a voice loaded with determination, "Number one – it's a free country. There's no law against enterprise, quite the opposite in fact, and there's certainly no law against telling the truth. Number two – it's up to Richard, not her, who he chooses to work with, so you can ignore her and her threats of litigation. Number three," she goes on, "when people try to put you down, they're either jealous or they feel threatened. She came to your house, saw what you're capable of – do you think for a minute she's able to design stuff like that? No, not a chance." She pauses and stares at me hard. "Look, you've got two choices. You can take a leap of faith in yourself and embrace this opportunity or you can do what I suspect you've done for a long time – underestimate your abilities and sell yourself short." She waits while I struggle with this assessment of my character before she goes on. "If it's good enough for her, Maggie, it's good enough for you and frankly, I wouldn't give a monkeys what she thinks. It's time to start looking after numero uno." Lecture almost over, she sits back to take her place as the third person to wag a finger in my face this week, every man jack of them spot on. "This is solid gold, gift-wrapped and offered to you on a plate," she throws in for good measure, "do you think it was co-incidence that you ran into me that day outside the lawyers' office? No, it was serendipity, meant to be."

No it wasn't, it was the Claptrap Cavalry, but I'm not about to argue the point.

"So, are you up for it or not?" she says. Who am I kidding, this is something I've dreamt about forever, my Holy Grail, and I need to stop resisting. *Never refuse the slap on the back, it's the only one not guaranteed.* I'm part excited, part wary and totally terrified but I know there's only one acceptable answer to her question.

Acceptable to *me*, that is.

"You can put away the thumb-screws," I tell her, "I think I can do this."

Elated, she smiles, leans forward and squeezes my arm. "Excellent. Every job will be unique," she says, "so he'll want you to quote room by room. If you think of a figure and treble it, you'll still be nowhere near McQueen's prices. And he has loads of contacts in the trade so he'll get you more work too. Go have a think, work out some details and talk to me before you go home."

"I will," I say, and stand up to leave.

"And think up a proper business name. It's so much more professional."

"No need," I tell her with absolute confidence, and another piece of my jigsaw plops into place. "I'm going to call myself 'The Drape Doctor'."

Friday, 5th September, 11.30am

I spent the whole night building a business in my head. I've been on the internet since six this morning and so far I've advertised for workers and designed a business card, I've even got a logo. I'm pulling the front door closed behind me to leave for the office when I hear the house phone ring out so I rush back in and pick up.

"Oh. Mrs McCardle."

"*Felicity.* What can I do for you?" Given that she's a lost cause, who can be bothered dealing with the woman?

I'll tell you who – me.

"Erm…well…yes. Just wanted to inform you," she blusters, a quaver in her voice, "the prestige contract I mentioned with the multi-national hotel chain? City Interiors put in a tender and I'm sure to get the commission." A silence hangs on the line.

"I see. And you're telling me this – why?" Another shorter silence.

"I want to let you know that, as promised, I will NOT be sub-contracting any of the work to you. Now good day Mrs…"

"Hang on," I shout. "Just so you know, I also tendered for that contract just yesterday under my trade name, the Drape Doctor, and the company awarded it to me verbally last night."

"But how did you…that's ridiculous, you're just a trumped-up seamstress, you can't possibly cope with running a business. You're making it up."

Guess what? When the crap hits the centrifuge, she ain't so cool.

"The general manager's name is Richard Armstrong, we had

dinner last night and I'm in business as of today."

"How dare you," she spits, furious. "This is deliberate, you've done this to sabotage me because I withheld the fee for those damned curtains. I should never have told you about that job, you've stolen it from me. Well I hope it was worth it because I'll be speaking to my solicitor and this time he'll sue you for everything you own."

"I didn't approach Richard, he approached me. Head-hunted me, in fact. And they're not multi-national, nothing like it. Plus, it strikes me that when you made this call you didn't intend to speak to me, did you? You assumed I'd be at work so you could sneak one of your malicious little messages onto my answering service. That makes you a liar, a coward *and* a bully. Call here again and it'll be me speaking to MY solicitor." And without waiting for her response I cut her off with the press of a button.

You know what they say – if you cut deals with snipers, at some point you're likely to stop a bullet so I figured I might as well get in a few pot shots of my own.

Game, set and match to me, Felicity. Cheers m'dear, I could never have done it without you.

Sunday, 7th September, 7.30am

Mmm, I can still taste the champagne, although I was careful not to over-refresh at last night's surprise Five-0 birthday bash. I know exactly how I got home and here I am, in my own bed, on the right side and stark, bollock naked.

I stretched awake over an hour ago, one foot dangling over the mattress edge, and I've lain here ever since, reliving it all in my head. How I went along with Mum's 'taking you out for a meal' ploy; how the taxi took us to Cat's and everyone jumped out shouting 'surprise'; how I should get a Golden Globe for my fake heart attack; how I love my new puzzle pieces and the future they depict.

I know that dratted mirror is waiting for my sprint to the loo so that it can burst my bubble, but it's wasting its time. The reflection in the glass will always say Maggie's less Elle MacPherson, more Tinky Winky, but she doesn't care and neither does the person whose sweet smell loiters on her skin.

Eau du Man, don't you just love it?

No hands on ha'pennies here, if Ken could see me now, in our bed, with a bloke and not giving a stuff, he'd be well miffed. Shame on you, Maggie McCardle.

Well, fuck you Ken. See? Works every time.

Fists balled I turn over and rub the sleep from my lashes. "Good morning, you," he murmurs all low and husky into my ear, and my heart does a pirouette.

"Hi yourself," I say, and squidge around to meet two smoky eyes.

One foot in Sleepy Meadows, my arse.

"Com'ere," he says, offers me the crook of his arm, and wraps me in a heartfelt hug. I close my eyes, lay my head on his chest and breathe in his sweet, sweet scent. "So," he says, looking pleased with himself, "did you have a good time?"

Geezus, what does he expect, a fly-past?

Oh. He means the party.

"You bet your bippy," I tell him. Now, this is more like it. No struggles, no firebombs and no seesaw, just a quiet feeling of security.

Nice.

I've made an executive decision – I won't be defined as someone's staff, someone's girlfriend, someone's wife. I made the mistake of looking at what I wasn't instead of what I was – an almost-golden, post-marital late bloomer with a wodge of experience tucked into her backpack and an opportunity to start again. Gus wasn't partner material, he was a stepping stone and my two fingers up at Ken. That's the trouble with lightning, the flash can blind you for a while.

I've changed. The teenager who nursed a crush on John Davidson wasn't the same girl Ken met and married and neither am I. I'm not the woman he left either. I'm new. Improved. Updated.

Refurbished; rebranded; relaunched.

Wonder who I'll be next time around?

He pulls back, his smitten eyes twinkling. "How's about I take you out for an early dinner, keep the celebration going? I'll need to go home and get changed first but we could nip into town later on."

I smile. "Sure, why not?"

"Great," he grins, "and I can talk you through your business plan." Oh yay. And I can talk him through *my* idea that he put in a bid to supply Richard with the custom-made furniture he needs. I award myself a congratulatory nod and snuggle down in his arms again.

Oh yes, I like these new puzzle pieces very much indeedy.

"My Mogs," he whispers, his voice thick, and buries his face in my hair. "By any chance did we have some...unfinished business?"

Fifty; a man in my bed; fire in his eyes. What's to resist?

Bottoms up, Johnny boy, I'll drink to that. Slange var, everybody!

Sunday, 7th September, 5pm

"*Tah-dah!*" I sing and strike a pose at Mum's door. "Am I a vision of sartorial elegance or what?"

Mum's face is a picture. "You'd better come away in," she beams and steps back to let me sashay through her front door. She scans me from my grey fine-knit tunic and dusky pink scarf to my black dress trousers, pewter pumps and bag, her eyes lingering on my boobs which are sallying forth thanks to the power of state of the art built-in scaffolding. "You're a bit overdressed for a Sunday afternoon."

"I have a date," I announce but she doesn't look surprised, not surprised at all. She folds her arms, jabs tongue into cheek and smirks. "Did you catch that? I have a date," but she's still smirking and it's obvious I'm missing something. "What's going on, Mum?"

She gives me a shrewd look. "Now you're going to tell me it's with John."

"Wha – how did you know? You were at the party for less than two hours and he didn't arrive 'til after you left."

She grins and beckons me with a finger. "Because I invited him. C'mon, I've got something to show you in the bedroom," she says, her hushed tone underlining the need for secrecy, and takes off along the hallway with me wondering what in the name of God she's on about. She throws open both wardrobe doors to reveal row upon row of stacked shoe-boxes filed within. She pulls a black box off the top row, removes the lid, lifts out a slim package swaddled in carrier bags and holds it aloft for my benefit.

221

Head spinning, I sink onto the bed, both hands clasped over my mouth. "No. Ho, no no no. Please, Mum, tell me you didn't."

"Oh, but I did," she says, puts the box down and commences unwrapping the package. "Took me ages to lever the blasted thing off without leaving a knife mark, I was starting to think it was pensioner proof." The seconds stream past, each one stumbling over the last in its hurry to be gone. "But if he ever finds out, let's just kid on it was the hand of God."

Like I'd ever own up to any of this.

"But what made you think he'd take the bait?"

She shrugs. "I saw the way he looked at you in the shop and I just knew. A mother does. And don't think I've forgotten how devastated you were all those years ago. But this time the drawbridge had been up too long, Maggie. So I put on my dippy old dodderer head and did something about it. That bloke Gus gate-crashed my plan but he was just a chancer, I knew you'd figure him out. It might not come to anything with John either, but I had to give you the chance. It'll all work out as it should, so don't worry. Oh and, sorry about the single bed thing, I needed him to know you were on your own again."

My mind picks up the pace and pedals a bit faster. The puzzle pieces are shape-shifting to slot perfectly into their once-tight spots. *Oh crap.* Embarrassment-by-Parent is a rite of passage for a teenager, but I had no idea it would all kick off again when I hit fifty.

She re-wraps the moulding, places the package in my hand and curls my fingers into a grip around it. Blank-faced, I gawp at the offending article. "Keep this somewhere safe, never let him see it," she says, hugs me and plants a kiss on my cheek. "Happy Birthday, my lovely Maggie."

Hang about – this wasn't as simple as yanking off a moulding. To hell with BAFTAs and Golden Globes, she's a top notch contender for an Oscar. She lied about the delivery men refusing to take it back; cajoled me into making the phone call;

kept him talking until I arrived to inspect the thing – who is this manipulative minx I call Mother? Hot, fat tears blur my eyes.

My mammy loves me.

Still awed by the stunt she pulled I drive home to wait for John, the evidence squirrelled away in my car boot. Dream Hug notwithstanding, I'm certain now that things will go my way. Why? Because she's my mother and she said so, that's why.

And that's more than good enough for me.

***

John looks smooth and confident, his long legs sheathed in brand new denim topped off with a pale blue shirt and dress jacket. I'm sporting Jackie-O shades on my head, rich bitch-style. Sitting at our window seat in L'Amuse Bouche, perusing the over-priced dessert menu, we are the epitome of middle-aged coupledom.

If only I could get a word in.

He's talking with his hands, laying out the landscape on the white of the tablecloth. "It'll be brilliant, Maggie. My floor manager can run the shop when I'm not there. It makes perfect sense, I source the furniture, then give you my ideas for curtain styles and you do your thing. Perfect."

You give me *your* ideas?

"Whoa, hold up, John, it's not as if it's a dead cert, I only mentioned it over the starters. I haven't even spoken to Richard yet, he might have invited other suppliers to bid for the contract."

"Not yet he won't. According to you the McQueen woman was set to supply both furniture and curtains, and he only ditched her at the end of the week. No, I think he'll be impressed with the deal I've got in mind, especially if I get in first." Picking up on a degree of scepticism from my side of the table he leans forward and pats my hand. "Don't worry, Mogs, I know how these things work."

At this point the waiter ambles up with an enquiring smile to take our order, but without consulting me John waves him away. *Please, don't do this* I want to scream but I can't; instead I smile and try not to let my rancour reach my face. *He's excited. His business isn't any more recession-proof than the next guy's, so this is a huge leg-up. Bear with him.*

I attempt a change of subject to diffuse the red mist that's emanating from my very bones. "You said you'd help me with a business plan."

He knocks back half a glass of water. "No worries, I started work on it this afternoon. Needs your numbers as far as money's concerned, of course, but you can give me those later. I'll lay down the basics first. Should be ready to show you by, say, middle of the week."

My heart booming in my ear, I grope for the right words. "I think you've got the wrong idea here, John, I don't need you to organise the whole shebang, I've pretty much got the entire thing square in my head." Outside, the evening sun slides behind a cloud.

"Maggie, I've been doing this for years, believe you me, I know what I'm talking about. Self-employment is tough and there's so much to learn…" And so it begins, his wall of sound. I can't hear him through the cold, dank cloud of anger swamping my brain but I pick up key words and phrases here and there – consumables; tax deductibles; in the lower percentile; a corner of my workshop.

Hang on, did he just say…

"Why would I rent a corner of your workshop?"

He spreads his hands to indicate it's a no-brainer. "Because I've got the space and you won't get a fairer price, of course. I'll be on hand to give you the benefit of my business know-how and you can stay in the loop with what Richard and I are up to."

He waits while I sit there in stony silence, my thoughts

hurtling down a desperate track, then dips his head and runs a hand through his hair. "Think about it, Maggie, you don't want a tuppenny ha'penny cottage industry, nobody rates that. My name and premises will lend your little sewing venture credibility."

My little sewing venture?

The final piece clicks into place and for the first time the whole picture is right there, clear as day. Brace yourself Johnny boy, this is no teenage Tallulah you're messing with, she's a mature woman going through a change of life to trump any menopause so watch out.

"John – I need you to stop, right now."

He snorts. "But why?"

"I realise you mean well but I prefer to do my own thing."

His eyes show the sting of offence. "But I thought..."

The self-same waiter strolls up and puts pen to pad yet again to take our order.

"Bill, please," I request and he nods and retreats. John looks as if I've slapped him hard. I take a breath to give the words time to gain credence on my tongue. "Sorry, John, but here's the thing. I haven't mentioned you to Richard yet, you don't even have his contact details. So stop behaving as if you're some high-end luxury brand and I'm the Tesco Savers version."

The grey of his eyes clouds over. "Oh. I thought this was a joint venture, thought we'd be working as a team."

Even I think my laugh is on the dry side. "You must know a different spelling for the word 'team', John." I lift the napkin from my lap, dab the corners of my mouth and drop it on the table. "This was supposed to be a date including a tête-a-tête about the business plan you offered to help me with," I tell him, and make it sound kind. "For whatever reason you did the man thing and took over. Then when I mentioned the possibility of putting a bit of work your way, you assumed the role of top dog and left me behind. To be honest, I don't need a business plan, I just didn't want to offend you. I have the premises, the equipment, and the contacts, but you didn't know that 'cos you didn't ask. Sorry, but this is my jalopy and from now on I'm hogging the wheel." He stares as if he doesn't recognise the person sitting opposite, as if trying to gauge whether I meant what he thinks I did; my eyes relaying that I did, I definitely did.

At that same moment the waiter brings the bill on a plate and I drag it across the table towards me and take a second to scan the bottom line. When he sees the purse in my hand John scrapes his chair back and leaps to his feet. "No, this is all wrong. I invited you out, remember? Please, Maggie, stay for dessert and talk."

With a gracious smile, I drop three twenty pound notes onto the table. "No thanks. The starter and main course were quite enough and it's my treat, John. This part of my puzzle's mine, all mine, and I won't let it be swallowed up by your jigsaw." He looks at me as if I've lost my marbles but I'm not about to explain myself. "Now, if you'll excuse me, I've got a business to set up." Those grey eyes flecked with regret, he looks as if he's swallowed his tongue, or wishes he had. I pull in a steadying breath, pick up my coat and bag and, for the second time in four days, walk away from a man and keep going, out of the building, out of his life, determined not to look back.

When I reach the street I stop, close my eyes, and assess.

Nice one, Project Me, you did a bang up job.

There was no sudden, out-of-the-ether pivotal moment; I worked this one out for myself. I see no airy-fairy celestial army waiting in the wings to rush to my rescue, only gut instinct jabbing at my intuition, giving me the heads up, and for once I paid attention. My dream hug was exactly that – a dream, prompted by my sub-conscious. I can't believe it's taken me a lifetime to assert myself and put my own needs first. Why didn't I realise, when it comes to puzzle pieces, you don't stumble over happy endings, you design and build your own? My project achieved more than a social relaunch, it upgraded me from passenger to driver and then some.

A swirling in my gut, a blend of endorphins infused with adrenaline and euphoria, forces my face to smile, my feet to skip, my heart to soar. I'm refurbished, rebranded, relaunched and geared up for the next phase. So what if passers-by slow up to stare, I don't care. From now on this golden girl's determined to take whatever life throws at her and grasp the thistle for herself so watch this space.

C'mon, life – bring it on…

The End

Fantastic Books
Great Authors

Meet our authors and discover our exciting range:

- Gripping Thrillers
- Cosy Mysteries
- Romantic Chick-Lit
- Fascinating Historicals
- Exciting Fantasy
- Young Adult and Children's Adventures

Visit us at:
www.crookedcatbooks.com

Join us on facebook:
www.facebook.com/crookedcatpublishing